Seduction Island

Also by Lorie O'Clare

PLEASURE ISLAND

Seduction Island

Lorie O'Clare

APHRODISIA

KENSINGTON BOOKS

http://www.kensingtonbooks.com

APHRODISIA BOOKS are published by

Kensington Publishing Corp.
119 West 40th Street
New York, NY 10018

All Kensington Titles, Imprints, and Distributed Lines are available at special quantity discounts for bulk purchases for sales promotions, premiums, fund-raising, and educational or institutional use.

Special book excerpts or customized printings can also be created to fit specific needs. For details, write or phone the office of the Kensington special sales manager: Kensington Publishing Corp., 119 West 40th Street, New York, NY 10018, attn: Special Sales Department, Phone: 1-800-221-2647.

Aphrodisia and the A logo Reg. U.S. Pat & TM Off.

ISBN-13: 978-0-7582-3448-3
ISBN-10: 0-7582-3448-1

First Kensington Trade Paperback Printing: November 2009

10 9 8 7 6 5 4 3 2 1

Printed in the United States of America

Seduction Island

1

Jordan Anton squatted on the edge of the volcanic rock and stared at the white foam as it raced up the sandy beach. It receded into crystal clear, bright blue water. Coral reefs added to the magnificence of the view. Too bad the small island was nothing more than a dried-up old volcano.

Jordan picked up a loose rock and hurled it at the ocean. Prisons came in many shapes and sizes. At least this one offered a view.

He jumped the three feet to the sandy ground and walked the length of the rocky wall. Beyond the thick grove of some erotic-looking flowering plant, a worn path led away from the beach. He started up the path, taking in the thick trunks of what might possibly be a hybrid of a palm tree. If he were in Montana he would know the names of the trees around him.

Jordan wondered how many Antons had been sent to this island when they didn't meet the approval of Pierre Anton, his grandfather. He would only be here a month, through all of January, and the terms weren't completely unbearable. But he was here against his will. He would be here in this warm tropical paradise, while everyone at the ranch endured the frigid winter.

He paused, tucking a thick black strand of hair that had come loose from the ponytail at the nape of his neck behind his ear. The long hair bothered his grandfather, but then, everything about Jordan bothered Grandfather Anton. Which, of course, was why Jordan was here.

"Why bother with a Harvard degree if you aren't going to use it, boy?" Grandfather had asked him more than once during their last visit.

Jordan wanted to ask exactly how he was *not* using his degree. There was knowledge in his head that hadn't been there before going to Harvard; life experience and memories that he wouldn't have had if he hadn't attended the Ivy League school. Jordan didn't have any regrets. He wasn't sure why it bothered Grandfather so much that he went to help Aunt Penelope with her ranch in Montana. His grandfather, of all people, should see and understand that Jordan was yet again learning and gaining life experience and memories by helping out on the ranch that his aunt would otherwise lose after divorcing her husband.

Of course, since she had divorced an Anton, more than likely Grandfather Anton didn't want her ranch to make it.

Jordan could spend weeks trying to understand the mind of someone like his grandfather. Or he could put those thoughts out of his head and figure out what the incredibly gorgeous woman standing no more than ten feet in front of him was doing on this island. His grandfather had spelled out the terms of their agreement very clearly before Jordan flew to the island. He would meet Tory, a Sicilian princess who possibly came from more money than the Antons. His grandfather wanted to merge the families, a business deal in his eyes, loosely called a marriage.

Jordan had no intention of marrying anyone but knew if he

didn't agree to come here, spend a month with the princess on the pretense of possibly announcing an engagement, Grandfather would make it hell for Aunt Penelope and her ranch.

Princess Tory would arrive tomorrow, which meant the sexy little thing wandering from the castle was one of the hired help, probably taking advantage of her boss not being here and exploring. He hadn't been scheduled to arrive until tomorrow.

He finished tucking the strand behind his ear and watched her studying the bark of the tree she stood in front of. "What are you doing?"

She jumped, yanking her hand back from the tree she was about to touch as if it might bite her, and turned and stared at him, wide eyed. In the next moment she regained her composure, straightened, and narrowed her gaze at him.

"I'm not sure that's any of your business. Who are you?" she demanded, obviously clueless as to whom her employer would be while on this island.

There were advantages to people not knowing his identity. It gave him the opportunity to learn their true nature before revealing his name and watching the fake appreciation and respect gloss over their face like it did every time he mentioned his last name.

"I asked you first." He hid his smile when she appeared frustrated, obviously realizing she didn't have the upper hand with him.

Jordan moved closer, admiring her long brown hair that was pulled back in a ponytail. His guess was it fell close to her ass. And he'd bet she had a nice ass, too. The curves he saw from the front view were beyond mouth watering.

"I seriously doubt you have permission to be away from the castle. And I don't approve of breaking rules to gain information." She had an American accent, probably northeast—New York or one of the nearby states. The way her hackles rose, turning her dark blue eyes almost violet, proved she knew how to defend herself.

Definitely not old money. Not to mention, if she were from his class, or the class his family so proudly held on to, she wouldn't be out here without an escort. Jordan wouldn't put her much past twenty-five at the most. No rings on her finger, not even a school ring. Maybe he'd run into his social organizer, although Grandfather boasted that the reputable social organizer ran only in the best of circles. Jordan seriously doubted his grandfather would hire a social organizer who shopped at Wal-Mart and not Neiman Marcus.

"Sometimes there are advantages to breaking the rules." He decided not to ask further who she was, doubting she'd confirm anyway. The anonymity on both sides allowed him to see her in her natural form. It would go away soon enough and she'd start kissing his ass. At least for a little while he could enjoy the fiery temper he doubted she'd let him see otherwise.

"Not that I can see." She turned, walking away from him, along the path she'd probably taken from the castle. "And if you believe there are, I doubt you'll hold on to your job for long."

Jordan liked playing the rogue. In truth, he didn't feel he was playing too much. But his damn last name and supposed "position in society" got in the way too often to allow him to interact with another person like this. Especially a gorgeous woman. Hell, when was the last time a lady walked away from him?

"What's life, if you don't take risks?" He caught up with her easily enough. Although it didn't bother him a bit that the path wasn't really wide enough to walk alongside her. The view of her backside was as extraordinary as he'd imagined.

"A safe place," she said tightly, her ass swaying beautifully in her snug, new-looking blue jeans.

"You must know how to take risks if you're here," he pointed out.

"You'd be surprised what I know."

"We might surprise each other with our knowledge."

"Huh," she snorted, picking up her pace. "I know your type."

The path curved around thick foliage and sloped up and down as it brought them closer to the large castle, now visible ahead of them. It was an anomaly, the only structure on this small island, and probably built during a time long forgotten. Jordan wouldn't be surprised if it were the selling point when his grandfather decided to pick up this little rock surrounded by the Pacific, and not too far off the coast of New Zealand.

He remained a couple paces behind her. "Do you, now? And what is my type?"

"The type I'm not interested in," she said, her arms swaying on either side of her. He liked how her long thick ponytail flowed from side to side, matching the soft curves of her hip and ass as it moved to a tantalizing rhythm.

"You don't know anything about me. How do you know if you would like my type or not?" he asked.

She stopped, the edge of the path just ahead of her, where it broke off into the well-maintained gardens surrounding the castle. He had been amazed when, upon his arrival just a few hours ago, he'd learned that a skeleton crew maintained the land and castle. There were only a few household servants, and there had to be a gardener, with as magnificent of a view the yard around the old structure provided, although he hadn't spotted any outdoor staff yet.

Jordan snapped his attention from her ass to her face when she spun around and shoved her long ponytail over her shoulder. He decided he liked how the spaghetti strap to her halter top almost crept off her shoulder, aiding in showing off her small bone structure and slender shoulders.

She shoved a nicely manicured finger into his chest. "I know what I need to know about you," she hissed, stepping close enough that he could see cobalt flecks bordering her irises. They helped her blue eyes darken when her emotions were running strong, as they obviously were now. "You are the one who thinks acting like a badass will impress a girl, make her take a risk, invite an adventure. You think you can play me, take what you want, and then gallivant on to the next pretty girl who strikes your fancy."

"Ouch." Jordan noticed she said "girl" and not "lady." That would definitely make her not Harvard. Probably not Yale or Stanford either, although he wouldn't swear to the latter. He also concluded she wasn't from New Zealand, although her American accent had already given a hint to that. Kiwis were usually pretty friendly folk, and this woman came equipped with a double-edged dagger. He hated admitting his intrigue. What he did know was he couldn't let her see it, or she might very well hand him his head on a platter. "You've pegged me wrong, my lady," he drawled, using his best Montana accent. "And as well, you've offered me a challenge. One I'm up to, I might add. For now, though, I'll bid you good day." If only he wore a hat. Tipping it in parting would play the part out perfectly. Instead, Jordan stepped around her, forcing her to jump to the side to avoid brushing against him. "I'm sure we'll see each other again very soon." He picked up his pace, heading to the castle, and as an afterthought, opted to head to the back of the building instead of the front. Making it look like he would enter through the servant entrance, or possibly even head to the stables, would keep her guessing.

Soon enough she would know who he really was.

* * *

Amber Stone walked down the wide hallway, her tennis shoes making a dull thudding sound on the glossy stone floor. Beautiful, ornate carpets, which were narrow and probably cost more than any paycheck she'd ever earned, silenced her footsteps when she walked over them. She paused and looked into a dimly lit library. Its tall bookcases filled with hardback books appeared ominous, as if all the secrets they held weren't for her. Amber never understood anyone who would willingly sit in a boring room all day reading a book, when everything anyone needed to learn came from experiences in living, not in fantasizing about someone else's life.

She hurried past the room, turning and hesitating at the glass doors, which closed off a room she wasn't sure what to call. Amber imagined royalty sitting in there, passing the time of day in accepted boredom while servants took care of their every need. It was a life she couldn't imagine, and honestly didn't want to try.

Walking quickly, she reached the far corner of the first floor of the castle and pushed open the thick wooden door, immediately inhaling something sweet mixed with the mouthwatering smell of coffee.

"Please tell me there is a fresh cup available," she said, smiling at the older woman who turned curiously and stared at her.

"Coffee, ma'am?" The woman's gray hair was thick and bundled up on her head. Her accent sounded Irish, making her the perfect cook for this kitchen, which stole Amber away to another time.

"Oh God, please. But I'm not a ma'am. Just call me Amber." She reached out and touched the woman's cool, soft arm when the cook hurried around the corner of the island counter, wiping her hands on her apron and then reaching for a cabinet. "I can get it. Just tell me where everything is."

"I don't think . . ."

"I insist. Whatever you're making smells so good I don't want to interrupt you. And I don't need to be waited on," she added firmly. "I can get my own coffee."

The back door opened with a bang, causing Amber and the older woman to jump and turn to acknowledge a man, probably close to the cook's age, hurry in so quickly he slid to a stop. "You wouldn't believe . . ." he began.

"Jesse," the older woman scolded at the same time the man spotted Amber and clamped his mouth shut. "Mind your manners," she added, lowering her tone as if she didn't intend for Amber to hear her. "There is company in the kitchen."

"Lord, I'm not company." Amber opened two cabinets before finding enough coffee cups to serve an army. Grabbing one of them, she admired the white, eggshell porcelain as she walked over to the industrial size coffeepot and put the cup under the spout. "My name is Amber Stone. I take it you're Jesse," she said, glancing over her shoulder at the older man who stood planted where he'd stopped, staring at her with watery brown eyes. "And your name is?" she asked, nodding at the older woman.

"I'm Cook," the older woman informed her, returning to her task of kneading out dough.

"Cook, huh." Amber carried her cup around the island, set it down, then spotted a stool up against the far wall. She dragged it noisily to the island and propped herself on it. "You've got a name, don't you?" she pressed.

Cook folded the dough in half, pressed with the balls of her hands, then repeated the process.

Amber glanced at Jesse, but he still hadn't moved. Obviously these two didn't get a lot of visitors. Their social skills sucked. Amber sipped the coffee and hummed her approval.

"I don't want to call you Cook. What's your name?"

Cook straightened, her eyes as pale a brown as the man's behind her, although their accents were very different. "It's a name you want, is it?" she asked crossly. "Fine, then, you'll have my name. It is Anne Marie Francis Margaret McGillicutty."

"Wow, that is one hell of a name," Amber said, hoping she sounded sincere. She glanced at Jesse. "Do you have as long of a name?"

"Nope. Just Jesse," he said, still not moving.

"What do your friends call you, Anne Marie Francis Margaret McGillicutty?" Amber asked.

"Cook," she said, returning to her dough.

Amber stared at Cook's thick gray hair, which was loose around her temples in spite of many hairpins attempting to keep it in place. Then, laughing easily at the comical situation, and wondering for the one hundredth time what the hell she was doing here, she wiped her eyes, still laughing.

Cook looked up at her, stopped her kneading, stared for a moment, and then broke into laughter as well. As if that were his cue to relax, Jesse hurried around the island, grabbing a cup and helping himself to coffee as well.

"How long have you two been here?" Amber asked, feeling the tension in the large, spacious kitchen fade as she brought her cup to her lips.

"I've worked for Mr. Anton for many years." Cook informed her. "Arrived the same day you did, yesterday."

"You're kidding. This place is in immaculate condition, the gardens gorgeous. Who takes care of the place?"

"I'm sure he sent in a crew to make it look like this before Jordan arrived," Jesse told her, walking over to the stove, lifting the lid off a pot, and breathing in the steam from it.

"He?" Amber asked.

Cook and Jesse looked at her pointedly. "He," Cook stressed. "Mr. Pierre Anton, our boss. Your boss, too. He told us you would be arriving tomorrow, though—assuming you are the young master's social organizer, Miss Stone?"

Amber nodded. "He just hired me but I asked if I could come out a day early to get settled in." She figured it might be worth trying to get any information out of these two concerning the mysterious Pierre Anton. She'd never been offered a job in quite the way he did, or with a job description like this one. And she'd been working since she was fourteen.

"You asked him?" Jesse asked, rubbing his gray hair as if trying to comprehend what she just said.

Cook's look was stern, as if Jesse's question was somehow rude. Her expression softened when she focused on Amber. "If you've come to discuss the menu, we can do that after dinner."

"The menu?" Amber frowned.

"The menu," Cook repeated. "You know, all the meals that will be served to you, the young master, and the princess."

"Oh, of course. Well, I'm sure whatever you decide will be fine. Whatever you're making now smells delicious."

"You are the social organizer, aren't you?" Cook looked at Amber like she'd grown a second nose. "Are you always so indifferent about the food served at your events?"

"Of course. Show it to me after supper. I'll approve it." Amber stared at her coffee cup, trying to think of something effective to say to cover her blunder. She'd been insane to think she could pull off being a social organizer. The servants in this castle knew more about her job description than she did. "I wanted to take time to get familiar with everything before our guests show up. But if you want me to go ahead and start my duties today, that's fine."

"That's what I came in here to tell you." Jesse suddenly sounded excited. "He's here already."

"Who is here?" Amber asked, more than willing to direct the conversation away from her.

"Jordan Anton, Pierre's grandson. I just saw him out in the stable with the horses."

"Oh really?" Amber jumped up, her stomach immediately twisting with nerves. The entire reason she'd been sent to this island was to provide the entertainment for Jordan Anton and his fiancée. Not that she had a clue how to do that, but she had successfully bluffed her way through the interview with Pierre Anton. And she would bluff her way through introducing herself to the millionaire's grandson. If she'd pulled the wool over the senior's eyes, junior wouldn't be much harder to convince. "So much for a day to prepare," she said, downing her coffee and walking her cup to the sink. "Where are the stables, Jesse?"

Amber ignored the comments from Cook about her attire not being appropriate. Jordan Anton would understand she didn't start working for him officially until tomorrow. She would keep the introductions simple, she decided, heading down the stone path Jesse had indicated led to the large, stone building behind the castle. It didn't look like any barn she'd ever seen before.

Amber didn't get why Cook thought she should put on a dress to enter this place. It had been all she could do to find nice summer clothes to buy during the dead of winter. She'd been excited to use her clothing allowance although every one looked at her like she was crazy when she wanted halter tops and shorts when it was snowing outside.

She pressed her hand on the large wooden door that was already open and breathed in the pungent smell of horses and manure. Everything smelled so different here than it did in Brooklyn, New York. But then, Amber wasn't sure she'd ever inhaled air that wasn't laced with factory smoke and carbon monoxide.

"Hello?" she called out, edging into the barn and looking warily into the nearest stall at the giant beast that glanced her way, looking bored. "Do you know where Jordan is?" she whispered to the horse.

Amber had never seen a horse in real life, and this creature was a lot bigger than she thought horses were supposed to be.

"Hello," a man said, walking around the horse, who continued staring at her with incredibly large brown eyes. "Beautiful creature, don't you think?"

Amber licked her lips, which were suddenly too dry as she took in the man she'd met while exploring the island. For a moment she wasn't sure of the meaning of his words. He stroked the side of the horse, his hands large, with long fingers and nails cut short. She imagined his touch would be rough, yet calming and confident. There was something about this guy, with his black hair pulled back in a ponytail and his relaxed, roguish stance, that screamed trouble in the worst of all possible ways. Yet he was compelling. Granted, annoying, too. But there was enough of a challenge in his eyes that she prayed he would spar a bit better this time without running away.

"I don't know a lot about horses," she admitted.

"I'm sure you know when something is beautiful." There was a drawl in his tone that was too soothing to be fake. Yet she couldn't grasp why someone who sounded like they were from the Wild Wild West would be across the world on this island.

"What one person might view as appealing another might find terrifying," she countered.

"True," he said, turning his attention to the horse. "Bess here isn't terrifying. She and I are becoming quick friends."

Amber almost asked why they were only now becoming friends, but decided she'd be smarter to focus on her job and not provoke a conversation with this man. He had trouble written all over him.

"Are you the only one out here?" she asked.

"Not anymore," he said, leaving the horse and approaching her.

Amber instinctively took a step backward. He took her arm, though, appearing indifferent to her balking, and guided her past the horse and deeper into the smelly barn.

"Now, tell me you don't find him gorgeous," he said, stopping in front of the last stall.

It was dark this far back in the barn, the only light streaming in through the two large doors opened at the other end. Amber jumped when the black creature in the stall lifted his head, meeting her gaze with a defiant look that gave her chills.

"Oh, my," she whispered, unable to stop herself as she stared at the large, sleek-looking, inky black horse.

"Put your hand here." The man reached over her shoulder, pressing his hand against the side of the horse. "Then calm, gentle strokes."

Amber was overly aware of the man touching her backside, his hard body like a steel wall pressing against her shoulder and her hip. She shifted her attention from the horse to his arm, noticing dark hairs on his forearm that she bet would tickle her flesh if he pulled her into his arms.

"Like this," he said, his soft baritone next to her ear when he took her hand in his and placed it on the horse. He kept his hand over hers, stroking the horse with her hand. "That's how you make friends."

She wondered if he meant with the horse or with her. "What's his name?" Her voice cracked and she cleared her throat, telling herself she should pull her hand from underneath his, but her body ignored the instructions. She wasn't about to show any interest by asking his name again.

"I don't know but can find out. Would you like to ride him?"

"I've never been on a horse," she admitted easily enough. She wasn't sure the thought appealed to her.

"We need to change that. It's obvious he likes you. I'll teach you to ride."

"I don't think—" she began, not seeing how riding a horse would help her to be a better social organizer.

"Don't run from something because you don't know about it," he told her, tightening his hand over hers when she tried pulling free. "Especially when your fascination is so apparent."

Amber yanked her hand from under his. The quick movement must have startled the horse, or possibly annoyed him. He raised his head, looking down at her with very large eyes. The whites of his eyes in contrast to his black coat made him look exceptionally pissed. She jumped back and the man wrapped his arms around her, stilling her.

God, the dark hairs on his forearms did tickle her, sending a rush of excitement over her body, while goose bumps traveled across her flesh just as quickly.

"Shh," he whispered in her ear. "What most people don't understand about horses is their intelligence level. Believe me, he reads you as well as I do. He just registered your fear when he moved, which confused him. And I'm sure he detects how aroused you are at the moment, too, which probably is annoying him because he's stuck back here without a female horse to enjoy."

"How dare you," she snapped, struggling to get out of his arms.

The horse moved in his stall, stepping back and forth while making a sound in his throat. Amber wasn't sure if the horse was agreeing with the dark stranger, who pressed against her backside, or announcing him an ass.

"Would you rather I lie to you?" he whispered in her ear, keeping one arm tightly around her waist while moving his other hand up her front. His fingers grazed over her breasts, causing them to swell, suddenly feeling heavy with need, while her nipples puckered painfully. "Would you not be interested in knowing how the first time I saw you I turned harder than stone? Before I said a word to you I ached to touch you, learn every inch of your body while exploring your mind at the same time."

There was something interesting about his vocal inflection. He held on to a drawl, reminding her of a ranch hand who possibly spent his entire life around horses. But there was a New England, almost aristocratic edge to his words, too, barely detectable but coming through more noticeably as he whispered in her ear, torturing her flesh. He cupped her chin, turning her head so she was able to see how deep his dark blue eyes were. She swore if she stared into them long enough, she'd understand the very depths of his soul. One thing she noticed, as she slipped deeper into his compelling gaze, was there was more to this man than just a hired hand who lived his life caring for animals and doing menial labor.

It crossed her mind that her month on this island, carrying out a job she knew damn good and well she wasn't qualified to do, might be more pleasant if she consented to a sordid affair with one of the servants. Especially one like this man with his powerful body and incredibly smooth way of speaking and manipulating her body so it was ready and eager to agree with his proposition before her mind could even wrap around it.

"No, I'm not interested in knowing that," she said, the words slipping out of her mouth from years of habit kicking in. It was second nature to turn down the advances of any man who came on to her strong and fast. Any man like that was a guaranteed heartache. She reminded herself firmly that she didn't have time for this, especially over the next month while she tried pulling off a job description that was more foreign to her than the damn horse who watched them with vague interest. Pulling off this job would give her enough money to put a down payment on a home, to finally own something. She ached to create roots, lay down a foundation, and quit throwing money away on rent.

Amber twisted in his arms, and was rewarded for her efforts when his cock stretched against her hip, hardening and throbbing while he continued staring down at her with his compelling blue eyes.

"I'll let you go," he informed her, although he continued holding her firmly against him, cupping her chin while his finger moved slowly along the length of her jawbone. "But first tell me why you're lying to me."

Amber smiled. Maybe being a social organizer, pretending to know what filthy rich people did for fun, was grossly out of her league. But handling this ranch hand, this rough and ready man, was definitely something she knew how to do. Just knowing he would willingly bend her over and fuck her right here and now should have her beating his chest, scratching and clawing until he let her go, and then running as far away from him as she could get. It was her pride, though, that had her relaxing in his arms, continuing to hold his gaze, and going as far as to lick her lips, although when he had her this close to panting, she couldn't moisten her dry lips.

"I'm not lying. Just because you've successfully discovered I'm a healthy young woman who is capable of sexual reaction doesn't mean I'm like that horse watching us. I wouldn't fuck someone simply because they're presented to me." She licked her lips again, liking how he watched her, searching her face and then settling his gaze on her mouth while she continued speaking. "I'm sure your horses are as intelligent as you profess, but what makes them different than most people—or at least, from me—is in order for me to fuck someone, the attraction must be mutual, not just physically, but also emotionally. Now, let me go, please."

He released her, although he didn't look appropriately chastised. Instead, when he lifted his focus from her mouth to her eyes, crossing his arms over his chest, the flicker she caught in his gaze created butterflies in her tummy. She held her breath, watching his lips part, and realized that, although free to walk away from him, she anxiously waited to hear what he would say next.

"Meet me here tonight at midnight and I'll prove to you I can stimulate your mind as well as your body." He walked away from her for the second time, while she memorized the view of his tall, muscular backside and focused on it even after he disappeared from her view.

2

Jordan turned his thoughts to his grandfather. It was the best way to make his hard-on disappear so he could walk through the castle and not risk any of the staff catching him with a raging boner. He pulled open the heavy door leading into the back hallway, immediately dragging the smells from the kitchen into his lungs.

"Excuse me, folks. Would you mind bringing me coffee and something to snack on," he asked, his announcement causing the two people in the kitchen, an older man and woman, to jump to attention.

"Yes, Mr. Anton," the older woman said, her Irish brogue a friendly sound as she quickly wiped her plump hands on her apron. "Would you like me to push supper back until later this evening? Or does seven P.M. suit you, sir?"

Jordan didn't pause, heading across the kitchen and toward the hallway to the stairs. "Whatever you arrange with my social organizer is fine with me," he called over his shoulder. "Coffee would be great. Maybe a shot of whiskey." He hit the stairs before suggesting they bring him the entire bottle.

He would give this much to his grandfather, he thought, running his hand over the smooth wooden banister while he headed up the wide staircase to the second floor. The castle was impressive as hell. Only Grandfather Anton would be able to sniff out a rock like this island and turn it into such a captivating paradise. He reminded himself it was still a prison, Grandfather's idea of an isolated sanctuary where he could take his time and convince Jordan to behave the way Grandfather Anton believed Jordan should.

Pausing at the top of the stairs, he took in the long, wide hallway before him. There were a handful of closed doors on either side, spread apart enough from each other that very large, heavy-looking old pictures didn't clutter the walls. The floor was carpeted in a thick forest green, which possibly covered an old stone floor that Jordan would have found more appealing and appropriate in keeping with the natural setting of the old castle. He walked down the hallway, aware that his footsteps didn't make a sound, and how easy that would make it for someone to leave his room at any time and not make their presence known to anyone else in the castle.

Jordan's room was the first door on the left, the room he'd chosen for himself after inspecting each of them this morning. Letting himself in, he felt the change of temperature quickly from having left his balcony doors open earlier. Leaving his bedroom door ajar for the servant, he walked across the room, which was large enough to be a studio apartment and not just a bedroom. The king-sized bed would look a hell of a lot more appealing if he weren't planning on sleeping in it alone tonight. Pausing at the large mahogany desk that faced the open doors to the balcony, Jordan booted up his laptop, which he'd placed in front of the computer already provided for him in the room. There was no way he'd use that thing. Jordan wouldn't put it past Grandfather Anton to install tracking devices on it. There were cameras all over the island. So far, the barn seemed the only place not heavily monitored. He looked up at the piece of duct tape on the ceiling, covering the security camera discreetly hidden there. It was still in place. Jordan had agreed to spend the next month here. He hadn't agreed to having his every action monitored and scrutinized while here.

He pressed the power button at the same time someone rapped on the door. "Sir? Your coffee?" the older woman with the Irish brogue announced herself.

"Come in." He sat down, aching to tell her she could drop the formalities around him. Jordan had lived two years now without being treated like he was royalty, and he hadn't missed it a bit. "Will you set it on the table, please?"

She gave him a curious look before placing the large round tray, which couldn't be light but that she handled with ease, where he asked. "Miss Stone confirmed dinner at seven," she offered, pouring coffee from a white porcelain pot into a tall, slender matching cup and then bringing it to him. "She's approved a delicious menu. Your grandfather arranged for the kitchen to be generously stocked. I know you'll love the meals she's lined up during your stay here. Miss Stone is a charming young lady, wouldn't you say?"

One thing Jordan had learned at an early age, growing up in a house staffed with more servants than there was family, was that servants seldom rambled on with idle conversation because they were bored.

"I didn't catch your name," he said, ignoring her question, although unsure that charming would be the best adjective to describe Miss Stone. Seductive, alluring, and most definitely a challenge he meant to conquer came to mind. The staff wouldn't gather information from him to use to piece together a soap opera over the next few weeks while they watched him being forced into an engagement he had no intention of being part of. More than likely there was already speculation on whether he'd fuck both women while he was supposed to be here to get to know only one of them.

"Forgive me, Master Anton. Everyone calls me Cook. Your grandfather has called me Cook for as long as I remember. My given name is Anne Marie Francis Margaret McGillicutty. When I worked for him in Arizona the nickname came about and it's stuck ever since."

"I see why he calls you Cook." Jordan grinned and noticed color wash over her plump cheeks.

"Now, if you don't look just like your grandfather did twenty years ago," she chirped, winking at Jordan.

It would have been more like forty years, since his grandfather was seventy and Jordan was thirty, but he didn't correct her math.

Cook moved to Jordan's bed, fluffing pillows. "And I hear we're expecting royalty tomorrow. Do you know what time we're to be receiving your pretty fiancée?"

The icons on Jordan's laptop appeared on the screen as Jordan considered correcting Cook. Part of his grandfather's stipulations were that everyone believe he'd met Princess Tory Alixandre prior to coming to this island, and Jordan wouldn't be the first one to break the rules.

"I believe she'll be here at noon," he said, although he would bet Cook already knew that. "Do you have her wing ready for her?"

Part of the conditions Princess Tory insisted on while staying on this island were that she have private quarters, and that her servants have rooms next to hers.

"All the rooms were cleaned before we arrived but I haven't inspected her wing yet. It will be ready before she gets here. We just arrived here ourselves yesterday," Cook added quickly, returning to the tray she'd brought up. Her back was to Jordan as plates clinked against each other. "So how did the two of you meet?" she asked, apparently planning on pressing Jordan for as much personal information as she could.

"On an island." He grinned at her again when she stopped, facing him with a plate in hand, and let out a delighted sigh as she misinterpreted his answer. "How many servants are here?" He turned the conversation once again and decided at the same time he was ready for Cook to leave.

"If that isn't the most romantic thing," Cook cooed, placing condiments next to a plate with a sandwich and fresh fruit. "And there is just me and Jesse here but don't you worry. Oh, and Sara. They say she's been on this island for years."

"That's a very small staff of servants."

"It's how your grandfather wishes it," she said, pushing out her ample chest. Cook didn't meet his gaze but instead surveyed his food and then turned her attention to his room. Walking over to the open doors to the balcony, she closed them and then searched for her next task. "The Princess is bringing her own servants who I'm told will take care of her wing while she's here. I've got the kitchen and the cleaning and Jesse will help me when I need it as well as chauffeur and maintain the yard."

"Chauffeur? Where would he drive anyone? There isn't a town or anyone else on this island, for that matter."

"If you and your lovely fiancée want a drive to enjoy the island, Jesse will do it," she insisted.

"I'll keep that in mind." He thought about asking who was in charge of the horses but was ready for Cook to leave. She would stay and answer his questions all day, all the while searching for more information, if he didn't dismiss her.

It was his turn to get some answers, and for that, he needed to be alone. "And I'll be downstairs promptly at seven," he told her, turning to his laptop.

Cook took the hint, picking up the tray and heading to the

door. Jordan glanced over his shoulder when she closed it behind her, sighing and reaching for his coffee.

Grabbing his cell phone as it rang, he clicked the icon on his computer to pull up his chat program.

"Jordan, how are you?"

"Aunt Penelope, what time is it there?" He glanced at the clock in the corner of his screen and tried subtracting the hours.

"It's the middle of the afternoon but I wanted to make sure you arrived safely. So far all of my hands are working fine. But they don't know how long you're going to be gone. Are you sure you can go through with this?" Aunt Penelope understood him more than his own mother, and even though he and his aunt weren't related by blood, he often felt a closer kindred spirit to her than he did to his mom.

"We've been through this, Aunt P. I wish you'd quit worrying. And I arrived here fine. It's a gorgeous island. You'd love it here."

"I don't know about that." Her laughter sounded tense. "It's way too far from my ranch."

Jordan imagined her standing in the living room, possibly looking out her front window, her hair tousled, and wearing the sweatpants she always wore. His aunt was a pretty woman, although after her divorce she quit trying to act the part. It would take a while for her to bounce back after forcing a husband out the door for his continued infidelity.

"That it is," he agreed, enjoying hearing her voice. "You shouldn't worry about the hired help, though. I can keep up with the books if you scan everything into the file I set up for you before I left. It will be just like setting them on my desk. And I'm fine. The month will fly. You know that. I'll be back in no time. Don't you dare give my job to someone else."

"If you see out the month, the conditions are you get married to royalty. And somehow I don't see a Sicilian princess enjoying living out her days here. If you don't marry her, you have to go to work for Grandfather," she added, the bitterness in her voice apparent. The moment she'd learned of the ultimatum, she'd hated Grandfather for it. "Coming back here isn't part of the deal."

"Don't hire someone to replace me, Aunt P. Please," he stressed. "I've got a month to figure out the best way out of this. And worst-case scenario, I walk away from all of the family."

"You won't walk away from them for me, Jordan. I won't allow it."

"You're getting yourself all upset and I told you not to worry. Don't you dare let that ranch fall apart while I'm gone. You can't afford to pay me overtime to get it back on its feet when I get back," he emphasized, intentionally snapping at her. "And you know damn good and well I wouldn't be walking away from my family. I plan on coming home to my family in a month. Now, get in the Suburban and drive around the ranch. Keep your appearances up and that will be enough to keep everyone working like they always do."

Her laughter was melodic yet sad. "There are times when I wonder how much Anton blood actually runs in your veins, Jordan."

"Flattery will get you everywhere, Aunt P," he told her, smiling while he logged in to his chat program and then watched the offline messages appear on his screen. "Now, do as I say. You know you can call with any questions or problems. We'll get through this. I'm going to get some work done before the fireworks start tomorrow."

"Okay," she said, yawning in his ear.

"Have a good evening, Aunt P. I'm here to tell you, tomorrow isn't that bad." Technically, he was a day ahead of her and made light of the difference in time zones between the island and Montana.

"Good night," she said, not laughing at his joke, and then hung up the phone.

Jordan blew out a breath. Putting his phone next to his keyboard, he stared at the sandwich Cook had brought him. He was no longer in the mood for it. In the back of his head, he'd known over the years since he reached adulthood that it was a matter of time before the Antons would disown him. Regardless of his last name, or how thick his blood was or wasn't, he couldn't play by Grandfather's rules. And Grandfather didn't allow any family member to not adhere to the reputation he believed all Antons should uphold.

Jordan stared at his offline messages, three of them from two ranch hands and a lady in town that he occasionally spent time with. He hadn't told her he was going to be gone for a month. Running his fingers through his hair he yanked out his ponytail holder and stood, combing his hair with his fingers and redoing his ponytail.

Opening the doors that Cook had closed to his balcony, he ignored the chime of his laptop informing him he'd received an instant message, and stepped out onto the balcony. Jordan's family wasn't perfect. Hell, they were worse than most of the soap operas his aunt watched. But they were his family.

"Figure it out, Anton," he grumbled under his breath, leaning on the edge of the sturdy railing and staring at the large yard in front of the castle and beyond, where the drive disappeared amidst rocks and trees leading to the ocean.

He straightened, staring beyond to the endless ocean that faded into the sky. Maybe he would have been smarter to tell Grandfather Anton to get the hell out of Jordan's life and refuse to come here. The ranch had been about to go under when Jordan moved in with his aunt two years ago. They'd worked hard to overcome the debts his Uncle Jorge had created. And Jordan was proud of how far they'd come. The ranch wouldn't make his aunt rich, but it was her land, free and clear, and today it was breaking even.

Jordan couldn't help thinking that their success was a good part of the reason Grandfather suddenly became interested in his life. That and his mother, who loved her country club lifestyle, ached to brag about her son the way other members of his family bragged about his cousins. She prayed daily, Jordan didn't have any doubt, that he would follow his father's footsteps and enter into the family business.

Jordan couldn't see himself ever donning a suit and sitting behind a desk deciding which business would go under and which would make it another year. The family business disgusted him.

His computer chimed again and Jordan entered his bedroom, shifting his thoughts to the compelling Miss Amber Stone. He needed to Google her, learn what he could about his social organizer. Grandfather would have hired the best, and if he intentionally chose her because of her looks, Jordan would soon learn the truth to that. He wouldn't put it past Grandfather to arrange for Jordan to spend time with a young woman on the pretense of marriage, but then throw a gorgeous employee into the loop to challenge Jordan's scruples.

Jordan sipped his coffee, knowing he'd have to get an appetite for the sandwich later. He wouldn't be going down to dinner at seven. Miss Amber Stone would be more likely to show up at midnight if she didn't know who he was. He'd rather seduce her anonymously. Just thinking about her smooth skin, her petite, curvy body, and all of that long, thick hair drained all blood from his brain to his cock. He stared at his laptop screen, not focusing on it, as he imagined how he'd take Amber in the barn later tonight.

Chat boxes now covered his screen and he studied them, noting the time as he did. He would wait an hour and then let Cook know he wouldn't be down for dinner. The most recent chat box, which was front and center on his screen and above the others, grabbed his attention. The name on the top of the box was *Anton_Admin2000*.

"Crap," he complained, reading the message in the box.

Your Grandfather wishes you to call at your earliest convenience.

Jordan X'd out the box, read the instant messages from the others, and X'd out each of those. Two of his workhands sent messages from their phones, both comments about the ranch. He grabbed a small notepad from his laptop case, jotted down a few notes so he could address their concerns later, and then grabbed his phone.

Mary Rhodes was a good lady, and he shouldn't ignore her message. They were casual lovers at best, and right now he had bigger fish to fry. That is, if he could catch them first. He X'd out her box after reading the message she'd sent from her phone as well. More than likely she instant messaged her friends from her phone while sitting at the combination diner, country store, and post office in Big Timber. He would have told Mary he'd be gone for a month, but Mary saw most of the ranchers and a lot of the ranch hands. Asking her not to mention that Aunt Penelope's ranch-hand supervisor would be gone for a month might mean asking more than she could do.

Taking his phone to the comfortable-looking chair alongside his large bed, he relaxed, putting thoughts of Mary out of his head. It had been a couple of months since he'd taken her out, and if she were hinting for another date, he would avoid answering her for as long as possible. The news would get out soon enough that he wasn't on Big Sky Ranch.

Placing the dreaded call, Jordan set the notepad and pen on the table next to the chair and then put his phone on speaker.

"Anton Enterprises," the secretary answered on the second ring.

"Pierre Anton, please."

"Mr. Anton doesn't take phone calls," she informed him, her voice clipped and indifferent.

"This is his grandson, Jordan Anton."

"One moment, please," she told him, using the same tone.

Jordan sat through the silent hold, his thoughts again drifting to Amber Stone. What was she doing right now?

"Pierre Anton's office." Grandfather Anton's right-hand man and primary bully, Pablo Diego, spoke with a husky voice that broke up through the speakerphone.

"Pablo, it's Jordan. I received your message on the computer."

Pablo didn't answer, more than likely watching Jordan's grandfather, who'd probably raised his hand for silence. Grandfather enjoyed making anyone around him wait for an audience. It was all about the power trip.

Jordan's thoughts wandered as he shifted his attention to his closed bedroom door. It had been longer than he remembered since he'd sat in the middle of the afternoon and done nothing, as he was doing now. And he didn't like it. Amber didn't strike him as the kind of woman accustomed to doing nothing either. She was a working woman, more than likely having built her reputation by putting in long hours and appearing tireless at all times. Would she exert the same energy sexually? What he'd seen of her so far—her craving to explore, boldness that covered her shyness—had him dying to find out.

"Jordan, my boy, how are you doing?" Grandfather Anton's voice boomed through the speakerphone.

Jordan tapped the button on the side of his phone to turn down the volume, just the sound of his grandfather's voice reminding him of the seriousness of the game he was about to play. Even relaxed and jovial, the power in Grandfather's tone wasn't missed. Jordan wondered how terrible his life would be if he just allowed the old man to disown him.

"Doing good," he answered easily. "The chartered flight from New Zealand went smoothly. You hired a good pilot."

"Of course," Grandfather said, as if the thought of anyone on his staff being less than perfect had never crossed his mind. "And Miss Stone, what do you think of her?"

"Miss Stone?" Jordan asked, deciding at that moment that he would allow his time with her today and tonight to be off the clock. He would also learn if there were security cameras along the paths on the island. "Is she here?"

"She arrived on the island a few hours ago, this morning your time."

"I'll seek her out, then," Jordan offered.

"Good. If she doesn't meet your needs for a social organizer I'll need to know within the next twenty-four hours. Princess Tory arrives tomorrow afternoon and you'll need to give a good show for Her Highness." Grandfather's tone lowered, the joviality disappearing when he continued. "Jordan, this is the chance of a lifetime, boy. I hope you see that I wouldn't do this for any of my other grandchildren."

Then why him? He wouldn't ask. What was the point?

"Your mother is heartbroken that you're throwing away your Harvard degree playing ranch hand. You're thirty years old, my boy. It's time to grow up."

"I'm grown up, Grandfather."

Grandfather's laugh bordered on dangerous. "Don't cross me, Jordan. Anyone else in the family would kill for this opportunity. The Alixandre family is one of the most prominent Sicilian families. Their royal line dates back centuries."

In other words, Grandfather wanted to marry Jordan into the Mob.

"Your marriage to Princess Tory will unite two of the most powerful families on this planet," Grandfather boasted, as if the event were already sealed. "I want to hear from you immediately after you've met Princess Tory. Keep an open mind, boy. You already know she's gorgeous. Take your time getting to know her and understand she will probably be terrified flying to an island away from her home to meet a man who very likely will be her future husband."

"I know how to be a gentleman," Jordan said, barely able to keep the disgust out of his voice. They weren't in the Dark Ages. Arranged marriages were a thing of the past. And in spite of Grandfather stressing that all of this was his and Princess Tory's choice, Jordan wouldn't be surprised to learn Grandfather had already arranged where the wedding would be held.

"I'll also be curious to hear what you think of Miss Stone," Grandfather added.

Jordan frowned. "I'm sure she'll be very capable of doing her job," he said, trying to figure out Grandfather's interest in the social organizer.

"I want to know what you think of her as a woman," Grandfather stressed.

"Why would it matter?"

"Because she is equally as beautiful as Princess Tory." Grandfather didn't elaborate. "I've got to go, my boy. There are people waiting." The line went dead without another word.

Jordan stared at his cell phone for a moment and pondered his grandfather's game. He had said both women were equally beautiful. Did Grandfather believe Jordan might fall for Amber over Princess Tory?

Dropping his phone on top of his notepad, Jordan stood slowly and stretched. Grandfather would be grossly disturbed to discover he didn't know his grandson as well as he thought he did. Jordan had no intention of falling for any woman. Not here on the island or on the ranch. But that didn't mean he wouldn't take the time to get to know both women better. It was Grandfather's idea to put him on this island with two women.

The terms of the agreement didn't state he *had* to marry at the end of the month.

Jordan wasn't going to marry anyone. All he needed to figure out was a way to get out of the alternative if he didn't. There was no way he could work for Anton Enterprises. His grandfather's corporation specialized in buying out businesses and then closing their doors, dismantling them and creating new, more organized companies that answered exclusively to Anton Enterprises. No way would Jordan spend the rest of his life putting hardworking people out of jobs.

Cook was obviously put out when Jordan informed her he wouldn't be down for dinner. After entering his room again, loitering way too long, and leaving him with a formal five-course meal on a round table that a gentleman named Jesse set up for her, Jordan was alone again. And restless.

There was no cable TV on the island, but Jordan found an extensive DVD collection under a large, flat-screen TV attached to the wall in an adjoining room to his. There was a billiards table, too. He wasted a few hours in the room before wandering outside his quarters, taking a different path through the castle and exploring a bit. The architecture was amazing, every room incredibly decorated and full of personality. It was impossible to believe there were only five people on the island right now including a staff of only three. A large staff had to have maintained this castle at one time and Jordan wondered where they were now.

A back staircase took him to a wing he hadn't explored before. It appeared to be part of the castle used strictly to entertain. He found very large stained-glass doors that were heavy as hell, but after pulling one of them open, Jordan stared into a ballroom that made him swear he'd just been swept back to a previous century. Incredible chandeliers, each as large as a small car, hung well over his head. If he were more of a romantic, he could probably induce his imagination into seeing many couples swinging around the dance floor, moving to the music of some accomplished quartet.

There were other rooms outside the ballroom, a coatroom about the size of his bedroom upstairs, and a kitchen that would make Aunt Penelope turn green with envy. There was also a foyer, its marble floors so shiny and dust free he started wondering at the accuracy of Cook's statement when she informed him there were only three servants on staff here.

The courtyard outside had so many flowers growing in large pots the air was filled with their perfumed scent. It was make-out central out here; with so many secluded locations, bordered with small trees and flower gardens, a couple could disappear and never be spotted by mingling guests. Something to keep in mind, he pointed out to himself. Especially if his social organizer decided to take advantage of all the castle had to offer.

It was a decent hike past the courtyard and around to the backside of the castle. The old stone barn was an ominous shadow in the darkness. But the scented air, mixed with the smell of salt from the ocean and various fragrances from tropical plants surrounding him, created a surreal atmosphere. Throw in some fog and it would be the ultimate setting for seduction and lovemaking.

Jordan always thought it would be hot as hell to fuck a willing lady in the barn back at the ranch. Unfortunately, he didn't know many willing ladies. Mary and he had had sex a couple times over the two years he'd lived there, but both times at her apartment. Mary dreamed of big cities, yet was born and raised in a small town. She had no desire to see the wonders of his ranch, or any other ranch in the area.

Pulling his cell phone off the clasp on his belt, he checked the time. It was barely eleven; he had a good hour before

Amber would show up. And he bet she'd be there. Amber was as willing to seek out an adventure as he was. He guessed she came here for more reasons than a great-paying job. Realizing he'd forgotten to Google her, he made a mental note to do that as soon as he returned to his room.

"How are you doing, girl?" Jordan asked the mare in the first stall as he entered the barn.

Not bothering with lights, he moved through the large structure, stroking the brown filly's neck as he made soothing sounds and breathed in the familiar smells that reminded him of home. His grandfather would have a stroke if he learned Jordan was more comfortable in the barn than he was in the exquisite castle.

"Who's there?" a woman demanded behind him as he moved past the empty stalls to the large back horse in the corner.

Jordan squinted in the darkness, glancing in the direction of the unfamiliar voice. "I'm here. Who are you?" he asked the darkness enveloped around him.

Light flooded the barn, blinding him momentarily while the large horse behind him whinnied his complaint.

"It's okay, boy," Jordan assured him, moving to the stall and speaking quietly to the horse while searching the barn. "Apparently our company would rather watch than be seen," he added, loud enough that whoever was in the barn with him would hear.

"What is there to watch?" the woman asked, her strong Kiwi accent strict and confident.

Jordan spotted the woman standing at the end of the stalls. "There you are," he said, smiling at her. "Do you tend to the horses?"

"Among other things." She tilted her head, brushed a wisp of gray hair behind her ear and hooked her thumb in the belt loop of her jeans.

Something about the woman immediately made him think

of Aunt Penelope. He didn't like the thought that she was on her own on the ranch right now, and possibly could be put in a similar situation to this woman at the moment.

"I'm Jordan Anton," he offered, walking to her with his hand extended. "And you are?"

"Sara, Sara Bird. This is my island."

3

Amber fisted her hands at her hips, fighting the urge to march right back to the castle. Outrage steamed inside her, making her shake, but she held her ground. Standing outside the barn and listening to the servant talk to Jordan Anton pissed her off more the longer she listened. How dare the rogue lead her to believe he was one of the hired help. And then proposition her.

She wasn't sure if she was angrier with his deception, or the fact that she possibly would have fucked him. Or possibly it was both that pissed her off. Shifting her weight, she listened to Sara talk, finding herself drawn into the friendly accent, as well as to the history lesson she offered Jordan on the castle and the island. Another time, once she'd calmed down, Amber would seek Sara out and learn even more about the history of this place. Never in her life had she dreamed such an incredible castle, which was apparently as old as it appeared, actually existed anywhere other than in fairy tales and movies.

"What's the matter, Bess?" Sara asked, her tone softening as she made clucking sounds. "You're edgy, girl."

"Maybe she's telling us we have company." Jordan stepped

outside the barn, apparently closer to the door than Amber had realized, and smiled at her. "There you are," he said, grabbing her arm and dragging her into the lit barn. "Sara, meet my friend, Amber."

"Are both of you going to ride?" Sara sized Amber up with a quick look. "Bess is easy enough, but Lord is spirited. He'll let me ride him but I won't be responsible if he throws you."

"I don't ride horses," Amber stammered, trying to pull her hand free from Jordan's firm grip.

He wouldn't let go. "I admit I inspected the barn thoroughly earlier today. I was impressed with your saddles. We'll ride Lord together."

"I don't know," Sara said, frowning as Jordan marched farther into the barn, still holding onto Amber. "If you're not a really good rider."

"I am," Jordan said without hesitating.

"Lord doesn't always take well to strangers," Sara continued.

"We've already become great friends." Jordan let go of Amber's hand and lifted a heavy-looking saddle into his arms.

"Enjoy your ride," Amber stated, marching out of the barn. "Sara, it was very nice meeting you. I look forward to more time."

She didn't even realize Jordan had put the saddle down. "Not so quick, my dear," he growled, wrapping his arm around her waist and pulling her against him. "Tell me," he whispered. "Are you afraid of the horse, or of me?"

"Neither!" she hissed, fighting to twist in his arms, but stilling when Sara watched them curiously. "I don't care for deception," she whispered, tilting her head to glare into his incredibly handsome, chiseled features.

His amused grin outraged her even further. Worse yet, it hit her with annoying clarity that as much as she ached to slap that pompous smile off his face, she couldn't. For the next month, she would be working for Jordan Anton, arranging his social life for him and his fiancée.

"Good night, Mr. Anton," she began.

"Sara, would you mind saddling up Lord for us?" Jordan asked without looking over his shoulder. Instead, he took Amber by the arm, walking her out of the barn. "Give me a minute to assure Miss Stone that I'm an expert rider and that she's in good hands with me."

Amber wasn't sure if Sara snorted her disgust or chuckled in amusement. Either way, she disappeared into the barn while Jordan led Amber by the arm under the moonlight.

"Why the sudden change of heart?" he asked after walking her a short ways from the barn. "You came here to see me and now you wish to leave?"

"When I came down here I didn't know you were Jordan Anton," she accused, yanking her arm from his grip and then hugging herself, as she squared off and faced him.

"So if I were a different man you'd saddle right up with me? Is that what I'm hearing here?" He still had that annoyingly disgusting, smug look on his face.

"I'm saying you intentionally did not tell me who you are," she snapped, but then threw her hands up in the air. "This conversation is pointless. Enjoy your horse ride because I assure you that will be all you're riding tonight."

"If that's the case, then you shouldn't have any problem agreeing to just going on a horseback ride with me," he answered, his tone too smooth, too sure of himself.

Knowing who he was didn't change her opinion of him, Amber decided. Jordan Anton was cocky and arrogant and probably believed he could do no wrong—obviously to the point where he didn't mind playing with people. Amber never did like people like that. It sucked that he was so drop-dead gorgeous. His good looks were wasted on a shallow, spoiled rich boy. She understood him all too well.

"I wouldn't go horseback riding with you no matter who you are," she told him honestly. At the same time, she gave herself a strict reminder that it was imperative she end this potentially disastrous evening on a smooth note. And if there was one thing she was really bad at doing, it was sucking up to people. Taking a slow soothing breath, she offered what she hoped was a believable smile. "Enjoy yourself, though," she told him, trying once again to retreat to the castle.

This time Jordan didn't grab her arm. Instead, while Sara led the giant black horse out of the barn, Jordan moved closer to Amber, brushing his fingertips over her bare shoulder.

His tone lost its cockiness. "If you won't ride with me because I didn't take the time to properly introduce myself earlier, then please allow me to do so now."

"That has nothing to do with it." She held her head high and still barely stood taller than his shoulder. Looking at him straight on gave her a delicious view of his Adam's apple. His black hair was pulled back in a ponytail that curled against his collar behind his neck. She imagined he'd look like a knight riding from his castle on that horse with his hair down. The image in her head damn near made her lose her train of thought. "I don't know anything about horses," she admitted, deciding the truth was her best argument here.

"You'll ride on the horse with me. All you have to do is trust me." With his final words, he scooped her off the ground.

Amber was taken off guard. Jordan's strong hands pressed underneath her breasts, and if that didn't shock her, being lifted into the air as if she weighed nothing and finding herself straddling the largest horse she'd ever seen in her life scared the crap out of her. Not that she'd seen many horses.

"Oh God!" she cried out, twisting over the smooth leather saddle.

The horse protested along with her, his large eyes growing even larger when he lifted his head, making a sound that couldn't be good. She didn't even know where to grab when it side-stepped, obviously as thrilled to have her on his back as she was to be there.

"It's okay, boy," Sara assured the horse, hurrying to the front of the animal.

Before she could grab the reins, though, Jordan slid onto the horse behind Amber, moving onto the creature with more grace and skill than Amber would have guessed a man his size capable of doing. He mounted the animal like he did it every day, adjusting himself behind her and then placing one large, warm hand over her belly while grabbing the leather straps in front of her with the other.

"I'll brush him down and feed him when we get back," Jordan informed Sara, and then made a clicking sound with his mouth.

The horse broke into a trot and they left the barn and Sara, whose parting words were impossible to hear.

Amber wasn't sure which was worse: The fact that she was on a horse and moving really fast, or that Jordan pressed her against his chest while his muscular thighs brushed against hers, his incredibly virile body touching her everywhere.

"Is this so bad?" His rich baritone brushed over her ear, caressing her oversensitive flesh while the wind blew in her face.

"I don't know." She was way out of her element.

When he started laughing, shifting behind her, Amber stiffened, certain she felt something hard and long press against her ass. Since she'd never been on a horse, and the smooth leather saddle was quickly making her rear numb every time the horse moved, she wasn't sure exactly what she was feeling. Not knowing her way around a man didn't sit well with her, and she would have said as much, except the land around them was flying past her; her eyes were watering as the cold, salt-filled air clung to her face; and a very large creature was between her legs.

"Amber."

"What?"

"Open your eyes."

She blinked, then dared move her hand from the death grip she held on the big round thing at the front of the saddle, and pressed her fingers to her cheeks to rub away the tears. She wasn't crying, but the air made them water.

"I'm fine," she told him, not knowing what else to say.

"Relax and you'll be even better," he assured her. "You're in very competent hands and trust me, everyone should experience the joy and freedom of riding a horse at least once in his life."

He sounded like he meant it.

"I appreciate your eagerness to share your passion."

Again he chuckled, the rich sound sending chills rushing over her body. "Relax," he whispered into her ear.

"I'm relaxed," she snapped, wondering if it was too soon to suggest they go back. "What? Why are we stopping?" She sounded breathless and stared anxiously at the darkness around them when the horse quit running.

Jordan adjusted himself again behind her, his long legs brushing against hers while he brought his arm up between her breasts and cupped her chin.

"We aren't stopping, just slowing the pace down a bit until you're comfortable in the saddle." His fingertips were calloused, like those of a man who worked with his hands all day.

"I think I'd be more comfortable if you weren't touching me everywhere."

Again that melodic baritone. Jordan's chuckle would be her undoing if all that roped muscle didn't push her over the edge first.

"So it's me who makes you nervous and not Lord? I can get off and walk alongside the two of you if you prefer."

"Don't you dare leave me on this thing alone," she snapped.

"Okay. Okay. But first things first. Lord is a male, superior and confident. Treat him as such, and the two of you will get along much better." He let go of her chin, dragging his fingers past her collarbone and once again between her breasts.

Amber shouldn't react to his touch, his body, anything about Jordan Anton. He was on this island to be with his fiancée. She blew out a breath, determined to get through this and chalk it up as insight into the nature of her employer for the next month.

"Take these," Jordan instructed, picking up the two leather straps that were attached to the horse's bridle. "They're the reins and are attached to his bridle. See?" he continued, placing the smooth straps in her hands and then keeping his warm, much larger hands around hers. "This is how you instruct Lord to go where you want him to go."

"I don't know where I want him to go," she said, looking between their legs at her hands inside his.

"That's okay. Lord can take us where he wishes."

"You're trusting a horse to guide us around this island in the dark?"

"I trust horses more than I do most people," he growled.

Amber stilled, pulling her attention from their hands and taking in their surroundings. She saw the beauty in the darkness for the first time since they'd left the barn. They were closer to the ocean than she realized. Dark waves lapped at a sandy beach as they moved along the edge of it. She breathed in the moist, salty night air, feeling it cling to her skin.

At the same time his comment registered in her mind, giving her insight into a man who was possibly a lot darker than he first came across.

"Why do you say that?" she asked, after a moment of riding in silence.

"Horses are intelligent. Trust me, Lord knows how to get back to his barn. He also senses how nervous you are and will keep at this pace until we allow him full run again."

"I'm not in any hurry to get to that." She admitted Lord's long neck and shiny black hair added to his beauty. And she didn't deny how beautiful he was; if only he weren't so incredibly big. When she shifted her attention to the ground, they were a good six or seven feet in the air. It would really hurt to fall off of him.

"Good," Jordan said, but didn't elaborate.

Amber suddenly worried he took her comment to mean she wasn't in a hurry to return to the barn. "Lord can walk back to the barn and I would be okay with that," she added, not wanting Jordan to think she was content being out here, alone with him, for hours.

Jordan didn't say anything but allowed the silence to drag out between them. Amber was acutely aware of the giant beast underneath her, of how her thigh muscles would probably ache like hell later from stretching her legs across Lord's massive back. More than that, she felt Jordan relax behind her, his body barely shifting to the motion of Lord as they walked along the beach, which seemed to go on forever.

She fondled the straps in her hand, feeling Jordan's hands relaxed against hers. He was a mystery, and admittedly not what she expected out of him so far. The rogue playboy attitude suited him perfectly. Although being unfaithful to a fiancée, or trying to be unfaithful, wasn't a characteristic limited to the rich. Amber couldn't even say how many married men had tried seducing her over the years, most of them very open about the fact they were simply looking for something on the side.

"Are you enjoying yourself?" he asked, breaking the silence.

He startled her out of her thoughts. "Oh," she said, letting the one word slip out without thought. "Sure. I guess."

"Not what you expected when you came to the barn tonight?"

Amber pondered her answer. "Obviously not," she admitted. Riding a horse, literally, had been the last thing on her mind. "I'm not sure what I expected."

"Oh really?" He didn't believe her. "I propositioned you, set up a meeting time, which you met, and you weren't sure what you expected?"

"I planned to honor the meeting, just to make it easier to work here over the next month."

"You believed having sex with me would make it easier to be here for a month?" That amused edge was back in his tone.

"That's not what I meant." She wasn't sure she liked how easily he got her dander up. Usually, she managed more control around men, no matter their walk of life.

"Then what did you mean?" He was rubbing his thumb along the outside of her hand, the slight movement proving more of a distraction than it should.

Not to mention roped muscle flexed against her legs, and if she relaxed just a bit, packed, steel chest muscle was searing hot across her back.

"I meant that if I hadn't shown up, running across you later would prove a distraction when I would need to focus my thoughts elsewhere."

"You would be wondering what you missed." He took what she said wrong and then continued running with it. "Or possibly you would worry I might stalk you, playing the rogue who would chase after the one who got away."

"You've got the rogue part right," she mumbled under her breath.

"What was that?" His body stiffened around her. "Is that what you think? That I'm no good?"

He grabbed her elbows, turning her and forcing her to slide in the saddle so that she struggled against his hold. Lord sidestepped, protesting loudly the struggle on his back.

"Is this a show to impress me and prove me wrong?" she demanded, sliding more until she panicked and clawed at the air when she was certain she'd fall off the horse and land hard on her back. "All you're doing is confirming what I already saw as the truth."

Jordan moved with a calm swiftness that stunned her. Lifting the leather reins with one hand, he clucked with his tongue and whispered to the horse. At the same time he brought his arm around Amber, pulling her against him. She still felt like she wasn't centered on the horse, with one leg hanging farther off and the other sticking out in the air on the other side. But letting go of his shirt, which she hadn't realized she'd grabbed ahold of, and pulling herself back onto the horse, seemed a feat she wasn't sure she could pull off at the moment. Instead, she hung precariously, staring at Jordan's perfectly chiseled features. It was no wonder his confidence level soared beyond anything anyone could tolerate. Not only was he damn near the best-looking man she'd ever laid eyes on, as he soothed the horse with words soft enough to calm a baby he prevented Amber from falling off the large animal and quite possibly severely hurting herself.

"I'm not the despicable man you believe me to be," he said after a moment, shifting his blue eyes that looked more gray at the moment to her. He penetrated her with a compelling stare, as if he possessed some hidden gift to reach deep into her soul and learn what made her tick simply by gazing deep into her eyes. It was unnerving at best and she blushed, feeling the heat spread over her flesh, traveling quickly until it swelled between her stretched legs. The seam of her jeans rubbed against her crotch, adding pressure to the swelling. Jordan studied her face, his features relaxing. "I'm honestly curious to know what action on my part convinced you I was no good."

"Oh, I don't know," she said, regaining her composure

when he placed the ball in her court. Certainly he wasn't so full of himself that he didn't realize how despicable his actions were just being out here with her. Especially when he continually implied something sexual could exist between them. "Possibly it could be you're hitting on the woman you hired to be your social organizer for you and your *fiancée*." She stressed the last word and let go of his shirt, reaching for the saddle and then forcing herself upright and forward once again on the horse. "How do we turn him around? I'm done with this charade."

"I didn't hire you, my grandfather did," Jordan said, his voice softening to a deadly tone.

If he weren't directly behind her and she could see his face, Amber would guess her accusation, as true as it might be, pissed him off.

"You didn't know you would have a social organizer while on the island with your *fiancée*?" Again she stressed the word.

"Yes, I knew. Grandfather arranged for you to be on this island when he made arrangements for me and Princess Tory to be here."

Amber noticed Jordan no longer held the reins. In fact, his arms weren't around her at all, but behind her. Other than his legs brushing against her outer thighs, he wasn't touching her at all.

She fingered the leather straps, wondering if maybe she shouldn't touch them either. Lord would respond to any tug from the straps, and she didn't know all the signals. He continued walking, his body moving underneath her like a warm, solid muscular wave flowing from between her legs to her tailbone and then back again. If anything, Lord's fluid, relaxed movement as he continued along the edge of the beach nearest a wall of tropical trees and foliage indicated he possibly understood the tension between the two humans on his back. Amber imagined the horse probably put them out of his head, instead focusing on whatever horses thought about as he enjoyed a nighttime stroll under the bright moon.

"How do you justify your behavior when you know the woman you're going to marry is showing up tomorrow?" More than once in her life Amber had been accused of being a bit too direct. But damn it, sometimes people needed a good smack upside the head for them to see the obvious.

She would wait out the silence, in no way offering him any help in coming up with a believable answer. As aware as she was that his arms were no longer around her, and in fact as little of him was touching her as possible, Amber wouldn't allow herself to regret no longer having all that roped muscle brushing against her. She would never claim to be perfect, but one thing she wasn't was a cheater. Jordan was sexy as hell, a distraction at the least, but he belonged to another woman.

"If you knew in your heart that I wasn't engaged, would you still find me despicable?"

His question threw her off guard, but only for a moment. "I'm not going to play games, Jordan. We're adults here. There is no subtracting a commitment you've made simply to offer convenience to one evening."

"There is nothing convenient about this conversation," he growled.

"I'm sorry if the truth hurts," she added, staring at her hands and running the leather straps between her fingers.

"The truth is more painful than you know." He was angry.

But that was too damn bad. His anger was his issue. She wouldn't enable him. Even when it hit her to change the subject, lighten the mood and talk about something less awkward and unpleasant, she bit her lip and said nothing.

"And I'll ask you one more time. Not for convenience's sake. You made it clear before we left for our ride our evening wouldn't be sexual. But if you believed I wasn't engaged, would you still find me despicable?"

"I never said you were despicable."

"Would you find me unappealing?"

"You're not unappealing."

"Good enough."

"What is good enough?" she demanded.

"It's actually not good enough, but for now it will have to do." Jordan's serious manner, his not touching her, and the matter-of-fact attitude he'd assumed with this conversation offered light to a side of him Amber hadn't seen when they'd first met. "Knowing your only reason for thinking me a rogue is your belief I have no scruples because of an engagement."

"And you think it's okay for someone to seek out something on the side?"

"Absolutely not."

"Then why are you trying to do it?"

Again he was silent. Amber blew out her frustration. This conversation wasn't going anywhere. If she did get him to admit his actions were wrong, it wouldn't stop his behavior. A cheater was a cheater.

"I think we should head back now," she said, no longer enjoying the ride. And oddly enough, for a few minutes there, she had to admit she was getting used to being on Lord's back.

"I'm not so sure." Jordan shifted behind her and then reached around her, taking the reins from her hand. "You seem to have relaxed since we left the barn. I'd hate for my unscrupulous behavior to ruin your opportunity to learn the love of riding horses."

She dared glance over her shoulder. Jordan stole her breath with the intensity of his expression. If she didn't know better, she'd swear she stared at a man hardened with conviction. It unnerved her. Amber always believed herself a good judge of character. Maybe she didn't have the education most had. Hell, she had less than most. But she had street smarts. And she could spot a criminal, or a shyster. Up until that moment she would have pegged Jordan a player who pouted over being called on it.

"We agreed prior to our ride that this night wouldn't be sexual, remember?" she said, studying his face as she spoke. There were so many layers to this man, a nature that went so far beyond his perfect bad-boy good looks. "Therefore your actions aren't unscrupulous."

"Just my desires?" he countered immediately.

"Well, that would depend on what your desires are," she whispered, tingles immediately rushing up her spine and spreading over her body when he moved slightly and his chest pressed into her back.

His face was too close to hers. And those eyes, now more gray than blue, probed so deeply inside her she felt the quickening in her gut as she lost herself in them.

Jordan's hands moved in front of her. There wasn't time to shift her attention and see what it was he was doing. Apparently he switched the reins from one hand to the other because his free hand moved to her face, gripping her chin and preventing her from looking away.

But when his mouth covered hers, searing her with a heat that robbed her ability to think, there wasn't any doubt what his desires were. He parted her lips with his tongue, tasting her and offering her a taste of a man hell-bent on a mission. Amber lost herself in the kiss, drowning in the power, determination, and raw, unbridled lust that filled her as his mouth moved over hers.

It took more effort than it should have to break off the kiss. And she hated herself for that, despised her weakness. The only thing she could do was strike out, release her frustration over tasting something she couldn't have, in the only way she knew how.

"Damn you!" she yelled, twisting and raising her fist at the same time. Anger peaked inside her and she aimed directly for his face.

4

Jordan moved fast enough to grab her fist, but the outrage burning in Amber's eyes turned them a compelling shade of violet. He'd never met a woman so willing to unleash her emotions. As easily as he had seen her lust and curiosity a moment before, he now saw her fury, and damn near felt it, too.

"Whoa, girl," he cautioned, gripping her fist in his hand while noting she was stronger than he had imagined. He exerted some effort to keep her from connecting with his face.

"Don't you talk to me like I'm some damn horse!" she hissed.

It didn't surprise him a bit when Lord didn't take kindly to her comment and tossed his head to the side, whinnying his complaint. Jordan held onto the reins firmly, knowing that, with much more of an outburst out of Amber, they'd be getting more of a ride than either one of them had anticipated this evening.

As quickly as Amber tried to strike him, she yanked her hand away from him. "Let go of me." She kept twisting, confusing Lord.

"Stop it, Amber," he ordered, releasing her and gripping the reins.

Amber didn't stop. In fact, she twisted away from him, putting her hands on the horse and pushing. "No. I will not stop it. Let me off this horse. I don't want anything to do with you, Mr. Anton. Let me off, now!"

Jordan had to choose: either grab her or control Lord. Sara hadn't been lying when she told him that Lord was spirited. Jordan sensed the power rising in the horse and knew the animal was very close to releasing it if they continued fighting in the saddle.

Amber wasn't a large woman. She wasn't tall and she weighed next to nothing. But she made up for it in attitude and feistiness. Jordan worried for a moment that he had more than he could handle. He had bonded with Lord earlier. Horses were enough of his life to know when he'd made a friend. That didn't mean Lord couldn't be spooked. As the horse sidestepped, complaining loudly as he tossed his head, Amber slipped out from under Jordan's arms, half jumping and half falling to the ground.

"God damn it, Amber, come back here!" Jordan urged Lord around.

Amber scurried to her feet, limping at first. If she'd hurt herself getting off Lord, he'd have her ass. What kind of fool woman would simply fall off a horse like she just did? She seriously acted like she'd never been around a horse at all.

"It's a long walk back," he said, feeling Lord's uneasiness when he reined him in alongside Amber.

"Go away. Leave me alone," she ordered, picking up her pace and marching over the sand. At least she wasn't hurt.

"You know I can't do that."

"Apparently there are a lot of things you can't do," she snapped, tossing her hair over her shoulder as she continued walking as fast as she could back toward the barn. "Well, I can't do this either. I'm leaving. Find another social organizer."

Amber took off running, her brown hair flowing behind her, and her firm, round ass in her jeans making his mouth water. There wasn't any way he'd leave her alone, especially when it was his actions that had pissed her off. Apparently Lord felt the same way. Without instruction, he picked up the pace, easily keeping in stride with her.

Jordan never hated his grandfather more than he did right now. But at the same time, he wasn't too pleased with himself either. Amber was irresistible. Few women fell into that category with him. There were plenty of gorgeous ladies out there, and more than one had learned who he was and applied their best seductions to him.

Maybe it was because Amber wasn't trying to seduce him. Although he knew interest when he saw it. And, in spite of what she said, Jordan had a hard time believing she'd showed up at the barn with absolutely no intention of fucking him.

When she had looked over her shoulder at him just a few moments ago, her dark blue eyes so heavily laced with lust, he'd reacted without giving it any thought. And God damn! Amber tasted better than anything he'd ever tried in his life. There was no way he would let her go with just one kiss. Jordan didn't doubt for a moment she ran from him now because she knew the same thing.

"You can't run all the way back to the barn," he called out to her, Lord's hooves pounding in the sand and the breeze passing by him as Lord kept pace with her, creating a rushing sound in his ears.

If she answered him, he didn't catch it. Jordan seriously thought about scooping her up, holding on to her when she fought him, and simply getting them back to the barn. Lord had spirit; Jordan saw that. But he was also as intelligent as any horse back at the ranch. The horse proved it now, keeping pace with Amber when some horses would have been spooked and raced to the security of their stall.

Jordan patted the horse's neck, leaning forward as he did. "We're not going to let her get away with this, are we, my friend?" he whispered.

Lord shook his head, whinnying loudly. The damn fool woman ran harder at the sound of him. Again, Lord paced her without instruction.

"You see the spirit in her, too, don't you?" Jordan patted Lord's neck, caressing it as he straightened.

Amber ran as if she did it every day, holding out and not slowing down. Her long brown hair fell in waves down her back, swaying with her body. For a petite thing, without an ounce of fat on her, her muscle tone outdid some of his ranch hands who worked physically all day. Obviously Amber worked out, keeping herself in good shape. Maybe she was one of those gym junkies. Which simply added another quality to the list of what appealed to him about her.

And made him despise his grandfather all the more. The deal stated he was to simply remain on the island a month, court Princess Tory, and announce an engagement or come back home and work for Grandfather.

He wouldn't be going back home if he did that. Grandfather had offices in New York and in Arizona. Jordan seriously doubted Grandfather would consider opening an office in Montana so Jordan could stay there. Of course, Grandfather wouldn't see the appeal of the Big Sky country. Honest, hardworking people lived there who looked out for each other, took care of each other, and didn't stab each other in the back. That breed of people meant nothing to Grandfather Anton.

Jordan knew telling Amber the truth—that he wasn't engaged, that in fact he'd never met Princess Tory before and would be laying eyes on her for the first time tomorrow when Amber met her—would resolve this entire matter.

Or it would make her even more livid for his misleading her in the first place. But he hadn't misled her. Grandfather had. Grandfather, or one of his bullies, had created a fake picture for Amber to lure her to this island and agree to work for him for a month. And Jordan didn't doubt for a minute that Amber would be paid a generous sum of money to complete her tasks. Why else would she have left the high-society life Jordan imagined her living, catering to the rich and famous, to come to a remote island off the coast of New Zealand and exist with just two other people and a skeleton staff during her stay here? Hell, this would make one memorable reality show. Not that Jordan ever got into watching those things.

If Jordan told her the truth and Amber turned her rage on Grandfather, the jig would be up. Jordan saw that and grew as angry as Amber was, thinking about it. He wasn't a social organizer and never wanted the job, but he imagined Amber's approach to entertaining would be a lot different if she believed she were handling a couple in love as opposed to two complete strangers.

It would blow up in his face soon enough. Amber would learn the truth as soon as Princess Tory arrived. But then she would know the truth because of circumstance, not because he told her. In which case, she would be outraged that he hadn't told her, and made her run all the way back to the barn, and at his grandfather for misleading her.

Amber and Lord stopped at the same time, pulling him out of his thoughts. She bent over alongside him, pressing her hands on her legs and breathing hard. Her hair was tousled around her and when she straightened, still panting, she grabbed it at her nape and struggled to comb it with her fingers.

"If I sit on . . . on Lord," she began, gesturing at the horse and breathing heavily as she shot him a furtive glance. "Can you hold the reins and swear to keep it in control so it won't run away with me?"

"Absolutely." Jordan hurried off Lord, noting the horse made no attempt to move but stood motionless without any commands. Lord might be as perfect of a horse as Jezebel, his Thoroughbred back home.

Amber stiffened, pressing her hands against his chest when he grabbed her waist. "I'll ride the horse, but you'll walk alongside it, making sure it doesn't run away," she ordered, her dark blue eyes full and round as she stared at him, not blinking.

"First of all, it is a *him*." Jordan watched her frown and then pucker her lips. God, he ached to taste them again. Keeping himself from getting a raging hard-on when he damn near had Amber in his arms was almost impossible to do. But he needed her to see he wasn't the unscrupulous cheater she believed him to be. Since telling her wouldn't work, his actions would need to speak louder than words. "Lord senses you're distraught, and in fact has kept by your side without my instruction."

Amber shifted her attention to the horse, giving him a more compassionate look than she offered Jordan. Immediately he envied the damn horse.

"Fine. I'll ride *him*," she decided, taking her hands off Jordan and turning to face the horse. "You promise to keep him from running away."

It was obvious she didn't know how to mount Lord. And when Lord turned his large head and gave Amber a scrutinizing once-over, Jordan didn't doubt for a moment the horse would decide she wasn't riding alone if Jordan didn't step in and help her into the saddle.

"It's not adjusted for you," he said, coming up behind her and again putting his hands on her hips. "You can't get your foot in to hoist yourself up without upsetting Lord."

He wasn't going to wait for her to argue. Amber didn't have a clue about horses. But he was a patient teacher and Amber picked up quickly, in spite of her hot-tempered nature.

Lifting her into the saddle gave Jordan a mouthwatering

view when she stretched her leg over Lord before sitting in the saddle. Unwilling to stop himself, Jordan let go of her hips and then gave her firm, round ass a good swat before she sat down.

"Hey!" she yelled, twisting and glaring down at him.

"Just keeping you on your toes," he said, biting back his smirk. "Besides, things aren't always as they appear."

"What's that mean?"

Jordan brought the reins forward, rubbing Lord's nose and whispering a promise that he'd take him out on a good hard run to make up for this night. He had a feeling both of them would need to burn off steam after this outing was over.

"It means you don't understand me as well as you think you do."

"Is that so?"

"That's so." He hated that Amber so clearly saw the deceit that made the Anton name what it was. If anything good came out of this month, he prayed it would be Amber putting Grandfather in his place. Not that Jordan didn't ache to do it first. "You think I'm a lowlife for kissing you because you believe I'm engaged to another woman."

"And your point is?" she asked dryly.

"That you don't know the whole picture," he informed her, wondering at this point if it even mattered whether he told her the truth or not. Amber didn't appear to be cooling down, even after running harder than Lord did.

"So I suppose here is where you enlighten me," she said, sitting upright and staring straight ahead.

Jordan studied her a moment longer before focusing on his footing when the ground grew rockier. He trudged along the beach, keeping pace with Lord. The next card he played could have a huge effect on the next month.

"No," he decided. "Here is not where I enlighten you. I will ask you to keep one thing in mind."

"What's that?"

"This evening I've learned a lot about you. Your values and high standards will get you far in life."

She snorted, sounding like she didn't believe him. Again he glanced up at her, and this time caught her staring at him.

"You may feel you've learned a lot about me this evening, but trust me, you don't know shit about who I am."

"Come in," Amber said the next morning as she stared at herself in the mirror. "What do you think of this dress?" she asked Cook, when the older woman entered Amber's bedroom.

"It's absolutely beautiful." Cook slapped her hands together, parading around Amber.

She felt like a stupid doll, all dressed up for breakfast. But then, she'd never met royalty before and didn't have a clue how to act, or what to say or not to say. And it sucked that she couldn't ask anyone for advice without blowing her secret out of the water.

"I'll admit a secret to you," Amber said, facing Cook and deciding part of the truth was better than none of it. "I've never been hired to work for royalty before."

"Neither have I." Cook grinned, showing off a dark hole where a tooth was missing. "But I wanted to make sure you knew you'd be dining with Master Jordan Anton this morning. He requested the two of you have breakfast outside on the terrace."

"Oh, did he?" Amber couldn't let Cook see her disgust. It would be his one last chance alone with her before his fiancée arrived. "What time does Princess Tory get here?"

"She will be at the landing pad at noon. Jesse will drive her to the castle. You'll have plenty of time to change before she arrives."

"Change?" Amber swirled in the bright-colored dress that swooshed around her knees. What the hell did someone wear to meet a princess? "You know, you've got it made, Cook," she said, staring at the older woman's reflection. "You get to wear the same thing all day."

Cook laughed, squeezing Amber's shoulder before heading to the closet. "There's a slight chill in the air this morning. Maybe a sweater over that would make breakfast more enjoyable for you."

Cook had way too much fun playing dress up with Amber before she decided Amber was presentable for her breakfast with Master Anton. Amber imagined Jordan liked his title, being referred to as "master" all the time. Regardless of what proper society might dictate, she wasn't going to call him master of anything.

Sitting at the beautifully prepared breakfast table a few minutes later and nursing coffee, she stared at the ocean that disappeared into the hazy sky and wondered for the hundredth time how she would pull this off.

"Cook, I'm glad I caught you," Jordan announced from behind her, making his presence known at the same time Cook appeared with a large covered platter she rolled to the table on a silver cart. "When Princess Tory arrives today, I think it would be proper if Amber makes the introductions."

"Introductions?" Amber shifted when Jordan paused at the table, but then barely heard Cook's response as she gawked at the man standing next to her.

"That sounds like a perfect idea," Cook agreed, and started taking lids off the dishes she'd rolled up next to the table.

Jordan wasn't wearing jeans today but khaki slacks that hugged his hard ass and accentuated his long legs. The blue, open-collar shirt finished off the image she was sure he was trying for, which was money. Lots and lots of money. His black hair looked damp and recently brushed. If it weren't for the ponytail curling under at his nape, he'd be the perfect image for some money magazine. As it was, his long hair simply gave him more of an appealing aura.

Amber snapped her mouth shut, telling herself not to drool over someone else's man. "What do you mean, introductions?" She met his gaze head on when he sat across from her at the table.

"It won't be hard to do." Jordan nodded and smiled when Cook poured his coffee. "Princess Tory will enter the castle and you'll present her to me."

"How sweet." Her appetite disappeared and was replaced by a lump as she stared at the food Cook began piling onto her plate. Apparently, Jordan Anton's personal social organizer wasn't expected to eat like a bird.

"You don't have to go for sweet," Jordan informed her, either missing her sarcasm or intentionally ignoring it. She would opt for the latter. "In fact, after breakfast I believe walking you through it might make it easier for you."

"You don't trust me to know how to present your fiancée to you?" Amber noticed that his eyes, although still that deep gray color, held enough hint of blue this morning to put her on guard.

"If I didn't trust you, you wouldn't be here." Jordan was all business, buttering toast while Cook presented him with a plate of bacon. "Princess Tory will no doubt enter with her ensemble. You will approach her, curtsy, of course, and then I'll be behind you at the other end of the hall. All you really need to say is, 'Princess Tory, I would like you to meet Jordan Anton,' or something like that."

He looked up at her when he finished speaking and it took her a moment to realize he'd stopped spreading butter over his toast. In fact, everything seemed to quit moving around them. The stillness settled in, allowing her to hear only what he had just said repeat itself again and again in her head.

"'I would like you to meet'?" she repeated, while bits and pieces of their conversation from the night before came back to her. "You've never met her before?" Her voice cracked and she cleared her throat, looking down at the bacon, eggs, toast, and bowl of fruit, a variety of which she didn't recognize, placed before her.

"No. I've never met Princess Tory," he offered, looking more pleased with the information than he should.

She looked up in time to see Cook disappearing into the castle through glass doors that remained opened. Amber shook her head, still registering the knowledge she'd just been offered.

"How is she your fiancée then?"

Jordan crunched into his toast, leaning in his chair while bringing his coffee cup to his mouth. He held it there, watching her over the rim while chewing and then swallowing. "Technically, she isn't. This time on the island has been arranged for us to get to know each other."

"You have a month to decide if you're going to get married?" All her life she had dreamed of being rich, of having enough money she wouldn't have to worry about dealing with a landlord, or deciding which utilities she needed the most. But she never knew it might mean an arrangement like this. "Being rich sucks," she said, but then wished she hadn't announced her thoughts on the matter out loud.

Jordan laughed easily, looking too damn good with the morning sun reflecting off his inky-black hair. "I won't argue that one."

"None of this changes your rogue status," she informed him, enjoying watching his grin fade and his eyes darken until they looked like a thunderhead ready to explode. Let him get angry at the truth. It still remained a fact. "You grossly misled me last night. In fact, before last night."

"I told you already, I had nothing to do with hiring you. All the information you were given about what to expect on this island came from my grandfather."

If he thought her knowing he and the princess were strangers would make it okay for them to fool around, he would be set straight soon enough. He continued speaking, though, before she could tell him as much.

"And I wasn't the only one holding secrets last night, was I, Amber?" he asked, lowering his voice while raising one eyebrow. "Even in your anger, you were still intrigued."

The way he stared at her, never pulling his attention from her eyes, created a heat inside her that swelled in her womb. The throbbing need between her legs was more obvious than all the sore muscles she'd woken up with this morning. And it was wrong. She didn't deny her attraction to him. There were many gorgeous married, or otherwise taken, men out there. Acknowledging their good looks was one thing; wanting to fuck them so badly she couldn't keep her thoughts straight was another.

"I haven't been dishonest with you," she began, worried he had somehow discovered the truth about her.

Jordan gulped down more of his coffee, finished his toast with a few quick bites, and then pushed his chair from the table. Amber was more than relieved he wasn't in the mood for all this food any more than she was. When he extended his hand, silently implying she stand and take it, she had half a mind to slap it away from her. But holding to her story—being a social organizer who was accustomed to moving in these types of circles—Amber placed her hand in his and allowed him to take her chair and move it so she could stand. It would be rude to do otherwise and she needed him to believe she was a real social organizer. There was no way she would screw up the opportunity to make all the money she would earn at the end of the month.

"Come with me," he told her, putting his free hand on the small of her back while continuing to hold her other hand in his.

It was too easy to get the sensation there was no one else in the castle other than the two of them. Jordan led her through the glass doors at the opposite end of the terrace from where Cook came and went.

"Are you learning your way around the castle yet?" he asked, letting go of her hand as they walked side by side down a wide hallway she'd ventured down the day before.

His left hand remained firmly in the middle of her back, though, creating a heat where he touched, which made her flesh sizzle as the sensation rushed over her body.

"I feel like there are lots of places I haven't even explored yet. The castle is so huge." Keeping the conversation casual, telling herself she was walking alongside her employer for the next month, helped keep her grounded.

"Keep an open mind as you explore. It's been my experience so far that every room has a different story to tell and if you hurry in and out you might miss something important." Jordan took his hand off her back when they entered the large foyer.

Amber studied his profile, shifting and causing her open-toe sandals to squeak on the marble floor. Jordan was taller than most men. And at five foot three inches, she was shorter than most men. But Jordan: his presence filled a room. It was more than his at least six foot stature, broad shoulders, and a confident, if not somewhat cocky, gait that reminded her of the lead cowboy in the old movies her uncle and grandpa used to love watching. It was more than his good looks, though, more than all that raw sex appeal. Something about his nature, about his insistence that she see him as a good person, even when the odds were stacked against him.

Amber thought about that as he walked through the large

entryway to the double doors with inlaid stained glass that led outside. Last night he could have told her he didn't know Princess Tory. He could have made her believe there was nothing wrong with his advances toward her. And if he had?

She forced herself to quit watching his tight butt as he reached for the door handle, and instead scowled at the floor. If he had, she might have fucked him. God, she still wanted him and it was still wrong. Regardless of whether he knew Princess Tory or not, he'd agreed to come here to meet her, not Amber. And the princess was flying across the world, just as Jordan and she had, on the grounds of spending time with a man who quite possibly might be her future husband. Both parties knew this. Amber's job wasn't to throw a corkscrew into all of this and make a mess out of things. Her job was to see to the entertainment, make sure the both of them had fun, and damn it, that was what she was going to do.

"Amber," Jordan whispered.

She jumped, snapping her attention from the floor up to his face. When did he end up inches away from her?

"What?" She pressed her lips together when he cupped her chin, holding her face so she couldn't look away from his.

Jordan's eyes were gray again, the hints of blue barely visible. She'd never met anyone whose eyes could change color like that. And the way he searched her face, concern mixed with something else, something dark and unnerving. Chills rushed over her flesh, although she was anything but cold at the moment.

"You were a million miles away and I was talking to you."

"I don't think I was that far away," she said, stepping out of his touch and crossing her arms over her chest, hugging herself when she immediately craved having his hands back on her. "And I'm sorry. I was preoccupied thinking about what event to plan for the two of you first. What did you say?"

He cleared the space between them, brushing his knuckles down her cheek. "I said I can't wait to taste you again," he whispered gruffly.

Amber blinked, not ready for his bluntness. But when she tried looking away he grabbed her, pulling her into his arms, and devoured her mouth. He crushed her body against his, impaling her while bending her damn near halfway over. Amber dug her fingers into the corded muscle of his shoulders, which flexed under her touch. His body was warm, solid, and so strong and powerful. But his mouth scorched her senses, sending her plummeting into a whirlwind of need and desire so powerful she couldn't pull out of it.

This wasn't what they were supposed to be doing. She'd just lectured herself on how she wouldn't have sexual thoughts about Jordan. Yet he tasted so good, kissed her better than any man had ever kissed her before. The swelling and throbbing that had plagued her since last night burned throughout her, stealing the rationale she had held on to a moment before and replacing it with a craving so carnal, so incredibly strong, the only thoughts in her head at the moment were how they could fuck each other before the princess showed up.

Which was wrong. So damn wrong.

"Now that I have your attention," he growled, his lips moist and soft as he moved his mouth over hers.

Amber blinked, allowing him to straighten her but then realizing she still held on to his shoulders.

"We're making progress. You didn't try to clobber me this time," he added, his grin beyond sinful and radiating with pure male satisfaction.

"I should," she said, hating how her voice sounded so laced with lust.

"I don't think so." He created a bit of space between them, but then stroked the side of her head, brushing her hair with his fingers as he moved it behind her shoulders. "I do think we need to pick up where we left off just now, as soon as we're clear on how we're going to greet the princess."

"You know we can't do that, Jordan." She fought to get her heart to quit pounding in her chest. The heavy pulse also throbbed between her legs, her clit swollen and so sensitive she didn't need to move to know her panties were soaked. "Truth be told that was what I was thinking about when I wasn't paying attention to you."

"You were ignoring me because you were thinking about fucking me?" He tilted his head and a lone strand of black hair fell loose from his ponytail, bordering his face and making her fingers itch to move it.

"No," she said, trying to make herself hate that smug look on his face when in fact he looked too damn sexy for his own good. "I was ordering myself to focus only on providing entertainment for the two of you so you will have fun together instead of . . ." She let her words fade away, knowing if she told him how much she was drooling over him, he would use it to get what he wanted.

Letting him know it was what she wanted, too, wouldn't do either of them any good.

"No. I'm not here to make things worse for the two of you. I'm here to make them better." She walked around him, her sandals slapping against the marble floor and creating an echo as she headed to the front door. "So, the doorbell rings and I answer it, let her in, and then say, 'Hey princess, this is Jordan Anton. I sure hope you two get along great.'"

Jordan chuckled behind her. "Did my grandfather meet you before hiring you?"

"Huh?" She turned around, her hand still on the long, narrow door handle, the cool metal doing little to soothe the fever burning out of control inside her. "As a matter of fact, he did. Why do you ask?"

"Because you're hardly his style."

"What's that supposed to mean?"

"Grandfather prefers proper ladies, women who are a statement with either their money or their good looks. You, sweetheart, are perfect in my eyes, but hardly what I would picture Grandfather hiring to cater to my needs."

"Maybe that's why he hired me." She didn't like his implication that she was rough around the edges. And she knew Jordan meant just that. He was old money, no matter how relaxed and easygoing he was when he was alone with her. Amber fought the panic rising inside her, refusing to accept that she couldn't pull this off. The amount of money she would make at the end of this month would help her buy the home she and her family had rented for years, finally own a piece of this earth that no one could take away from them. "Maybe your grandfather wanted you to have a social organizer whom you would like. After all, you're the one who is going to be with me for the next month, not him."

Jordan's expression sobered so quickly it scared her. She stared at him, her heart beating just as hard as it had when he'd kissed her, while he seemed to grow before her, his hands balling into fists.

"You're right. And I was a fool not to figure it out immediately. Grandfather probably guessed I had no intention of proposing to some Sicilian princess. I bet he hired you on purpose, thinking that next to you, I would be more impressed with her money and refinement."

5

If anything came out well from the morning, it was Amber winning their argument and convincing Jordan that the initial introductions should be made after Princess Tory had a chance to settle in her room. After all, a lady liked to look her best when being introduced to a man. And since the princess had traveled so far to get here, Amber knew she would want to at least freshen up.

Other than convincing Jordan to do things her way, the morning might possibly have been the worst day of her life. There was nothing better than having it rubbed in her face that she was a lowlife. No matter her new wardrobe and her continued efforts to appear confident and sophisticated, Jordan's simple comment earlier stung more than any insult ever slammed in her direction.

There was an attraction between the two of them; it sizzled in the air anytime she got close to him. But Jordan saw her as less than equal to him. He would fuck her. Hell, he might end up being the best piece of ass she'd ever had. That wouldn't change his nature, though, his inability to look beyond social classes.

Leaning back in her chair at the desk in her bedroom, she glanced at the clock and then stretched her legs, wiggling her toes and focusing on the color of her polish that matched her fingernails.

"Somehow you've got to pull this off," she told herself, shifting her attention to the computer screen. "You've taught yourself everything you've ever needed to know, accomplished tasks you were supposedly not skilled to do, and this job is no different." She'd left Jordan over an hour ago, after rehearsing how introductions would take place in the room she'd spotted when she first got here. Turned out it was called a parlor, and Jordan was incredibly amused when she described it as the room where rich people sat content with being bored.

Her lecture didn't lift her mood when she returned to her task of searching Web sites, while trying to figure out what Jordan and Princess Tory's first date should be like. She hated feeling sick to her stomach when she thought of Jordan spending time alone with this woman—this princess. Amber hadn't even met the princess and already she didn't like her.

Her cell phone buzzed, and then started ringing. Amber pushed herself out of her chair and moped as she walked barefoot over carpet thicker than anything she'd sunk her feet into before. After digging her phone out of her purse, she glanced at the number and then answered it before it went to voice mail.

"Hello," she said, praying her voice sounded cheerful.

"Well, you don't sound like you're on the other side of the world," her mother said, sounding happy but tired. "How's my baby girl doing?"

"So far, so good. How's everything going there? Are you doing okay?" Focusing on any problems at home sounded a lot better than trying to figure out how to entertain Jordan and the princess.

"Everything is fine. I just woke up from a nap and Karma helped me figure out the time difference between you and us, so I hoped it was a good time to call."

Amber quickly subtracted the hours in her head. "It's Sunday afternoon there?"

"Yup. And already Monday morning for you," her mother said, while Karma, Amber's younger half sister, made a comment in the background. "Your sister says you can predict our future," she added, laughing.

"I predict she has to go to school in the morning." Amber rolled onto the incredibly large bed, which she noticed had been made while she'd been out of her room this morning. She would have to make note to be sure and clean up after herself, and put away anything that mattered to her every time she left her room. Not that she didn't trust Cook, but there was something about knowing another person could go through her things that didn't sit right with her. "Tell Karma she can call me whenever she needs help with her homework. And Bobby, too. Is he there?"

"Of course not. He's out running around with his friends. And you know as well as I do that it will be a cold day in hell before he calls anyone for help with homework. I swear at this rate, he might as well just get a job."

It was an old argument with her and her mother, and one Amber didn't feel like taking on at the moment. Just because Amber never finished high school and opted, instead, to go to work full time to help with bills so her family wouldn't get evicted, didn't mean she wanted the same thing for her brother and sister.

"Is Uncle John back yet?" she asked, changing the subject.

"He should be home by midweek. They extended his hours." Her mother suddenly sounded louder as she added cheerfully, "He's lined up for a bonus he hopes to get by the end of the month. If he gets it, I can probably cut back on the hours at the newspaper."

"You should do that anyway. It's too much work for you to get up every night and deliver all those papers." Amber was careful not to say her mother was getting too old to work so many hours every day. At forty-three, though, Jennifer Stone too often looked a lot older. "You need to start using your evening hours to make time for yourself."

"That will be the day," her mother said dryly.

"That day is coming, Mom. I told you that, when I get home, I'm going to have enough money to buy our home. No more paying rent every month to an asshole who won't even fix the leaks in the roof."

"At least we have a roof." Her mother didn't comment on the money Amber would earn.

"We're going to own our roof," Amber stressed.

"We'll see. Is everything going okay for you there so far?"

"Yup. I'll be meeting royalty here very soon." She glanced at the clock. "Actually I should let you go so that I can get ready."

"Take pictures for all of us," her mother said.

Amber didn't bother explaining again how she wasn't a tourist here. Already she'd messed things up by not being able to present herself to Jordan as comfortable and knowledgable with the rich and successful. She wouldn't fuck things up worse by gawking at royalty.

"I love you, Mom."

"Love you too, sweetheart. Call us when you can."

Amber promised to do that and then ended the call. She was to stay in her room until Cook called for her, letting her know Princess Tory had arrived. Walking over to the large balcony off her bedroom, she pulled open the French doors, but then remained planted where she was and watched a long, black car move slowly toward the castle. It was the same car, a limousine, that had brought her here from the landing pad.

Her mouth went dry when the car parked in front of the castle below and all four doors opened at the same time. Jesse got out of the driver's side, hurrying to the back of the car and opening the trunk. Two men Amber didn't know stood on both sides of the car, moving in unison and dressed identically in black suits. They assisted two young ladies out of the car. Both dabbed at their hair, and then moved next to each other, appearing to do nothing more than just stand at attention. Finally, one of the men bent into the car, extending his hand, and a frail young woman got out of the car, moving with such perfect grace there was no doubt who she was. Princess Tory had arrived.

Amber ached to move outside, to lean over the balcony and watch the party enter the castle. Princess Tory didn't move from where she stood just outside the car until the two men came to her side. They didn't touch her, but walked alongside her, making her look even smaller, like a child between them, as the group approached the doors to the castle as if they were a parade preparing to appear before their audience.

"Let the show begin," she mumbled to herself, hurrying to slide into her sandals and then head downstairs.

On an impulse, she kicked her sandals off her feet and hurried to her closet, opting for closed toe, black pumps. Doing a quick inspection in the mirror, she stared at her hair flowing past her shoulders. All the women who got out of the car had their hair piled on top of their heads. Amber hurried to the bathroom and dug through her overnight bag she hadn't unpacked yet. She owned two decent-looking hair clasps and now wished she'd taken time to buy something nicer as she fingered each of them, pondering her meager choices.

"Like there's anything you can do about it right now," she scolded herself, opted for the silver clasp, and then bent over, twisting her long hair and then sliding the clasp into the loose bun. She made quick work of spraying it into place and then reached for her perfume. Princess Tory might have class and finesse, but she wouldn't outshine Amber. Damn it to hell and back if her thoughts were wrong and her motivation out of line, but Jordan would notice her. She would damn well see to it.

She reached the stairs when a loud gong sounded through the castle, making her jump out of her skin and almost trip down the stairs.

"Graceful," she ordered herself, hating how damp her palms were, when she realized the sound she just heard was probably a doorbell.

Cook would answer the door, let the ensemble inside, and Amber would take over from there. She sucked in a breath, suddenly wishing she had something to drink. Her mouth was drier than sandpaper.

At the bottom of the stairs, she headed to the foyer, her shoes clicking on the floor and announcing her presence when she appeared in the open doorway. Too many heads turned in her direction at once. She didn't know what to say.

"Welcome," she choked out, forcing one foot in front of the other and staring at the serious expressions that looked anything but friendly. At least Amber didn't have to worry about which one was the princess. Her large body guards, or whoever they were, surrounded her so Amber could hardly see the small woman standing between all of them.

"Princess Tory will be shown to her quarters now." One of the tall men stared at her with a frown, moving slightly and completely blocking Amber's view of her as he spoke with a thick accent.

"Of course. I guessed she would wish to freshen up before meeting Mr. Anton." Amber cringed, wondering if she should have instead referred to him as "master." "Cook will show her to her room. I can wait until she's ready to come downstairs."

"You will escort us," the man corrected her, never blinking or taking his focus from her face. "The princess will allow an audience this evening after resting from her exhausting journey."

"Mr. Anton expects an audience with her soon," Amber told him, but then held her breath when all the men surrounding Princess Tory stiffened. The two ladies standing next to each other, a few feet from the men, lifted their gazes and stared at her for the first time. The room grew so silent not even the air drifted through. Amber's lungs hurt until she realized she held her breath and released it, sighing. "But tonight will be fine."

"Yes, it will," the man who played spokesman informed her, his accent growing thicker.

Amber narrowed her gaze on him, scowling silently and letting him know with a look that size didn't matter, and she wouldn't be spoken to as if she were a child. He wasn't royalty and she wasn't either, and if he thought himself somehow better than her when there hadn't even been introductions, he would learn quickly how inaccurate he was.

Amber spun around on her heels. "Follow me, please, and I'll show all of you where you're staying." Thank God she'd been snoopy. At least she knew the location of the wing where the lot of them would stay for the month. No way would Princess Tory see her as anything but professional and at ease in her role.

If it weren't for her years working in a secretarial pool with chauvinistic bosses who believed women should be dressed as uncomfortably as possible, Amber might not have been able to storm out of the castle in her heels after showing them to their rooms. Nonetheless, a few minutes later she questioned her judgment on stalking away from that rude and ridiculously stuck-up group, who entered their rooms and closed doors in her face without saying a word to her.

Halfway to the barn, she spotted Sara coming out of it. Amber wasn't in the mood for company, though, and headed into the flower garden instead. At the end of the gardens were the paths she had found her first day here. Opting for a different path from the one she took before, Amber followed it into the thick grove of tropical trees. Vines with beautiful, heavily scented flowers twisted around the trees. It really was beautiful here. She followed the sound of rushing water and paused after a short hike, kicking her shoes off and staring in amazement at the view spread out before her.

"It's beautiful," she whispered, staring at a waterfall that could be out of a fairy tale. Just what she needed to clear her mind, get a grip on what was going on around her and what she needed to do.

Footsteps sounded behind her. Amber met Jordan's gaze as he came through the trees. There was something in his expression—amusement, maybe satisfaction—that made her tummy do flip-flops. She imagined he was happy to find her out here alone. Amber straightened, not sure how she should react to him seeking her out.

"What are you doing here?" He tilted his head, searching her face and then looking lower.

Amber pulled her attention from him, glancing at her shoes she held in her hand, then returning her attention to the incredible waterfall that a moment before had offered tranquility and a chance to regroup.

"Apparently my services aren't needed for a while."

"Is that so," he said under his breath, moving in next to her and placing his hand on the small of her back, leading her closer to the edge. "What happened with Princess Tory?"

He held on to her when they stepped onto a smooth, rocky ledge that was flat and cool under her bare feet. Keeping a firm grip, he motioned that they sit. Amber's insides fluttered with too many reactions to his silent suggestion that they cuddle next to this amazing sight. He was getting very comfortable with her, and part of her mind screamed that she demand distance. But an overwhelming warmth traveling inside her, making her breasts swell and her nipples harden painfully, as well as a throbbing between her legs, made her anxious to play out the moment and see where it took them.

She knew exactly where it would take them.

"She's here," Amber said, sighing for dramatics as she sat on the cool rock and then tucked her dress around her legs, pressing them together while heat swarmed and made her clit throb with a need so strong she was acutely aware every time his body brushed against hers.

"And?" he prompted, sitting next to her and stretching his long legs out in front of him. The cowboy boots at the end of his straight leg–cut blue jeans made his legs look even longer. He leaned back on his elbows, his eyes holding a hint of blue when she looked at him. "No one came and got me. What happened?"

It dawned on her he was as alone on this island as she was. In spite of his status, or any prearranged deal made prior to coming here, there were only the few of them in the castle. She should have sought him out and let him know plans had changed. Since she hadn't, he'd set his own schedule. And his agenda had brought him here. Whether he sought her out or simply escaped the castle to clear his own head, he spotted her first and came to her. He wanted to talk to her—and possibly more. She wondered if he tried talking to Princess Tory and had been turned away. Jordan didn't look upset though.

Amber licked her lips, unable to keep her gaze from traveling over all that roped muscle pressing against his T-shirt and jeans. He'd changed out of the semiformal attire she saw him in at breakfast, making her wonder if this was more his usual style of dressing. If so, she liked it a lot.

"I saw her arrive in the limousine Jesse picked me up in at the landing pad."

"You saw her arrive? Where were you?" he asked, his gaze still pinned to her face.

"In my room. I saw her from my balcony."

"You went out on the balcony and watched them pull up?" He made it sound like doing so would be something bordering on atrocious.

"I wasn't out on the balcony. I had opened my doors. I was restless and felt caged in my room," she admitted, but didn't add she'd been scrambling online, searching for what types of parties and events the rich and famous attended under these circumstances. "When I opened my doors the car was driving toward the castle. It parked and from where I stood just inside the doors I saw all of them get out."

"So they didn't see you," he finished for her, nodding and looking at his boots. "How many of them were there?"

"There were two men—big men, like bouncers or something. Then there were two women. I barely saw the princess. Her people blocked my view of her. I couldn't tell you what she looks like at all."

"She's supposed to be gorgeous," he muttered, still focusing on his boots.

Amber stiffened, something hardening inside her at the thought of Jordan seducing the princess the way he'd been coming on to her. She didn't like the bile that rose in her throat. There wasn't anything to fight for, here. Forcing her attention to the waterfall, watching the water turn to white foam as it raced down jagged rocks across the cliff where they sat, she tried yet again to put any thoughts of a personal relationship with Jordan out of her head.

"That should make things easier for you," she said, praying she sounded sincere.

"I seriously doubt that," he told her, his tone not changing. "You're more gorgeous than the pictures I've seen of her, and I'm just to the point where I can have a conversation with you without being attacked."

She grinned, leaned forward and pressed her hands to her

bare legs as she stretched to see over the ledge where the water swirled. The mad rush of water around rocks that swirled into a bright blue pool was beyond breathtaking, dangerous yet incredibly enticing, if not hypnotic.

"Good luck doing that with Princess Tory. Those thugs around her make it impossible to even see her."

Jordan snorted and Amber itched to see his facial expression but pinned her attention on the water below them. "I'm sure that is probably intentional," he grunted.

"Why do you say that?" She snapped her head in his direction before she could stop herself. It seemed impossible to tone down her interest in him.

"I'm sure she's as thrilled about all of this as I am," he offered, lazily lifting his gaze to hers. His black hair was thick and silky looking, pulled back from his face and bound at his nape. She loved the unique color of his eyes, which at the moment were bright and attentive as he focused on her, giving her a glimpse of the man who was so different from how she had judged him the first time they met.

"I don't understand. Why would either of you put your lives on hold and traipse across the world to this remote island to meet each other? And even at that, to meet under the pretense that you quite possibly could marry? Your grandfather didn't give me any indication this was anything other than a done deal."

"I'm sure," he growled, but then simply studied her for a moment without elaborating.

It bugged the crap out of her how much she really wanted to hear his answers. She didn't say anything else, allowing the silence to grow between them. When he still didn't elaborate she shifted her body, once again putting her back to him, and stared at the water falling off the cliff across the ravine and plummeting to the rocks below.

"Do you have family you're close to?" he asked.

She was surprised by the question but didn't let him see it. "Too much so," she offered, adding a small laugh. She couldn't let him see how strongly he affected her sitting next to her like this. Since she couldn't get thoughts of fucking him—right here, right now—out of her head, the least she could do was act as if she didn't feel this way. "Why do you ask?"

"At holidays, or possibly birthdays, is it assumed you'll be with your family? Or can you say no without feeling guilty?"

"I get it. You come from a family where saying no makes your life hell."

"Exactly. But then take how it is with most families like that and multiply it tenfold."

"Sounds annoying," she grunted, focusing on a large rock that interrupted the flow of the water, causing foam to splash off it as it descended.

"I interrupted my life to come here," he threw in.

She chuckled. "Annoying," she repeated.

"So you understand."

She wasn't sure she understood anything about Jordan. And although his comment welcomed her to dig deeper into his life, ask more questions and possibly get answers to help her know the man next to her better, she didn't see what she would gain. Already he proved to be an incredible distraction. Learning more about him, taking time to understand what made Jordan tick, would probably make her like him more. She needed to think of him less, not become infatuated with him.

"Princess Tory will allow an audience tonight," she said, quoting the words the bouncer had told her.

"'Allow an audience'?" he asked, obviously put out by the choice of words. "That isn't how they said it."

"That's exactly how they said it."

"I see." He moved slightly.

It grabbed the attention of her peripheral vision and she

shifted her gaze, not her head, straining to see what he was doing. Jordan crossed one booted foot over the other. She jumped when his hand touched her back.

"Tell me, Amber," he began quietly. Her flesh sizzled with need when he dragged his fingers across her shoulder blade. "What would you do if your family announced they would disown you if you didn't meet and spend time with a man they thought would make you a good husband?" he whispered. His gravelly tone antagonized the need swollen inside her.

"My family wouldn't send me to an island," she told him, remembering how her mother had looked at her in disbelief when she'd come home from work after being propositioned by a man her boss had pulled her from her desk to meet.

"Wherever they sent you. That isn't important. What would you do if it meant so much to them that you meet this man that they told you they wouldn't speak to you again if you didn't meet him?" He tugged her shoulder, forcing her to shift her weight and meet his gaze.

His brooding expression made her itch to touch him, to stroke the lines of concern from the sides of his eyes. "My family wouldn't do that to me," she told him.

He nodded once. "Sounds like you have a family who loves you."

"I do."

It didn't surprise her when he pulled her down on top of him. But it should have surprised her when she didn't fight him. Instead, meeting the hunger from his kiss with a hunger of her own, she wrapped her arm around his neck, molding against his body when he laid back on the rock.

"Don't tell me no," he growled into her mouth when he rolled her over, coming down on top of her, and then ravishing her before she could answer.

He rested his weight on his arm, while his hand tangled in

her hair. But his other hand moved down her body, cupping her breast through her dress and bra and then torturing her nipple until she cried out into his mouth.

"Tell me you want this," he whispered, nipping at her lower lip and then placing moist kisses on her chin and down her neck.

"I think you know the answer to that." Her voice was rough, raspy, offering aid in answering his question.

"Admit you want me as badly as I want you," he growled, moving his hand down her thigh and then raising her dress until he cupped her pussy through her underwear.

She bucked against his touch, blinking and then focusing on him. Jordan stared down at her, his fierce expression determined and serious, stealing her breath as she drowned in his blue-gray eyes.

"Admit it, sweetheart," he whispered.

"I shouldn't, but I do," she admitted.

The look of satisfaction that washed over his face damn near made her come.

"Yes, you should," he growled, then lowered his face and nipped her collarbone as his fingers worked their way underneath her underpants.

He slid between her smooth folds. Good thing she'd shaved early that morning, although she'd argued with herself that she was being ridiculous to do so. Her efforts were rewarded with the ultimate male grunt of happiness when he moved his fingers over her soaked entrance, lubricating her even more.

The pressure inside her swirled to heights she wasn't sure she could handle. Grabbing his shoulders, digging into perfectly sculpted, hard-as-steel muscle, Amber wasn't sure if she held on or tried pushing him lower.

"My God, are you always this wet?" he asked, lifting his gaze to hers.

Amber managed to glare at him, deciding his question didn't merit a response. She seriously doubted his ego needed that much stroking.

"Are you always this inquiring?" she demanded, barely able to move her mouth. Her teeth were clenched together as he continued working magic between her legs. It was all she could do not to tremble and let go, allowing her orgasm release.

"Only when the person I'm with matters to me," he whispered, moving his mouth over hers again.

Jordan had a way of kissing that was as erotic as his touch. His lips were warm and moist and moved over hers with a skill that had the jury still out on how much of a rogue he might be. But damn, he appealed to her in ways a man shouldn't, especially a man who'd agreed to meet another woman here. And even more so a man who in a month she'd probably never see again.

Amber didn't play the field. Her heart couldn't handle the indifference of those who did. Jordan's actions were so smooth, his actions so perfect, she couldn't stop herself from reacting to him. Worse yet, now he knew beyond any doubt how he made her feel.

His fingers slid inside her and she cried out, turning her head and breaking the kiss as she gasped for air. The hard, smooth surface underneath her pressed against her head. She didn't care. Arching into him, she rode his hand, aching for him to touch that one spot that would send her over the edge. It no longer mattered that she hold back. The way he touched her, caressed her, and made her feel better than any man had ever made her feel put all her care for the moment to the side. Later she'd figure out what his motivations were, or if in fact simply fucking her was his only motivation.

"I think I know what matters to you," she said, damn near panting, as she managed to shift her attention back to his face.

"This definitely matters to me," he growled, his focus moving slowly down her body. "I can't wait to hear what you sound like when you come."

He thrust his fingers deep inside her, hitting that spot she'd been sure he couldn't manage with his fingers.

"Crap! Jordan!" She dug her fingernails into his shoulders, clamping her legs together.

"Come for me."

"I am . . . oh shit!" Amber kept his hand where it was, thrusting her hips as she rode out the intensity of her orgasm. She clamped down on his fingers, feeling her muscles constrict before managing to catch her breath and relax her fingers over his shoulders.

"That's it, sweetheart," he whispered, leaning in to brush his lips over hers. "God, you're beautiful." He sounded like a deadly cat, purring with satisfaction while he stared into her eyes. "I want you out of your dress."

Amber opened her eyes, his face blurring before her although she fought to focus on him. "Out here?" The thought had crossed her mind. It would be so fucking hot to ride him, knowing the risk of getting caught existed, even if it was a small one.

"Do you honestly think anyone is going to leave the castle to traipse through the woods?"

She doubted Cook or Jesse would leave; both were working. There was the woman in the barn, Sara, whom she knew little about. Then all the people who came with Princess Tory.

"Well, the princess wouldn't," she said, making a face at him. "I doubt she goes anywhere alone. In fact, you'd probably have an audience if you tried fucking her."

"Sounds kinky." The corner of his mouth curved, her only indication he spoke to get a rise out of her.

Amber raised one eyebrow, but then let her head fall back against his arm when he reached underneath and lifted her. His fingers slid out of her pussy, leaving her immediately aching for more and feeling incredibly empty. As easily as he relieved the pressure inside her, it already rose again, the throbbing in her clit a distraction when he eased the zipper of her dress down her back.

The material slipped off her shoulders, leaving the dress bunched around her hips, with her panties and bra barely covering her.

"I'm not getting naked out here by myself," she informed him, tugging on his T-shirt with two fingers.

Jordan didn't hesitate to peel it off, revealing bulging, roped muscles and a chest that put anything she'd ever seen before to shame.

"Do you work out every day or something?" she asked, taking in the well-defined muscles and his six-pack abs. The perfect amount of coiled black chest hair spread over his pecs. Talk about absolute mouthwatering eye candy.

Jordan stood, leaving her sitting at his feet, and grabbed hold of a nearby tree limb. "Pull," he instructed, lifting his boot over her lap.

Amber grabbed his boot, helping pull it off his foot, then did the same with his other.

"I guess you could say I work out daily," he told her, "with my job."

"What do you do?" She was doing what she told herself she wouldn't do: learning about him personally. But then fucking him was something she had said she wouldn't do with him, too.

"Run a ranch," he said, popping the top button of his jeans and then unzipping them.

"Oh." She wasn't sure what she'd pictured him doing for a living, but running a ranch was the last guess she would have made. "Where is this ranch?"

"Montana." He stuck his thumbs inside his jeans and boxers and slid them down his legs.

Amber forgot about pursuing the conversation when his dick popped free from its confinement and stretched before her, at eye level, as she sat on the rock at his feet.

Jordan was fucking huge! His cock was hard and stuck out before him, looking swollen and mouthwatering. "I want to touch you," she whispered, glancing up at his smoldering gaze.

6

Jordan clenched his teeth together when she wrapped her fingers around his shaft. Her hand was small, her fingers soft and cool as she ran them along his length.

"Woman," he hissed, unable to move his mouth to tell her more.

Her long lashes fluttered over dark blue eyes. "You're very big," she said softly, sounding in awe. "I guess you know that."

Admitting he knew that would put him right back in rogue status in her eyes. "I do now," he said, grabbing the side of her head and then fingering the clasp holding her hair.

Amber had gone to efforts to appear conservative and proper for Princess Tory. Jordan had already guessed that Amber wasn't thrilled about having to arrange events for him to spend time with the princess. He wasn't thrilled about having to spend time with the princess either. Especially after meeting Amber.

She'd captivated him all over again when he'd first spotted her walking ahead of him on the path. But he definitely liked her hair down better. Undoing the clasp, he pulled it from her hair, trying not to hurt her. She shook her head when he pulled it free, allowing her long, thick, brown hair to fall around her shoulders and past her breasts. She was too damn sexy for her own good.

His blood boiled in his veins, every inch of him hardening to where he could barely move when she leaned into him and pressed her lips over his swollen tip. Jordan watched her tongue dart out of her mouth and then stroke his length and swore his world tilted to the side.

Grabbing both sides of her head and tangling his fingers in her long, silky-feeling, wavy hair, he closed his eyes, enjoying every sensation tumbling over him when she closed her mouth around him and sucked him deep into her heat.

"Baby, you're fucking perfect." He held her head in place, thrusting forward and feeling her tongue dart around him when he sank deeper into her mouth.

Amber hummed her pleasure, her eyes closed as she sucked and stroked him with her lips and tongue. He wouldn't let her know how long it had been since he'd been with a woman. And he wasn't sure why he believed it, but something told him she hadn't slept with a lot of men. Not that she couldn't. Amber was quite possibly the most beautiful woman he'd ever laid eyes on. But the way she had resisted him when she believed him engaged proved she lived by a set of rules she didn't stray from—yet another compelling attribute that made her a perfect package.

She pulled her head back, her fingers wrapped around his shaft when she almost took him out of her mouth. Just as the air wrapped around his shaft, feeling cool after being in her hot, little mouth, Amber sucked him in deeper than she had before. The tip of him touched her tonsils and she gagged, her mouth constricting around him before she pulled him out again.

"Fuck!" he growled, his balls aching with the need to come hitting him almost too hard to control. "Don't do me in before I can return the favor."

Amber looked up at him, her lips moist and swollen and her dark blue eyes glassy with moisture. Her hair was tousled around her face and down her back. He was positive she was the prettiest woman he'd ever seen as he gazed down at her, watching the swell of her breasts press against her white silk bra.

"Can't handle it?" she teased.

"I'll show you what I can handle." The sound of the water below them mixed with blood draining out of his brain and created a rushing sound in his head when he squatted before her. "Stand up, little vixen," he growled, grabbing her waist and pulling her to her feet as he situated himself on the flat rock before her.

Amber presented a view to die for when she stood. He tugged on her dress, helping it fall to her feet, but then held on to her when she stepped out of it.

"I shouldn't let it get wrinkled." She hesitated, and then tried reaching to pick up the dress.

"I'll buy you new dresses," he rumbled, not wanting to take a minute from enjoying every inch of her perfect body.

He grabbed her underwear, tugging the silky fabric and gliding it down her hips.

"You don't have to do that." But she didn't mess with the dress, instead stepping out of her panties and grabbing his shoulders to balance herself. "I feel very exposed," she added, sounding breathless.

"You should feel very beautiful." He dropped her underwear onto her dress and pulled her to him, burying his face in her breasts while unclasping her bra behind her and then pulling it free from her, too.

He took only a moment before again dragging her over him, going up on his knees while holding her against him as he sucked her nipple, then teased it with his tongue. Large nipples on a woman were sexy as hell. Amber had good-sized breasts, too. And they were real. Their soft, round shape added to her sensuality. He could do this all day long and enjoy every minute of it.

Moving from one breast to the other, he feasted on her, taking his time so as to enjoy even more the moment he tasted her thick cream. As he dragged his tongue over her flat belly, kissing her soft skin until he reached her smooth, shaved mound, Jordan breathed in the rich aroma of her sex and grew drunk on the taste and smell of her.

"Part your legs, sweetheart," he ordered, his voice rough with a need that he felt would explode inside him.

Amber complied, spreading her legs and resting her fingers on either side of his head. As he used one hand to separate the smooth folds while cupping her ass with the other, Amber yanked on his ponytail, freeing his hair so it flowed against his shoulders. He hadn't guessed she was the kind of woman who would like long hair on a man. It was the one part of him he still held on to, possibly because he was unwilling to completely surrender the more reckless days of his youth.

Closing his eyes, Jordan loved her fingers combing his hair while he tasted her cream on his lips and tongue. When he dipped inside her, caressing the tender muscles that had so recently clamped down on his fingers, Amber staggered, crying out.

She wailed over him, scratching his scalp as she came again, soaking his face with her thick cream. "Jordan," she breathed, acting like she'd fall over onto him.

But he held her firmly, keeping her in place while lapping her juices. His dick was so damn hard he couldn't focus, could barely breathe, and he had a harder time moving than he wanted her to notice.

"That's it, sweetheart. Every drop," he growled, running his tongue from her opening to her clit and then sucking in the small hard ball of flesh until she spasmed.

"Shit!" she howled, trying to jump out of his arms.

They weren't so close to the edge that she would fall off, but nonetheless Jordan had no intention of letting Amber go anywhere. He gripped her ass with both hands, spreading the soft, round flesh, and stretched his fingers over her tight asshole, stroking it while he continued torturing her clit.

"I can't," she cried, bending over him so that her long hair draped past his shoulders. "Please, Jordan."

"You can, my dear," he encouraged her as he took her in his arms when her legs gave out. "And in fact, you are. You're coming for me so beautifully."

She moaned, not saying anything but relaxing in his arms when he cradled her against his chest. "I need to fuck you, darling," he grunted, his cock so swollen it made it damn hard to speak without growling.

"Do you have a condom?" she asked, her voice lazy with a soft drawl to it. Her cheeks were flushed and her hair tangled, adding to her sex appeal.

Jordan held on to her while fishing through his jeans pocket and producing the small package he'd stuck in there earlier with high hopes. He was real glad he'd thought to do so now, because returning to the castle in his current condition might have proven impossible.

Making quick work of spreading their clothes over the rock, he then placed her on top of them, watching as she reclined and stared up at him. He loved how her hair fanned over her shoulder and around her breast. Her full, ripe breasts swelled when she sucked in a breath, showing off her concave belly and smooth, narrow hips. The flesh between her legs glistened with moisture, and his cock danced eagerly, anxious to experience her heat around him.

Jordan ripped the package open, removing the condom and sheathing himself before kneeling between her legs. Amber spread herself open for him, bending her knees and running her fingers through her long, wavy hair while staring at him, her expression flushed. She was willing, though. He didn't notice any hesitation as she watched him, her dark blue eyes glowing with passion as she moistened her lips.

"Amber," he whispered, bending over her and pressing his lips over hers as he found her entrance and eased inside her.

She cried into his mouth, quickly moving her hands and grabbing his arms, digging in with her fingernails while he continued his journey deep into her heat. It took every ounce of strength he had not to plow as far into her as he could go. She'd commented on his size and, as tight as she was, damn near suffocating the life right out of him, Jordan wouldn't hurt her. Before he'd completely filled her, he paused, fighting to breathe while his balls tightened painfully, every inch of him on edge while he struggled to take it slow for her.

"Jordan, please," she begged into his mouth. "Don't stop."

"I don't want to hurt you."

She opened her eyes, staring up at him without blinking. "Fuck me, now," she demanded.

"Okay," he agreed, knowing once he started he wouldn't want to stop.

He thrust deep inside her, feeling the sting on his skin when she scraped him with her nails. She rolled her head to the side, crying out as so many tiny muscles constricted around him she damn near milked him dry before he could get started.

Her cries assured him she didn't want gentle. And once he let go there wasn't any turning back. As tight as she was, Amber took everything he could give her, constricting around his shaft when he impaled her again and again. He thrust deep into her heat, her silky soaked flesh pulling him in farther and clinging to him when he receded, only to dive deep inside her once again.

His heart pounded so hard in his chest while every ounce of blood drained straight to his cock. Jordan couldn't remember when he last felt harder than steel and so swollen he could barely stand it. When his balls constricted, tightening as the need to come became too strong to ignore, he straightened, moving to his knees so he could watch Amber when he came.

"Open your eyes," he told her, grunting as he slowed the momentum, wanting to feel her muscles around him for as long as possible.

Amber's lashes fluttered over her dark blue eyes. Her mouth puckered into a small, perfectly round circle and her cheeks were flushed. He loved watching her full round breasts bounce every time he impaled her. And her creamy white skin, so smooth and soft, glowed with a sheen of perspiration.

"Watch me," he instructed, gliding in and out of her soaked heat while adoring the view she offered.

"I am," she breathed. "I want to watch you come."

Her daring, open nature and willingness to speak her thoughts without hesitating appealed to him as much as the rest of her. As he swelled, feeling his release surge through him, Jordan knew without any doubt this wouldn't be the only time he fucked her. Whether his grandfather planned it or not, he also knew that being with Amber would make it impossible for him to ever touch Princess Tory.

Amber fidgeted with her dress as she stood in the hallway outside Princess Tory's private quarters. The princess and her entourage took up one of the wings on the second floor. Five rooms had been set aside for all of them. She shifted her weight from one foot to the other, feeling the strain inside her from fucking Jordan earlier, and continued waiting, as she'd been instructed when she first arrived, to escort Princess Tory to the parlor to meet Jordan.

Straightening as the door in front of her opened, Amber clasped her hands in front of her, but then released them, hating how nervous she felt.

"Tell me your name, my dear," an older man, possibly in his fifties, asked as he entered the hall and closed the bedroom door behind him.

"Amber Stone." Unsure what the proper way was when it came to introductions with royalty, she thrust her hand out, seeking his to shake.

"Miss Stone," he said, not taking her hand or even looking at it. "I am Carlos Rodriguez, the princess's personal chaperone. The honor is mine, my dear," he added in a rich, melodic accent as he bowed once before her.

Amber wasn't sure if she should bow also but before she could decide, he'd straightened and continued talking.

"Before long, Princess Tory will join us and we'll walk downstairs. I walk alongside the princess and you shall lead us. Please tell me now the itinerary for the evening."

"I'm here to take Princess Tory to the parlor. Jordan is waiting there, and is looking forward to meeting her," she added, although wasn't sure why. More than anything now, when she still sizzled inside from fucking him, Amber despised this task she had to do. And this was just the beginning. It was her job to organize events that would help bring this couple closer together.

"I'm sure he is," Carlos offered dryly. "The princess also requests knowing what will be served for dinner. There are a list of food items she will not eat."

"If you let me know what those are, I'll tell Cook to be sure to not serve them," she offered, thinking it would have been nice to know beforehand that the princess was a picky eater.

"That will be arranged."

Amber nodded. "Cook has arranged a Sicilian dinner she's very anxious to serve." Since she'd researched Sicilian recipes earlier, taking a handful of them to Cook, Amber was grateful she did that now, since it made it easier to describe what would be served tonight. "There will be grilled swordfish, with rice balls stuffed with meat—"

"I will let the princess know," Carlos informed her, cutting her off before she could finish describing the elaborate meal.

Amber had been impressed with how well the kitchen had been stocked. Cook had almost every ingredient on hand for every recipe Amber brought to her. The few items she didn't have, she'd simply grinned and told Amber she'd make do.

Carlos turned and opened the bedroom door, closing it behind him without saying another word to Amber.

"Rather rude," she mumbled, not sure what to do next other than continue to wait.

She didn't have to wait long, though. The door opened again and Carlos appeared with a young woman at his side. He was all business as he entered the hallway, the woman's delicate-looking hand draped over his forearm. He stared at Amber without saying a word, and Amber stared back. Since he wasn't going to make introductions, Amber knew how to do that herself.

"I take it you're Princess Tory," she offered, smiling at the young woman, who in fact was incredibly pretty, and also very young looking. "I'm Amber Stone. Just call me Amber. I'll be organizing the time you spend with Jordan. I have a few ideas already, but if there is any type of social activity you prefer, please let me know."

She sucked in a breath and studied Princess Tory, who stared at her as if there weren't a thought in her head. Her black hair was twisted beautifully around the top of her head. Strands that had been tightly curled fell around her face. She wore a little makeup, but not much, and her soft brown eyes were round and large. The princess didn't bat an eye and didn't respond.

Amber wondered if the woman even knew how to talk. Or maybe she didn't speak English. That would make all of this fun.

"Well, anyway," she mumbled, remembering Carlos telling her she would lead the way to the parlor. "Where I come from it's nice to say hi."

Princess Tory parted her lips, looking for a moment like she might smile. Amber didn't know whether to wait and see if the princess would speak, or to continue heading down the hall to the stairs. She decided to wait.

"Where I come from it's very nice to say hello as well." Princess Tory was very soft spoken, her gentle-sounding voice as melodic as her chaperone's when she responded. "We look forward to the entertainment you have to offer."

Amber grinned, noting Princess Tory was possibly a couple inches taller than she was, and although thin, just slightly more full figured. She didn't know Jordan well enough to know his preference in women, but Amber gathered, watching Princess Tory when she spoke and afterward when her nondescript facial expression returned, that she and Princess Tory were nothing alike.

"It's nice of you to say that. And I admit, I'm a bit nervous about all of this. I've never been in a circumstance like this before."

"It's quite all right," Princess Tory told her, using that same, soft voice that made her sound younger than she probably was. "We believe all of us might be slightly unsure of our behavior at the moment."

"Princess," Carlos urged.

"What?" Princess Tory actually frowned at him, showing her first sign of emotion since Amber met her. "Are we wrong to speak our minds at this point? I don't think so. We think our social organizer's mannerism is refreshing." Princess Tory proved that when she decided to talk, she could easily put people in their place. Carlos nodded once, resuming his solemn expression.

Amber took that as her cue. "If you'll follow me, please."

* * *

Jordan paced his bedroom, knowing he needed to get downstairs and meet the princess, but unable to cut his aunt off and end the phone call when she was so upset.

"I know it's not going to comfort you any to say he's just trying to make you nervous," he tried, doubting anything he said at this point would appease his aunt.

"No, it's not. And I'm not ashamed to say to you that your grandfather is an ass."

"You go right ahead and say it," Jordan told her.

"My ex-husband never owned this ranch. It has never been Anton land," Aunt Penelope continued, her anger seething through the phone. "He's got a lot of nerve contacting me and informing me I need to produce all financial records for the ranch for his accountant to look over and determine if Jorge should be made to pay me alimony or the other way around. The divorce is final."

"They're trying to upset you, Aunt Penelope. Don't let them do it." Jordan could ring his grandfather's neck for striking out when he knew Jordan was on the other side of the world and couldn't properly defend his aunt. "Tomorrow I'll call and arrange for a good lawyer to come out and talk to you. Right now I need to go meet a princess."

"All right, Jordan. Go meet the woman. Who knows, maybe the two of you will hit it off."

Jordan knew his aunt wanted him back on the ranch as badly as he wanted to be there. She didn't want him to like the princess.

"I doubt you have much to worry about. From what I hear I'll be lucky if I get anywhere near her. She has bodyguards who walk around her, blocking her off from the world."

Aunt Penelope snorted. "Sounds like the perfect wife," she grumbled.

"I'll call you really soon." Jordan said his good-byes and hung up the phone, wishing he had time right now to call

Grandfather and give him a piece of his mind. The rat had pulled a fast one, making an attack on the ranch now that Jordan was out of the picture. More than likely Grandfather guessed, or had figured out, that Big Sky Ranch could turn a profit if a few changes were made. Jordan was working on it and sure as hell didn't need Grandfather's greedy claws in the picture.

His frustration toward his grandfather didn't fade when he left his room, adjusting the damn tie he'd decided to wear, and headed downstairs to the parlor. He was ten minutes late, but the princess would just have to accept the fact that the man she was getting to know ran a business. And it wasn't an eight-to-five job. Nor was he the type of guy who smelled rank from old money and lounged around all day, or simply traveled, living a life of leisure.

"Where have you been?" Amber's heels tapped against the floor as she hurried to the bottom of the stairs. She'd changed dresses; and the forest green, figure-hugging piece she'd chosen was stunning.

"I had a phone call." He noticed the moment she took him in, appreciation making her bright blue eyes darken.

She didn't hesitate but reached for his tie when they met at the bottom of the stairs. "Princess Tory is in the parlor and her chaperone has already asked me twice why you aren't here," she whispered, straightening his tie and then stepping back to survey her work. "She doesn't talk much but I've noticed if you ignore the protocol Carlos seems to want in place, she will speak."

He had no idea what she was talking about. "You look gorgeous," he whispered, lowering his face closer to hers.

"You're supposed to say that to the princess." She was all business.

He thought about stealing a kiss but glanced over her shoulder at the cook and the older man by her side. They stood at attention outside the door and when he looked their way both snapped their focus back in front of them. It hadn't been that many years since Jordan lived in a houseful of servants. They would spy, gossip, and make his life hell if he didn't practice discretion. Life would be so much better once this month ended.

"Would you have me seduce two women?" he asked, keeping his posture straight and the appropriate distance between them but narrowing his gaze on hers when her bright blue eyes turned almost violet as she glared up at him.

"No, I wouldn't," she snapped, inhaling deeply, which helped show off her cleavage against the V-neck cut of her sleeveless dress. She'd piled her hair once again at the top of her head and wisps fell around her face and tapered the curve of her slender neck. "You're here for Princess Tory," she added, although her hardened expression didn't fade.

"No one runs my life but me," he informed her. "I might have agreed to spend a month here out of loyalty to my family," he said and finished his thought silently: as dysfunctional and backstabbing as they were. "But what I do while I'm here is my decision and no one else's."

Amber stared at him, not saying a word, possibly digesting his meaning. He ached to touch her. When she looked away first, gesturing for him to follow her, something told him she didn't quite buy his declaration. Jordan didn't have a problem showing her he would run his own life. After Grandfather's attempt to sabotage the ranch in Jordan's absence, any desire Jordan had to go along with his grandfather's game plan here on the island disappeared.

Jordan focused on Amber's narrow waistline and the way her ass swayed as she walked in front of him. She paused at the entrance of the parlor, turning so he stared at her profile. Her back was straight, her chin high, and her expression neutral, offering no indication of how she felt presenting a man she had just had mind-blowing sex with to another woman.

The servants remained at attention, probably more aware of how he eyeballed Amber than they would let him know. Jordan followed Amber into the parlor.

"Princess Tory, I'm honored to present Jordan Anton," Amber announced, her soft, sultry tone sounding sincere but her blue eyes dull, shut down.

Jordan didn't miss her body language, in spite of her exquisite presentation as she swept into the room, proving she could be a professional in spite of the rough edges he'd caught glimpses of since meeting her.

Jordan stepped around Amber, facing the young woman who didn't stand when he entered the room. Ignoring the older man who immediately came to his feet, Jordan bowed gallantly in front of Princess Tory, taking her hand when she offered it and bringing it to his lips.

"It's a pleasure to meet you," he drawled, meeting her gaze and noticing immediately how nervous she was—and how young.

Amber hadn't been wrong when she'd stressed Tory's youth. Jordan would guess her to be in her early twenties, and her cold, damp hand was limp in his as he pressed her fingers to his mouth—not kissing her, but going through the motions before releasing her and straightening, taking a step backward and acknowledging the chaperone.

"Jordan Anton," he said, lowering his voice and extending his hand to the older man, who greeted him with a firm handshake and a scrutinizing stare. "Your flight here was uneventful, I hope."

"The princess has had time to rest and is refreshed," the older man announced, as if all that mattered in the world was the young lady who remained silent in her chair.

"Jordan, this is Carlos Rodriguez, Princess Tory's personal chaperone," Amber announced, finishing her introductions and then stepping backward. "I'll return shortly to escort you to the dining hall." She continued backing up, then grabbed the French doors, closing them quietly and leaving Jordan alone with the princess and her chaperone.

Jordan breathed in a lingering waft of Amber's perfume, holding it in his lungs while visualizing how dark her eyes had turned a moment before when he'd asked her about seducing two women.

"Please, be seated," Jordan said with a wave of his hand to Carlos, playing the host and making himself comfortable in an upright chair facing Princess Tory. He studied her complacent expression and the way her black hair was twisted above her head with tiny curls hanging around her face and along her neck. "I'm sure this is a very awkward moment for you," he said, focusing on her large, round brown eyes that barely blinked when she stared back at him. "We're hardly in a time and age where two people are committed to something without having an opportunity to explore that commitment for themselves."

Princess Tory straightened, the dark blue silk dress she wore accenting her black hair. She was pretty—quite attractive, in fact. But she stared at him as if she'd turned herself off inside, accepting that she had to be here in body, but her mind was a million miles away. He would be insulted by her behavior if he didn't completely agree with the desire to be somewhere else.

"The only commitment here has already been fulfilled," Carlos announced as the doors to the parlor opened.

Jesse appeared, decked out in a tuxedo, and moved along the edge of the room to the bar. Ice cubes clinked in glasses while the servant made himself busy, probably tending to an order he'd already received for the princess.

"Agreed," Jordan offered. "We are all here. And now that we are, we will make the best of this month by relaxing and simply enjoying each other's company." Jordan stood, needing to do something to get that bored, if not incredibly displeased, look off Princess Tory's face. "Princess, let me personally make your drink for you," he suggested. "What suits your fancy?"

"The princess will drink iced water with a slice of lemon." Carlos sounded stern.

"Is she not of age?" Jordan asked.

"She will not be seduced by alcohol," Carlos snapped.

Jordan was getting real tired of everyone's first impression of him being that of a rogue. "There will be no seducing of any kind on my part, sir," Jordan informed him, lowering his voice and giving Carlos a shrewd look. Although technically a servant, the man was in a position where he was used to being a voice of authority. "If Princess Tory would like to sample a refreshing drink, I would be pleased to make it for her." Pulling his hard glare from Carlos, letting him know with a look who really was in charge here, he turned to Princess Tory, surprised to see her staring at him in awe. "Would you like to try a drink a bit more refreshing than iced water?"

"I do enjoy a good Cosmopolitan," Princess Tory said, her accent making her voice pleasant to listen to.

Jordan smiled at her, nodding once. "The lady has good taste," he informed her and moved over to the bar. The servant had indeed prepared iced water with lemon and a mixed drink that resembled a good bourbon. Jordan nodded at him to serve the drinks and then made himself at home preparing Princess Tory's drink and finding a beer for himself.

When dinner was announced, by Cook and not Amber, Jordan offered his arm to Princess Tory, who took it silently and walked alongside him to the dining hall. He'd never understood the practice of the wealthy having dining room tables so long speakerphones were needed to properly address someone at the other end of the table. Sitting at one end of the table with Princess Tory and her chaperone at the other, he felt as if he ate alone.

By the time dessert was served, Jordan was torn with calling it a night and making one last chivalrous effort to know Princess Tory better. She didn't appear to be an unpleasant person, although she was a far cry from being as attractive as Amber. But he sensed in her an unwillingness to explore any kind of relationship with him. If that were the case, nailing it quickly might put all of them out of their misery a lot sooner.

He stood, accepting coffee in lieu of dessert, and walked to her end of the table. "Come outside with me, my dear," he said, holding his hand to take hers. "The gardens are beautiful and very well lit. I think you might enjoy them."

Carlos stood, reaching for Princess Tory's chair before Jordan could.

"The princess won't need an escort during our walk outside," Jordan informed him, knowing there would be no getting to know the real woman behind the shrouded expression with her chaperone accompanying them.

"The princess is always escorted. It isn't proper otherwise," Carlos announced, puffing out his chest.

"It is proper here." Jordan took Princess Tory's hand, lifting her out of her seat. Jordan didn't allow her time to decide but picked up her coffee cup for her, handed it to her, and then guided her around the table. "Inform your chaperone to wait for you here," he said quietly, barely having to lean to speak close to her ear. Princess Tory was a couple inches taller than Amber. "Let him know we won't be more than ten minutes or so; a short walk around the gardens and then back to the safety of your chaperone."

"I don't require the safety of a chaperone," she informed Jordan, her expression changing for the first time since their evening began. She pressed her lips together, pinning him with a look, which was clear enough to read. She didn't like him. "Carlos, I'll be back in a minute," she said, waving her hand over her shoulder, and then freed herself from Jordan's grasp on her arm to walk ahead of him toward the glass doors leading outside.

"Tell me what you think about all of this," Jordan began after they walked into the garden and found benches arranged in a square. Jordan stood on the opposite side of them facing Princess Tory. "If we're to get to know each other, it might help knowing what each of us feels about this unique situation we're both in."

The princess smoothed her hands down her dress. She was definitely beautiful, although not petite like Amber. Her large brown eyes would mystify a man, captivate him and draw him in, eager to know the woman behind such sensual, round orbs.

She didn't wear a lot of makeup, but the liner around her eyes, a bit of color accentuating her high cheekbones, and a dark rose that she had somehow managed to keep on her lips during dinner, helped create a classy image. It was the way she pressed her lips together, though, and then slowly crossed her arms over her chest as she studied him that proved to Jordan she wasn't the least bit interested in him.

"Since you're asking, Mr. Anton," she began.

"Please call me Jordan."

"As you wish," she consented with a slight nod of her head, although she didn't state his name. "When I was informed of the level of your infatuation over a picture of me taken at the beach last summer, my opinion of you hasn't started on a very sound foundation."

Is that what she was told about him? Grandfather Anton was an idiot if he thought using that line on any lady would persuade her to consider dating a man. "I'm not sure I've ever been insulted more gracefully."

Again she nodded, as if they played a game of chess and she noted his action or comment and then played one of her own.

"If you determined me so shallow prior to even meeting me," he continued, "then why did you come? Certainly shallowness isn't a quality that appeals to you in a man."

"Hardly." Her Sicilian accent added to her beauty and grace. Although he immediately would have determined she was too young for the two of them to have many common interests, under different circumstances he might have viewed her an interesting conquest. Princess Tory walked slowly to the end of the stone bench and stared at a trellis covered with beautiful flowers, still showing off their blooms even at night. "I was intrigued as to what type of man would consider buying a wife." Her answer was as stiff as her profile, implying possibly her answer was rehearsed.

"Buying a wife?" Jordan coughed, unable to stomach a moment longer the pack of lies she'd been fed. "I assure you, Princess, I'm not buying a wife."

She sipped at her coffee, continuing to look at the flowers or possibly the darkness beyond the gardens. "There is a chill in the air. I believe I'll retire for the evening."

"As you wish." He wasn't in the mood to beg her to stay.

She didn't accept his arm when he offered to escort her back to the castle. Princess Tory walked in silence next to him, pausing when he opened the French doors for her, then stepped inside in front of him.

"I am ready to retire," she announced to Carlos, walking toward him and then falling into pace, accepting her chaperone's arm and disappearing out of the dining hall without so much as a good evening.

"Rude as hell," he growled, returning to the table and refilling his coffee.

There wasn't a chill in the air. In fact, the evening was rather warm when he returned outside and strolled through the gardens until he reached a tall black, wrought-iron fence surrounding an oblong, nicely lit swimming pool. Walking around the fence, he found the gate unlocked and let himself in.

He placed his coffee at the first table he reached and then returned to close the gate—so he'd have some notice if anyone approached. Pulling out his cell phone, he placed a call to his grandfather. Maybe it was damn near midnight where his grandfather was. It would serve the old man right to be awoken from his sordid nightmares to speak to his grandson.

The call went to voice mail, and Jordan cursed under his breath. Leaving messages on machines wasn't his style. But maybe if the phone beeped announcing a message, Grandfather's interest would be piqued and he'd listen to his voice mail.

"I find it very interesting that you would plant such heartless lies in the beautiful Princess Tory's mind, making it damn near impossible for me to establish any kind of relationship with her." Jordan spoke slowly, thinking his words through as he spoke. "The princess despises me, and I can't say I blame her. She believes me shallow for becoming so infatuated with a picture of her. As well, her opinion of a man who thinks he can buy a wife isn't high either. You've set this entire meeting up to fail and I'm not sure why you did that."

Jordan hung up, satisfied his message would come across loud and clear. Dropping his phone by his coffee on the table, Jordan tugged at his tie until he could pull it from his neck. Then, unbuttoning several of his shirt buttons, he considered stripping out of it as well when he heard the gate behind him rattle.

"Forgive the intrusion." The older servant, Jesse, pushed open the gate and then entered, carrying a small tray next to his head, flat on his palm. He brought the tray down when he reached the table. "I hope I'm not presumptuous in thinking maybe something stronger than coffee might be in order."

"You're a good man," Jordan told him, accepting the cold bottle of beer Jesse presented to him.

The servant still wore his tails and took a small bucket, stuffed with ice, off the tray and set it on the table. Several other bottles of beer were chilling in the bucket. Jesse was worth his weight in gold for understanding the situation and knowing exactly what remedy was needed at that moment.

"Will there be anything else, Master Anton?" Jesse asked.

Jordan's cell phone rang and he scowled at the number, his plan working perfectly, although he would have liked time to down a beer or two and get a good buzz going so he would be more numb before taking on the old man.

"You've more than earned your keep for the day, my man." Jordan saluted Jesse with his beer and then answered the phone.

Jesse nodded, retreating to the gate and leaving Jordan alone poolside with an incredible view. And a conversation with a man Jordan should respect and honor, instead of despise. And he did respect him. It wasn't right to hate family as much as Jordan did—though he'd wished over the years he could have a different family, one that loved and supported each other instead of stabbing each other in the back, Jordan was an Anton and always would be.

"I hope I didn't wake you," Jordan said instead of hello when he answered the call.

"I'm sure it was exactly your intention to do just that," Grandfather Anton said.

In spite of it being the truth, Jordan didn't comment but reclined in one of the chairs at his table and nursed his beer. "I take it you got my voice mail message."

"You're looking for excuses to get out of this, boy," Grandfather decided, instead of apologizing for planting crude and inaccurate innuendos about Jordan in Princess Tory's head. "The Alixandre family is very old and very established in Sicily. That girl comes from blood bluer than yours will ever be."

"That's no reason to insult her," Jordan said under his breath, then tilted the bottle back and downed a good portion of it. "She doesn't like me, Grandfather. And I don't blame her a bit considering the lies you fed her."

"You don't have what it takes to fix something as trivial as a misunderstanding?"

Jordan wasn't sure he wanted to bother. "I shouldn't have to attempt to make a go of this by kissing her ass," he said, knowing getting an apology out of Grandfather would never happen.

"If you don't have what it takes to impress the princess, I can have you flown out of there tomorrow," Grandfather informed him, his tone cool and cutting. "I can put you in our Arizona office for the next few months until you learn the ropes. But mind you, I'd start you out in a plush office with a very padded salary out of consideration to your mother. She wants the best for you even if you don't."

Jordan ached to tell his grandfather to go to hell. "I never suggested I was throwing in the towel," he growled, pulling another cold beer out of the bucket and then twisting off the cap. "There are times, though, Grandfather, when I wish you would show a bit more compassion when you decide to *help* someone."

"Compassion?" Grandfather spat out. "How many relatives do you know who would take care to give their grandsons a plush job with a six-figure income?"

"You know as well as I do I don't want that damn job," Jordan snarled.

Grandfather's laughter should have chilled Jordan's blood. He knew the old man was just warming up, though.

"Forget about that strap of land, boy," his grandfather snarled. "By the time you get home there won't be anything left of it."

"Don't you dare lay a finger on that ranch," Jordan hissed, pushing himself out of his chair with enough force to send it flying backward to the fence behind it.

"Damn shame you don't care about pleasing your own mother as much as you care for that piddly ranch." Grandfather would start attacking where it hurt now. His style was all too predictable, although that didn't make it any less dangerous. "There's nothing at that ranch for you, boy."

"If that ranch means so little, then why are you attacking behind my back?" Jordan growled. "Seems rather cowardly, Grandfather. Even for you." He downed half the bottle of beer, wishing he could feel a buzz from it. His anger soared inside him too much for anything to numb it, though. "If you had any balls, you'd wait until I was back at the ranch before making your next move. That is, unless you're afraid I might actually have the strength to defend myself against you."

Grandfather chuckled, his amusement sounding so sincere, as if he'd just been told a damn good joke. Jordan didn't doubt for a moment Grandfather Anton had been threatened more times in a day than most heard in a lifetime.

"I tell you what, boy. I'll make that deal with you. It might be a good lesson for you. And I want you to make note," Grandfather added, his calm raspy voice hitting a soft, cool tone showing how much he loved the act of verbal intimidation. "When I destroy that ranch, with you on it, you watch and see how it is done. Learn from the master, my boy. It will be a lesson well worth your watching."

"I'll do that," Jordan said dryly, knowing his grandfather expected Jordan to get off the phone and immediately start trying to prepare his defenses. Grandfather would watch his every move and prepare his counterattack accordingly. "At the same time, you can kiss your opportunity to have the Anton family married into bluer-than-blue money good-bye. I don't want anything to do with your sordid game."

Jordan hung up on his grandfather and fought the urge to

hurl his phone across the pool. Instead he slammed it down on the table, forcing ice in the bucket to settle around the remaining bottles. Glancing past the table, he stared at Amber, who stood on the other side of the gate, watching him, her expression a mask of shock and dismay.

7

Amber froze when Jordan noticed her. She'd considered sneaking away when he didn't first spot her at the gate. When she'd heard his half of the conversation and realized how much he despised his grandfather and, worse yet, how pissed he was to be put in this position, she'd found it impossible not to eavesdrop.

"I should have announced myself," she mumbled, hating feeling busted as he glared at her silently.

"Yes, you should have," he growled.

Still unsure whether she should enter the pool or turn and leave him alone, Amber didn't move when Jordan stood, walked over to the gate, and opened it. He took her hand, pulling her inside the gate and then closing it behind her.

At least she didn't need to decide what to do now.

He guided her to the table and let go of her hand to pull out a chair for her, then freed a bottle of beer from the ice in the bucket and twisted the cap off before handing it to her. He returned to his side of the table, relaxing his long, powerful body in the chair and nursed his beer.

Amber sipped at hers, trying to relax with his virile body across the table from her. Charged currents zapped the air between them, giving her chills and at the same time creating a rush of heat she couldn't control anytime she was near him. He'd removed his tie and unbuttoned several buttons on his shirt, allowing one hell of a view of his dark chest hair and the rippled muscles she knew traveled all over his body.

Downing more of the beer barely helped soothe her frazzled nerves. She stared at the swimming pool. The underwater lights created a tranquil and inviting setting. Unfortunately, especially now that he'd met the princess—although Jesse and Cook informed her their first meeting didn't appear to go very well—there was no way she could be seen with Jordan in any setting other than a professional one.

Unable to handle the silence any longer, Amber took another drink of her beer and set it down, turning and facing Jordan. She was surprised to see him already focusing on her.

"Tell me about this ranch," she suggested, noting the torn, yet outraged look in his eyes that made her wonder if talking to him at all would be wise right now.

Jordan downed his beer and put the bottle next to another empty bottle. Pulling another one free of the bucket, he snapped off the cap and gulped it while studying her. His gaze made her wary, and her heart started pounding in her chest. Jordan looked hell-bent on getting drunk. That could make this a very dangerous situation.

"Big Sky Ranch belongs to my aunt and I'm the foreman, or supervisor, over all the ranch hands," he told her. "How much of my conversation did you hear?"

"Probably more than I should have," she admitted. But since she had, and he knew it, it was impossible not to be curious. "Why is he attacking the ranch?"

"To prove to me he can. Grandfather believes that showing

others he's invincible will make them follow and obey without question."

"Is that what you've done up until now?"

The question surprised him. "Hell no," he growled, downing more of the beer and then putting it down on the table hard enough to make ice shift in the bucket. "And it's because I've never done as Grandfather's wished, up until coming to this island, that he's attacking now."

"I don't understand how he would attack a ranch," she admitted, fiddling with her beer bottle. His brooding stare made it too hard to concentrate.

"Take it down. Destroy it. Which would put good people, who've worked there for many, many years, out of jobs. Grandfather doesn't look at it that way, but I do. These people don't know anything else."

"I understand," she said, nodding and slowly scraping the label off her moist bottle. "A job is a person's life. Take that away and you take away every opportunity they have to accomplish any of their goals and dreams. And for some, depending on their age, or how many skills they have, taking their job from them can kill them."

"That sounds like firsthand knowledge."

Amber snapped her attention to his face, realizing she might have revealed more about herself than he could be allowed to know if she were to pull off her job here. And this job meant more to her than any she'd ever had. Already her mother didn't believe the money would be delivered. It was too much to hope for. And Amber understood that. Her mother had struggled all her life for what little they had, and had lived with it being yanked away from them more times than Amber could count. She wouldn't fuck this up. No matter what. Any action, any behavior, was worth it to go home with enough cash to put a down payment on a home her family could call theirs and that no one could take from them—ever.

"It is," she said, putting her beer down and then rubbing her wet hands over the skirt she'd changed into after her duties for the evening had ended. She tugged on her halter top and watched his eyes shift to her breasts. Instantly, they swelled, greedy to have his attention again. "My work as a social planner is my life."

He nodded, seeming to accept her answer. Amber did her best to exhale slowly. He couldn't see her serious sigh of relief.

"That ranch is all my aunt has," he offered.

Asking more questions meant digging deeper into the man she was already too seriously intrigued by. At the moment it was a major case of lust. She treaded in dangerous water pursuing this conversation but desperately wanted to understand him.

"You're here because of that ranch?" She didn't understand the connection and wondered if it would be safer ground discussing Princess Tory.

"No," he said, growling. "I'm here in spite of the ranch." His frown deepened and he downed more of the beer, then reached for the next bottle.

"Are you trying to get drunk?"

"Do you have a problem with that?" he snapped.

"Nope." She saw the demons he warred with and ached to help, to understand. Already she was drifting into territory so dangerous she might not be able to get out if she didn't shut up right now.

"I've worked at the ranch ever since my Aunt Penelope divorced my Uncle Jorge. The problem is, you don't divorce an Anton and survive it."

Good food for thought, she told herself, but then grabbed her beer, feeling danger closing in around her. Like she cared how his family treated their exes.

"My mother knew my helping Aunt Penelope could quite possibly get me blackballed so has made a show of her panic and concern. Needless to say, Grandfather has stepped up to the plate. He has no problem putting family members in their place, or destroying them. And the old bastard chalks it up as a lesson learned."

"Sounds like you might get the award for most dysfunctional family," she told him, trying to make light of it and grinning.

He didn't return the smile but instead watched her with eyes so dark her insides quickened as she lost herself, feeling him pulling her in when she couldn't look away.

"Am I scaring you?" he asked, almost whispering.

She should be terrified. "Not at all. We all have skeletons in our closets."

He did laugh then, although he sounded anything but amused. "And you've heard enough about mine," he informed her, leaning forward on the table and continuing to pin her with his intense stare. "Now tell me about yours."

"My ghosts?"

"You just said everyone has them."

"Oh well," she began, not sure what to say.

"Let me guess. You're from New York . . . Manhattan?"

"I'm from Brooklyn," she informed him, watching for any sign of disapproval. Instead he nodded, appearing intent on knowing more. "This job requires I travel a lot, though, so I'm not there much."

If she told too many lies she'd never keep them straight. It was best to be evasive and get the conversation off of her as smoothly as possible without being obvious.

"Speaking of which, tell me what you think of Princess Tory. I need to lay out your schedule for the rest of this week. I thought we'd start with quiet activities and once you two are more comfortable we'll move to something more elaborate. But if we throw a party I'm going to need lists from both of you as to whom you'd like to invite."

Jordan raised one eyebrow, not responding and then looking like he was ready to veto her entire idea. "Nice try changing the subject off of you," he informed her, swallowing more of his beer and then putting the bottle down. He slid his chair back and kicked off his shoes. "Let's go swimming. You can tell me your life story while we're in the water."

"I don't have a suit." She knew exactly what he had in mind when he gave her a knowing look. "That wouldn't be proper, Jordan. You've had too much to drink. And what if someone saw us?"

"Then they will know I'm getting it on with my social planner." He stood and stripped out of his shirt, dropping it on his chair, and then did the same with his slacks.

Amber gawked at his naked body, immediately drooling over all the bulging muscle flexing in his legs and back as he walked confidently to the edge of the pool. At the last moment, he tugged his ponytail holder from his hair, turned enough for her to see how hard his cock was, and tossed it at the table. It fell to the ground but he ignored it and instead faced the pool and dove in, causing the water to ripple but not splash as he went in, showing off how good of a swimmer he was.

Not only was getting in the water with him naked beyond dangerous, but letting him see she couldn't do anything beyond a doggy paddle would also be a bad idea. There'd never been time to learn how to swim when she was growing up. She'd held down a good thirty hours a week ever since she was fourteen.

Jordan sprang up on the other side of the pool, the top half of his body out of the water as he leaned against the edge with his arms stretched on either side of him. His black hair clinging to his neck and shoulders and tiny ringlets curled over his muscular chest as he smiled at her. Water clung to his lashes, making his eyes appear to glow as he gave her a devilish grin.

"You're coming in or I'm dragging you in, darling," he

drawled. Apparently diving into the water had washed a lot of his anger away. He still looked dangerous, but now for very different reasons. He stretched his arms over the water, moving closer to her, and with a look Amber saw he meant every word he had just said.

"You are not dragging me into that pool." She stood, moving behind her chair and watched him warily.

"Is that a challenge?" he asked, reaching the edge of the pool and then lifting himself out as if he weighed nothing. "You're going to have wet clothes if you don't strip out of them very quickly, my dear," he informed her, walking with ease toward her. He was tall, dark, and so damn good looking her mouth went dry and then suddenly so moist she damn near started drooling. "What's it going to be, my lady?" he asked, reaching her and brushing his wet hand over her cheek.

"Jordan, we can't keep doing this," she whispered, knowing at that moment without any doubt that she was going to fuck him again tonight.

"What? Go swimming?" he teased, taking the bottom of her halter top and easing it up her body.

"I'm not a very good swimmer." And she was even worse at telling him no. She didn't get it. In her twenty-seven years she'd never had a problem telling a man no. And Jordan wasn't the only gorgeous man on this planet.

"I am. I'll protect you." He pulled her halter top over her head and tossed it to the table. Reaching around her waist, which pulled her against his soaked chest, he found the zipper to her skirt as if he knew where it was all along. "All I'm suggesting we do is get into the water."

"Yeah, right." She stood in his arms, his wet chest hair torturing her nipples.

"Nothing will happen that you don't want." He eased her skirt down her legs and then let it fall.

"That's not fair," she complained, stepping out of her skirt and bending down to pick it up so it wouldn't get wet.

"We'll talk about you," he offered, taking the skirt and tossing it to the table without looking in that direction. Instead, he grabbed her panties and pushed them down her thighs.

"I don't want to talk about me."

He knelt in front of her, helping her out of her underwear. But when he pressed his lips to her abdomen, just above her pussy, she gasped, grabbing his wet hair and trying to pull him to a standing position.

Jordan didn't fight her, but stood, and then ran his fingers through her hair, finding her clasp and undoing it. "I want to hear about your family. Prove they are more dysfunctional than mine."

"My family doesn't hate each other." She regretted her words instantly when his gaze darkened and he stared down at her, as if trying to learn something about her. "I mean, we aren't perfect. A far cry from it," she added, trying to compensate for insulting him.

"What is the worst thing about them?"

Before she could answer, Jordan lifted her into his arms and walked to the pool.

"Jordan, no!" she cried out, wrapping her arms around him as tightly as she could. "I'll get in. I promise. Let me do it my way, please." She panicked, suddenly scared to death he would throw her into the water. "Jordan, please," she murmured, burying her face in his neck and clinging to him.

He eased himself into a sitting position next to the pool, adjusting her on his lap so that his cock throbbed against her ass. This wasn't a better position than being tossed in the water.

"Amber," he whispered. "Look at me."

When she lifted her face and stared into his, he kissed her. And he wasn't demanding and aggressive the way he had been earlier today and last night. Instead, the gentleness he applied, moving slowly and almost tenderly, drew a cry from her throat she couldn't stop. She relaxed into him, no longer clinging but resting her arms on his shoulders while leaning back and helping to deepen the kiss. Why the hell did he have to be so perfect in every way imaginable?

Jordan slid forward into the water and Amber tightened her grip on him.

"It's okay, sweetheart," he whispered into her ear. "It's shallow enough you can stand here."

Maybe *he* could stand here. Amber forced herself to relax against Jordan. When she stood, she bobbed up and down in an effort to keep her face and chin out of the water. Their height difference made it a lot easier for him to stand on his own than her.

Jordan once again lifted her into his arms, moved to the edge of the pool, and let go after Amber held onto the side, the heated water coming over her breasts. Sinking in the water until their faces were together, he again pressed. "Where do you live right now?"

"I live with my mom." Amber didn't want him nagging every bit of her personal information out of her. It would make all of it more memorable to him if she just offered enough information to appease him; then they could move on to better topics. "I have a half brother and sister who are about ten years younger than me. Then there's my uncle."

"All of you in one house?" He raised one eyebrow. The underwater lamp, built into the wall of the pool, created light between them, accenting shadows on his face and showing off his rugged good looks.

Amber moved her legs under the water, making scissor motions, and brushed her foot against his muscular leg. Its roughness, the coarseness of body hair, sent tingles rushing over her. She didn't want to talk about her family. It wouldn't impress him. She saw that already by his surprised expression.

"It's temporary." She shrugged, implying it wasn't a big deal. "It really is important that you share your thoughts on Princess Tory with me, though. How else will I know the best events to schedule for the two of you?"

Amber dared to glance into his face. Jordan watched her with eyes that were darker than usual. His black hair clung to his head and neck, showing off his neck and broad shoulders. As he shifted his attention around her face she couldn't help getting the sensation that he was trying to determine the sincerity of her statement.

"And my happiness with the princess is that important to you?"

"It's my job," she said.

"And the quality of work you do while you're here will be determined by whose report? I'm sure whatever I tell Grandfather will suffice."

"Any job I do, I do to the best of my abilities," she stressed. "I don't need anyone covering for me."

Amber pushed away from the wall, moving cautiously with her arms stretched out on either side of her. The water reached her shoulders, and waves caressed her neck and the back of her head when Jordan followed her. Her hair lifted off her back and floated around her in the water.

She felt herself lifted and then his strong arms wrapped around her waist as she suddenly moved with her back pressed against his body.

"I don't want you arranging events for me and the princess," he growled into her ear.

His breath scorched her flesh and she sucked in a tight breath. "That's why I'm here."

He flipped her around, causing the water to splash around them. But she didn't panic this time. Jordan's strong hands gripped her hips but then pulled her against him. She spread her legs and wrapped them around him while resting her arms on his shoulders.

"I'll agree to the charade of being entertained with one condition," he informed her, keeping her pressed against his body with one hand while moving his other hand in the water. Grabbing his dick, he pressed it against her entrance. "For every social engagement you arrange for me and the princess, you also arrange one for you and me."

Jordan slid his cock inside her. It glided deep, feeling like it eased deep into incredibly smooth, tight flesh. The water did something to accentuate and heighten the sensations, allowing her to feel him better. Every twitch, his length and width, stroked her insides.

"That's pointless." She arched against him, staring at him wide eyed while her mouth opened but she managed somehow to stifle her cry. Instead, staring into his dark, dominating eyes, she lost part of herself, of her battle to keep her distance. "Why?" she whispered instead.

Jordan cupped her ass, thrusting with his hips and creating waves around them as he drove deep inside her, hitting the spot that craved his touch the most.

"Because you appeal to me, and she doesn't," he said simply, his teeth clenched together while his facial expression hardened, and he impaled her once again.

Amber wasn't sure why she made her next move. But she leapt backward, like a fish out of water and anxious to return home. Diving to the side, desperately trying to get out of his hands, she hit the water full force, splashing it everywhere and then quickly sinking. Bubbles exploded in front of her face and her own hair blinded her when it floated like a net, trapping her and making it impossible to see which way to go.

She felt Jordan's dick slide out of her and immediately missed the sensation of him stretching and filling her. The emptiness inside her would have been terrible if she hadn't gulped water in, filling her lungs and making her cough. Which made her choke even further. She kicked furiously and waved her arms on either side of her; the surface couldn't be too far away.

Jordan's strong hands pinched her flesh when he scooped her out of the water, lifting her entire body completely into the air and carrying her to the edge of the pool while she continued coughing water out of her lungs as she almost hung over his shoulder.

"You really can't swim, can you?" He didn't set her on the side of the pool, but instead moved to the steps at the end of the pool and stepped out of the water with her in his arms.

A stack of white towels filled several shelves down from the tables and Jordan grabbed a couple, shaking one open with one hand and then placing Amber in a chair and wrapping the towel over her shoulders. He used the other towel to wrap around his hips, securing it and covering himself.

She stared up at him with blurred vision and hated how he glared down at her.

"What the hell did you do that for?" he hissed.

Amber shook her head, struggling to get her long, heavy wet hair out of her face and catch her breath after making a complete fool out of herself. She was as pissed at him as she was angry at herself.

"I didn't ask to go into the water," she pouted.

"You were perfectly safe in my arms, and you damn well knew that." His pressed his fists against his hips, still scowling down at her as if she were in need of some reprimand.

Well, she wasn't in the mood for it, any more than she was in the mood to lose her heart to him. "Jordan, just go. I can find my own way back." She wouldn't look up at him.

"Like hell. I was here first. I doubt you seriously think I'm just going to walk away from you anyway," he informed her, still sounding stern and too damn serious. "Now tell me why you leapt out of my arms when you seriously don't appear to have the first clue about water."

"Excuse me for never taking time to learn how to swim as a child."

"You're excused. Now, why did you leap out of my arms?"

"Because I didn't want to be there," she said.

"Bullshit!" He dragged another chair from the table around to face her and then sat in it. "I want to know what the hell is on your mind. And I want to know now."

"Quit being so damn bossy," she snapped.

"I'd ask nicely if I thought it would make a difference."

She shoved her hair behind her shoulder and then pulled the towel around her tighter, suddenly feeling a chill. Pressing her legs together, she studied his face. There was concern there, but also aggravation. It amazed her how well she felt she understood his expression and body language after just a day. But she reminded herself she'd only known him a short time, and he had no idea who she really was. Amber seriously doubted he'd give her so much attention if he knew she was merely a part of a secretarial pool, working a temp job. At the end of the month she'd once again be sitting at her desk doing tedious data entry. If she pulled off this month, she would be doing it with a hell of a lot of money in the bank.

"It doesn't matter how you ask, Jordan." She swallowed the lump in her throat and blinked back the burning in her eyes as she sucked in an uneasy breath. "We can't get this comfortable with each other."

Amber stood, walked over to the rack of towels, and grabbed another one for her hair. "You're going to have to try harder to get along with Princess Tory. And you aren't going to use me to compensate for the time you feel you're being forced to spend with her."

She tried walking past him but Jordan leapt out of his chair,

grabbing her and not caring when his towel slipped danger-
ously close to falling off his body.

"Like hell I'm using you," he informed her, his face tightening in anger as he narrowed his gaze on her. "Don't feed me a
line of crap, Amber. Because you don't believe this is just physical any more than I do."

"Let me go, Jordan." If he didn't he would see her cry. He
might not have anything to lose if this month didn't work out
the way it was supposed to, but she had everything to lose. And
she wouldn't let go of the first chance she'd had in her life to
have everything.

Jordan dropped his hand to his side and watched her when
she gathered her clothes and then wrapped the other towel
around her waist instead of her hair. She hurried away from the
pool and toward the castle as the first tear burned its way down
her cheek.

8

Amber entered the wing where the princess and her people were staying in the castle. After being here two days, it didn't appear that dining together was bringing Jordan and Princess Tory any closer together. Even steering clear of Jordan didn't seem to be helping matters much.

She paused in front of two large double doors, rapping on them with her knuckles, and then stepping backward when she realized the doors weren't closed all the way. Knocking on them had caused both doors to open slightly into the room.

"It doesn't matter what I think of him, now does it?" Princess Tory was complaining to someone. "I don't have any say over anything in my life."

"Only because you choose to let it be that way." A man spoke and it wasn't Carlos. The thick accent was soft, smooth, and soothing. "You can tell your father you will not continue like this."

"And be disowned? You don't get it, Raul. I don't know why you don't understand."

Obviously Raul's soothing tone did little to appease Princess

Tory. Amber stood frozen, unsure if she should leave or knock louder. Princess Tory hated this arrangement as much as Jordan did. Which made Amber's job even harder. Pierre Anton had checked in with her the night before and implied that her job would be considered done only if she managed to get these two together. She wanted to scream at the old man that she wasn't a matchmaker. Amber was understanding more on a daily basis why Jordan didn't care for his grandfather, and why he didn't stand up to him. The old man had a smooth way of talking and getting her to agree to what he asked. Not to mention he upped the stakes if she helped ensure a proposal, or at least an agreed engagement, when the month ended.

"I understand that if you go along with your father's wishes you'll be miserable for the rest of your life. Do you really want to be married to that pompous ass?" Raul demanded.

Amber stiffened, raising her fist to pound on the door, even if it did open all the way. Whoever this Raul was, there was no way he could know anything about Jordan. And obviously what he did know was very ill informed.

"I will not lose my fortune," Princess Tory announced coolly. "Jordan Anton also comes from money—*a lot* of money, Raul. Would it be so terrible to accept his offer of marriage? Within a year you and I could still be situated at the summer cottage in southern Italy. If I become pregnant, we could simply tell him the child is his."

"You are a wicked child, Tory," Raul growled.

A despicable one was more like it. Amber knocked hard enough to hurt her knuckles. And the door did indeed open farther, allowing Amber to catch a glimpse of Princess Tory walking into Raul's arms, before jumping back and looking at the door, startled.

"Marie!" Princess Tory snapped, walking away from the now opened doors instead of acknowledging Amber.

A woman about the same age as Princess Tory jumped up

from somewhere in the corner of the room and hurried to the double doors, grabbing them and attempting to close them on Amber.

"Wait, please." Amber wasn't going to be sent away. She'd done too much research over the past couple of days while hiding in her room, and she needed input. Approaching Jordan would be too dangerous, which left Princess Tory as her only option. "The princess wants to see me," she whispered, pleading with the young woman, who didn't appear to speak very good English.

Marie shook her head furiously, speaking in Italian and English while gesturing for Amber to back out of the doorway.

Amber grabbed the young girl's hand, holding it firmly in hers and then giving it a firm shake until Marie stared at her with large brown eyes while her mouth parted and formed a small circle.

"Enough," Amber ordered. "Announce me to Princess Tory now, or I'll push my way in and announce myself." She spoke slowly and softly, hoping Marie understood English better than she let on.

Apparently Marie did. She closed her mouth, her lips pressing into an agitated line, and then made a tsking sound in her throat before turning around. Amber didn't let her close the doors on her, but stuck her foot out. She stepped forward when Marie marched over to Princess Tory and started complaining in Italian and gestured wildly.

Amber moved into the room farther, clasping her hands behind her back. She wasn't sure if approaching Princess Tory in jeans and her sleeveless blue blouse, one of the new pieces of clothing she'd purchased with the clothes allowance she'd been given prior to leaving the states, was proper or not. Princess Tory wore a corset-style blouse that showed off her breasts rather nicely. Her figure-hugging skirt, which ended before her knees, was cut close at the waist, also showing off Princess

Tory's nice, youthful figure. Today her black hair tumbled past her shoulders in large, flowing curls that gave her a regal look.

Amber shifted her weight from one foot to the other, holding her own and enduring the rather displeased look Princess Tory gave her before waving her servant away. Marie mumbled something else in Italian, glaring at Amber before returning to her corner. She plopped down in a chair next to the other woman, the two of them apparently there for when Princess Tory decided she needed them.

Amber took the action to mean that Princess Tory would speak to her. Stepping into the room farther, she spotted Raul standing not very far from Princess Tory with his arms crossed over his thick chest. He was one of the men who'd escorted the princess into the castle the night she arrived. To Amber, his tan skin and black hair with equally black eyes helped give him a compelling, if not commanding appearance. Amber decided that, at most, he was her age. Somehow knowing no one in the room was older than she was added to her confidence and she moved closer to Princess Tory, pausing when she was several feet from her and Raul.

"Thank you for giving me a minute of your time," Amber said, lowering her head slightly out of respect although for some reason feeling it would be too foolish to bow. When Princess Tory didn't comment and simply stared at her, Amber decided to cut to the meat of her visit. "It's really important you and I speak," she added, deciding that playing at Princess Tory's frustration might be to her advantage. Brainstorming quickly, while watching the Princess for any sign of emotion to reveal itself in her otherwise bored expression, Amber chose her words carefully. "I've kept notes on the results of each meal you've shared with Mr. Anton," she began cautiously. "I believe discussing with you the next scheduled event, prior to arranging it, might be to your advantage in this delicate matter."

Raul whispered something to Princess Tory in Italian. More

than anything at that moment Amber wished she understood the language. Whatever he said caused Princess Tory to shoot her attention to him, and then a smile appeared on her face. She murmured something to him in return, and he nodded once, then turned and left the room through another door, possibly adjoining the room next door.

Princess Tory snapped her fingers and the two young women in the corner jumped to their feet. Both moved to their princess's side, and then moved with her to a corner of the room. There was yet another door, which Marie opened, but then both women hugged Princess Tory, speaking frantically in their native tongue. Each woman kissed the princess on either cheek before hurrying out of the room and closing the door behind them. Princess Tory turned to face Amber, her hands behind her on the door handles, and her expression triumphant as she smiled at Amber.

"You and I will talk," she announced, as if the idea were hers. "You are in charge solely of the entertainment and events I will partake in with Jordan Anton?"

"Yes, I am," Amber said, taking in the contents of the room and noticing a couch and coffee table on the opposite end of the room from where Marie and the other woman had sat. "If you will," she continued, gesturing to the couch, "we should sit and visit, know more about each other, and work together to make these events as pleasant for you as possible."

"Why do you care how pleasant they are for me?" Princess Tory walked over to the couch, but before sitting, picked up the phone on the end table next to the couch and made a quick call. After muttering just a few words, she hung up and then sat in a corner of the couch, stretching her arm over the back of it, and waving her hand as royalty would—or at least how Amber imagined royalty would—for Amber to sit in the upright chair next to the couch.

Amber moved to the chair, sitting and crossing one leg over

the other, then pressing her hands over her knees. "I'm not doing my job right if you aren't happy while you're here, Princess Tory," she said, hoping she wasn't slitting her own throat by offering this information. The princess looked like she might enjoy making people's lives hell if she were so inclined. "I understand that you aren't necessarily here by your free will."

"Who told you that?" Princess Tory snapped, but then stiffened and offered her bored facial expression when Marie and the other woman entered, carrying a silver tray and placing it on the table. Two cups of steaming, strongly flavored coffee were poured. After serving the coffee and small plates with some kind of cream-filled Danish, the women retreated, leaving them alone. "I never do anything I don't want to do. You must understand that right now," she stressed.

Amber nodded, deciding not to argue with her, and took a sip of her coffee. "Oh, this is good," she said, grinning at Princess Tory. "Did you bring this with you?"

Princess Tory was affected by flattery. "I bring my own coffee any time I travel."

"I don't blame you a bit. I should have done the same. The coffee here is good and all . . ." she added, intentionally letting her sentence drift off. Allowing the princess the upper hand, making her believe she was better than Amber, more organized, and that Amber was here to appeal to her for assistance in planning what would happen next between Princess Tory and Jordan, would hopefully get her to open up more to Amber.

"I will have Marie and Leona provide you with some of my coffee for your room," Princess Tory decided.

"You're very kind." Amber took another drink, thinking round one went to her. Now to learn more about Princess Tory. She needed to do something to make sure this month didn't turn into a complete disaster. "I accept that you don't do anything you don't wish to do," she began again, treading carefully while watching the princess's expression for any sign she might be pushing too far. "But I believe I'm right in guessing you haven't been very impressed with Mr. Anton so far."

Princess Tory sipped her coffee, taking her attention from Amber and instead fingering the pastry on her plate. Apparently she didn't wish to share her opinion about Jordan with Amber, which might be for the best. Amber didn't want to defend him. She wanted to think about him as little as possible, especially during a conversation with a woman who was supposed to marry him, if all went as both her and Jordan's families planned. All because of money. Even more reason for Amber not to think about Jordan. He would never be able to consider someone like her, other than as a woman to meet with secretly. Amber wouldn't live like that.

Clearing her throat when Princess Tory didn't answer, and letting her think Amber was disappointed with her silence rather than fighting to keep Jordan out of her head, she tried again.

"There are several different activities you and Mr. Anton can do together in an effort to relax the atmosphere between the two of you. It would help me, though, to know your interests. I don't wish to invite you to do something you don't enjoy with someone you already aren't comfortable around."

"That is very considerate of you. What do you have in mind?" Princess Tory asked.

"I think over the next week the two of you should engage in horseback riding, if you ride," Amber said, throwing out her ideas quickly. "You two can hike over the island. Or if you prefer you can be driven to one of the many beautiful locations on the island for a private picnic. You could go to the beach and swim there if you're inclined. Also, there are activities in the castle that might amuse you."

"Such as?"

"There are pool tables," Amber began.

Princess Tory frowned.

"Billiards," Amber corrected herself and Princess Tory nodded. Amber went on, "I've explored the castle thoroughly. There is an indoor swimming pool if you prefer that over being in the sun. There is a tennis court in the castle as well."

"You wish to exhaust the two of us," Princess Tory accused although her expression remained relaxed.

Amber decided to take her comment lightly and laughed, relaxing farther into the chair. "Honestly, Princess, I just want to make your time here on the island enjoyable. I am planning a party in a couple weeks. You must be comfortable around Mr. Anton to at least appear the happy host and hostess when guests arrive," she added, quoting a comment Pierre Anton had said to her the night before.

"A party?" Princess Tory laughed. "How will you throw a party? You will invite the servants to dance?"

"No. Already I have contacted both of your families to gather names and addresses of your friends so I can invite them to the island. The party will be festive and will include everyone you know."

Something akin to terror passed over Princess Tory's face. "You've contacted my family? Who have you contacted?"

Amber searched her memory, hoping she got the name right. "Lord Duke Alixandre." She hadn't been sure initially if she was dealing with two titles or if Duke was his first name. Fortunately, a friendly servant, who answered the phone when she called the Alixandres, and spoke decent English, had informed her the Lord's first name was Duke.

"My father," Princess Tory muttered. "You spoke with him personally?"

Amber nodded. "The gentleman who answered the phone sounded rather surprised that Lord Alixandre would take the call, but I spoke to him personally and he will have a list of names to me before the week is out. He sounded rather excited about the party and asked for an invitation as well."

Princess Tory's look turned wary. "Is my father paying you as well to insure the success of this engagement?" she asked, watching Amber carefully as she spoke.

"Not at all. And honestly, the whole thing seems rather odd to me."

Princess Tory put her coffee cup down and jumped up from the couch, looking like she might throw a serious fit. Amber braced herself, moving to the edge of her seat, more than capable of defending herself but reminding herself she wasn't dealing with a spoiled brat from back home.

"Thank you for that!" she announced, throwing her hands in the air in a fit of exasperation. "This entire ordeal is preposterous and simply my father's way of punishing me for looking beneath my social status," she announced, fisting her hands against her waist and narrowing her gaze on Amber. "But you might be able to help me. I would pay you generously on the side if you were to do something for me. Would you consider such a proposition?"

Amber left Princess Tory's wing less than half an hour later, wishing more than anything she had someone she could talk to. Princess Tory was a bitch. But at the same time, Amber didn't blame her completely for wanting the month to end in her favor. After storming through the castle, more than anything to burn off steam, she had to admit that, in the same position, she would also want this bizarre scenario to end in her favor. Although, Amber gave thanks for not being cursed with so much money in life she couldn't live it as she wished. If she walked away from this adventure with anything, it would be learning that being impoverished her entire life had its advantages.

She gulped in the warm afternoon air, laced heavily with the saltiness from the ocean breeze, when she headed outside and toward the stone barn. Today, Lord—the large black horse she'd ridden with Jordan her first night here—stood inside a tall fence attached to the barn. Amber paused at the entrance to the barn, not seeing anyone, but not feeling like announcing her presence, and instead walked to the fence. Lord immediately moved closer to her.

"Hi there, big guy," she whispered, hesitating in extending her hand. "Looks like you're enjoying your day."

The horse was magnificent, so tall and the sun radiated off his shiny black body. He lifted his head, glancing down at her with his large dark eyes, and she swore he nodded.

"I wish I could say the same. You've probably spent a good part of your life around the incredibly wealthy. How do you handle it?" She didn't move her hand off the fence when Lord moved his head, brushing his velvety nose over her fingers. "I don't see how you can take it," she continued, deciding that if the only creature she could unload on was a horse, at least he appeared intelligent and nuzzled against her. She dared moving her hand to the side of his head, stroking him the way Jordan had shown her when Lord had been in the barn. "They seriously do believe every problem can be resolved with money. And maybe they're right to an extent. But how do I take money from someone and then bad-mouth someone I care about?"

Lord lifted his head. He looked disgusted and she nodded. "I agree. It's wrong. And I can't do it. But there's got to be a way to help these two out so they can both leave here happy."

Lord made a whinnying sound and then nodded his head up and down. Amber stepped back from the fence, her heart suddenly pounding when Lord stamped his hoofs on the ground and looked like he might try leaping over the fence.

"What is it, boy?" she asked. Glancing around her, she wished she understood horses better. "I don't have anything to give you." Her palms were sweaty when she moved closer to the fence and once again put her hand on the top of it. "Maybe you see how ridiculous this entire situation is. Is that it, Lord?" she asked, forcing her hand to stay put when once again Lord nuzzled his nose against it. "People should be allowed to decide for themselves who they fall in love with. Although I guess you don't get to choose, do you?" She shook her head and made a face at the horse. "If you could choose, you'd probably want a lady horse as magnificent as you are, wouldn't you? But Princess Tory wants a man who her father doesn't approve of. She's willing to cheat and enter into a marriage without love and then keep her lover on the side. Jordan deserves so much better than that. But how can I tell him?" Amber lowered her head, staring at Lord's strong, muscular body through the fence. "Maybe he doesn't want to know. He was willing to see me on the side during this month. Maybe he'd marry the princess and then do exactly the same as what *she* plans on doing. And you know, nothing either of them does is any of my business. All I have to do is organize parties and keep my feelings out of their affairs. Why is that so hard for me to do?"

When she looked at Lord, wishing he could offer some paramount wisdom, the horse held his head high, staring past her to the barn.

"You think all of this is ridiculous, don't you?" She couldn't get Lord's attention and sighed, taking her hand off the fence and walking along the fence to the gate behind the stone barn. Entering into the shady area, the coolness quickly surrounding her was thick with the pungent smell from the barn. Lord paced her, reaching the gate before she did and then stepping anxiously, as if he believed she would open it for him. "I can't help you out any more than I can help out Jordan," she told Lord. "I can't give Jordan what he wants. And I can't give you what you want."

Amber wouldn't feel sorry for herself. She wasn't doing anything wrong. Princess Tory was adamant that Amber accept her offer to bad-mouth Jordan, state to Princess Tory's father that she found Jordan to be without scruples and rude, annoying, and any other terrible things she could think to say to him. Princess Tory even offered to pay Amber extra if she would tell Lord Duke Alixandre that Jordan had repeatedly propositioned Amber, letting her know he would have an affair with her while courting the princess. If Amber denounced Jordan publicly, Princess Tory would see to it that Amber was paid a very nice figure, enough money that, along with what Pierre Anton offered her for bringing the two together, she could buy a house outright.

Lord stomped his hoof on the ground, appearing impatient that Amber was lost in her thoughts and ignoring him.

"Sorry there, boy," she soothed, reaching her hand to his face but then jumping back when he moved quickly, raising his lips and showing off strange-looking teeth. "Hey, you don't need to be mean about it!"

"He's not being mean. He wants you to feed him." Jordan, speaking behind her, almost made Amber trip over her feet.

She jumped around, stabilizing herself by pressing her hand against the stone wall, and stared at Jordan. He leaned against the other end of the barn, one boot crossed over the other and his arms crossed over his chest. God, he looked sexy as hell!

"How long have you been standing there?" she demanded, worried that he might have heard her unload on a horse.

Jordan shrugged, pushing away from the corner of the barn. "Long enough," he suggested, piercing her with an intense gaze that suggested possibly too long.

He made a clicking sound with his tongue and Lord moved to him, reaching his head over the fence when Jordan patted his T-shirt pocket. "There something you want, boy?" he murmured.

Amber's heart raced in her chest as she watched him talk to the horse as if they'd known each other forever. If he lived and worked on a ranch, that would explain Jordan's familiarity with horses. It also should have made her think twice about coming here to find solace and comfort. Jordan was probably more at home around the horses than anywhere else on the island.

She watched him pull something from his pocket that excited Lord. Holding his palm out, Jordan kept it steady when Lord moved his lips in that funny way of his again, brushing them over Jordan's hand.

"Want to try it?" he asked her, glancing in her direction and looking incredibly calm and relaxed, as if they hadn't gone a couple of days without seeing each other and that the last time she'd seen him she hadn't raced away from him in tears.

"Try what?" she asked.

Jordan reached into his shirt pocket and Lord raised his head, whinnying loudly. Amber jumped, unsure which way to move but not so sure the horse wouldn't rise up on his hind legs. He looked ready to do just that and he was tall enough as it was just standing on four legs.

"Feeding him. He's got a sweet tooth," Jordan told her, then looked at the horse and winked. "Don't you, boy?"

"I don't think . . ."

"What? You'll carry on a conversation with him, but not feed him?" Jordan looked dangerous when he moved in on Amber, his black hair pulled neatly away from his face and his hardened features making her believe he was quite pissed and covering it up with his soft baritone and slow movements.

She ached to ask exactly what he'd heard her say, but pursuing that line of questioning would inevitably end up with him demanding any clarification he might need as to what he overheard. Amber wasn't going to go there.

"I don't have anything to feed him." She glanced over her shoulder while backing away from Jordan.

He wasn't going to let her go. Although he'd approached her cautiously, he suddenly lunged at her, causing Lord to jerk his head back and make a low, menacing sound that couldn't be good.

Jordan ignored the horse, instead lifting Amber off the ground and pulling her into his arms. "Don't try to run from me again," he whispered into her face, his eyes so gray they stole her breath.

"Why are you doing this?" she demanded. Fighting him was useless. He was a lot taller and a lot stronger than she was. Not to mention, she'd so desperately missed him touching her that when she crashed against his muscular chest she damn near came. Her husky whisper was probably as much of a giveaway to her feelings as the expression on her face must have been.

Jordan held her to him, not saying anything for a moment. He was angry. His entire body appeared tense enough that for a moment she didn't know if he'd keep her against him or send her flying.

"Why are you fighting it?" he asked, instead of answering her question.

Amber shook her head, so many possible answers to his question hitting her at once. "You aren't here for me," she whispered, not voicing any of the many reasons that popped into her head.

"Do you think I'm here for Lord?" he asked, keeping her pinned in his arms with her feet dangling against his legs.

"You know what I mean," she countered.

"I already told you I came to this island because it was the only way to get Grandfather off my back. It never was to get to know some princess better. Since you know this, then there must be another reason why you're avoiding me."

"I'm not going to be some fling that will be tossed to the side once your time here is over," she spat at him, and then struggled to get out of his arms.

"Is there some reason you wouldn't continue seeing me

once you return to the states?" he demanded, tightening his grip on her.

She couldn't free herself and sagged against him. It took more strength than she had not to place her arms on his shoulders. His face was inches from hers. And he held her against him as if she weighed nothing. He must have overheard her telling Lord her fears and concerns. Yet now he would torture her with that virile body of his pressed against hers, touching her everywhere, until she said to him what he'd heard when he shouldn't have.

"You accept that your family would put you in a position where you're to date a woman because of her status and how much money she has. Yet you question why I would think you wouldn't see me under circumstances away from here?" He didn't know her financial situation but there wasn't reason to give him the morbid details. "I don't come from the kind of family that your family approves of."

"Like that matters to me!"

"Obviously it does or you would have told your grandfather to go to hell and would have never come to this damn island," she yelled, unable to control her temper any longer.

Instead of tossing her to the side as she anticipated, Jordan lowered his mouth to hers, brushing his lips over her mouth. "I'll call my grandfather right now and tell him to go to hell if you'll return to my room with me to hear it."

"Jordan." He was taking the fight out of her.

Damn him to hell and back. For two days she'd managed to stay in her room, researching the kinds of parties thrown by the rich and famous. The moment she'd taken a break, found respite outside the castle, he'd found her. What sucked was she was glad he had. She'd missed this, missed being in his arms, feeling every inch of that hard body of his pressed against hers. And she'd gone nuts not feeling him caress her, bring her body to a boiling point in a matter of seconds. She'd missed his kiss.

Amber didn't instigate the kiss. She swore to herself she didn't. But when his lips pressed against hers and his tongue caressed her mouth open, her arms wrapped around his neck and she took all he offered. When he turned, pressing her against the rough stone wall and devouring her mouth like a starving man, she barely acknowledged the roughness scraping her backside as she tangled her fingers in his hair and fed from him.

"Come back to my room," he groaned, already pulling her from the wall and walking to the side of the barn.

"I can't." She struggled in his arms before they were out from behind the barn. No way could anyone from the princess's entourage see her with Jordan, especially after Princess Tory's proposition.

"You would go visit with Princess Tory but not feel it's appropriate to visit with me?" he demanded.

He allowed her to slide down his body, but kept his hands on her hips. She stared at her hands and how her fingers stretched over his T-shirt, which was taut against bulging muscle.

"What all do you know, Jordan?" she asked.

He moved his hand to her chin and forced her head back. When she met his gaze and those intense gray eyes of his, she feared the worst.

"What I don't know I have no doubt you'll tell me when you're ready," he informed her, then lowered his mouth to hers again in a searing kiss.

9

Jordan left the dinner table, once again disgusted and bored with the time he'd spent with Princess Tory. He'd noticed her manner toward him changing over the past day or so. Although the conversation always remained superficial, she appeared to be friendlier than she had been during their first meeting. He didn't trust her.

Amber had been close to panicked earlier behind the barn that he'd overheard her say something she didn't want him to hear. He'd arrived at the side of the barn in time to see her trying to make friends with the horse. She'd been talking to Lord, although Jordan hadn't paid attention to what she'd said. All he'd seen was her willingness to learn about something she didn't know, and to befriend a creature most experienced riders would have seen in a flash wasn't a horse to be reckoned with.

Amber didn't see that, though. Any more than she saw Jordan as someone to trust. Her inability to see his true nature when she so easily saw the beauty in Lord bugged the crap out of him. And told him one thing. Amber fought tooth and nail to keep her distance from him. But her mind and body screamed to do just the opposite. That, or possibly she saw something in him that he didn't want to admit existed. That put him in an even fouler mood.

He glanced in the direction of Princess Tory's wing but then headed the opposite direction toward his own room. Turning to take the hall to his bedroom, he paused when Amber stood against the wall outside his door.

"Lost?" he asked, and enjoyed the hell out of how her cheeks flushed a beautiful rose color.

"I can get lost," she retorted, pushing herself away from the wall.

"Like hell." He reached his bedroom door and opened it, then stepped to the side so she could enter ahead of him.

Her look was wary, but she hesitated only a moment before walking in before him. She wore a strapless minidress tonight with plain flat shoes. He loved the slender curve of her legs and couldn't wait to find out if she wore underwear under that one-piece dress.

Closing the door behind him, he had half a mind to unzip the back of it and put his curiosity to rest.

Amber walked away from him, farther into his room, looking around her as if inspecting his personal quarters. He remained where he was, giving her time, and waited until she faced him.

"I don't know what you heard me saying to the horse earlier today," she began.

"Nothing." He decided he didn't like her tormented expression and wanted to put her mind at ease. Obviously she'd worried since this afternoon about what he might have heard.

"Nothing?" she repeated.

He shook his head. "Why don't you tell me now."

She let out a tormented sigh, again taking in her surroundings. Amber wasn't nervous, but instead possibly plagued by something. He chanced walking away from his bedroom door, knowing he could stop her from leaving if she tried, and instead went over to the stocked wet bar in the corner of his room. He opened the small refrigerator and pulled out two beers, twisting the cap on each and then moving to her side.

She searched his face as she accepted the bottle he handed her and then again sighed deeply when she walked away from him.

"I think I unloaded my worries earlier today on a horse because I wasn't sure there was anyone else on the island I could talk to about it."

She wasn't making any sense, but Jordan had learned long ago that remaining quiet and allowing someone time to speak their mind often got him more information than if he bombarded the person with questions. He walked over to his couch, which was in the corner of his room, and reclined on it. Amber faced him but didn't join him, and he made himself comfortable, taking off his boots and then crossing one foot over the other on the coffee table in front of him. He admitted it did his ego good to glance up at her and catch her definitely drooling over him.

She cleared her throat. "It dawned on me earlier tonight that I didn't talk to you about these things, although I wanted to initially, because I was being selfish. Telling you what I know will help you. I didn't tell you initially because I knew what would happen if I was alone with you again."

At least she accepted she would make love to him tonight. Jordan nodded to the couch next to him. "Sit down and tell me what you know," he instructed, telling himself he wouldn't touch her until she had gotten whatever was bugging the hell out of her off her mind. As it was, she was too distracted to enjoy herself.

Amber obeyed, taking the other end of the couch and shifting her body so she faced him. It was hard as hell for him not to focus on the spot where her legs met when she crossed one over the other. Her dress rode high on her, exposing a fair amount of thigh. But when she let her shoes slide off her feet while taking another sip of her beer, obviously intent on getting comfortable, it was damn impossible not to get hard as a rock.

"I don't know how you know I went to visit with Princess Tory earlier today, but I did." She stared at him, searching his face, as if waiting for him to enlighten her. He wouldn't give her any answers and sidetrack her from what she needed to tell him. "Fine," she grumbled. "Don't tell me. I went and visited with her. We both know that."

Jordan took a long slow drink of his beer, watching when she sucked in a breath and her cleavage pressed against the straight cut of her strapless dress. Amber matched him, guzzling down a good half of the bottle of her beer. She drank like a pro, more proof that she was as far from polite, upper-class society as a girl could get. It was one of the many things about her he truly liked.

"I approached her because it's obvious how little both of you are enjoying each other's company." She chewed her lower lip, studying him for a moment, then put her beer down. "And your grandfather had a long talk with me last night, making it clear he would pay me even more if I could ensure that there would be a marriage proposal by the end of the month."

"Did he say whom I had to propose to?"

His question didn't hit her as quickly as he expected, proof something seriously tormented her. But then her jaw dropped and her face turned a beautiful crimson. She snapped her mouth closed, scowling at him, and then nervously reached for a strand of hair that tickled her neck. The rest of her hair was wrapped in a loose bun behind her head, and he couldn't wait to tear it free and watch it fall loosely around her naked body.

"I didn't ask," she told him curtly. "But I decided to ask Princess Tory what activities she would enjoy partaking in. We discussed riding horses, hikes around the island, or even playing pool or swimming."

"What was her response to all of that?"

"She accused me of trying to wear the two of you out."

He couldn't help laughing at her adorable scowl and continued laughing when she finally offered him a small smile.

"So are you here to ask me what kind of activities I would enjoy?" he asked, downing the rest of his beer while watching her over the bottle.

Again she blushed and then reached for her bottle, finishing off most of her beer. "I came here to tell you what she suggested I do."

Jordan got up to get them each another beer. "I'm listening," he told her.

"Princess Tory offered to pay me if I would inform her father that you propositioned me while on the island."

Jordan froze, his hand on the refrigerator handle. Outrage tore at his insides. The fucking little bitch would mar his reputation, destroy him if possible, in order to get out of this ridiculous situation. He admitted he hadn't seen that one coming and was glad he had his back to Amber for a moment to regain his composure before getting their beers and returning to the couch.

He again sat facing her, handed her a beer, and then opened his bottle. "Go on," he said, noticing she didn't bat an eye when he didn't open the beer for her.

Amber didn't look at her bottle when she twisted off the lid, proof she'd opened a fair share of beers on her own in her lifetime. "That's it. All I have to do is let her father know what a terrible person you are and she'll pay me more money than I've made in a year before."

It was on the tip of his tongue to ask her how much. But that wasn't the point here. Amber brought him the information, which was proof enough, he hoped, that she didn't plan on taking the bribe.

"What are you going to do about it?"

She shot him a look of surprise. Then, jumping off the couch, her minidress swirled around her slender legs when she hopped around the coffee table.

"This," she announced, holding her arms out, her beer in one hand. "I'm doing it now. I'm ashamed I talked to a horse about all of this instead of you in the first place," she admitted, looking appropriately chastised. Then, fingering the damp bottle, tugging on the label, she continued. "I avoided coming to you first for the wrong reason: because I was scared to see you." When she focused on him, her bright blue eyes appeared to glow with emotion. "And that's wrong. You're a good man, Jordan. Your reasons are your own for being here. And I won't have some cheap tramp hiding behind her royal title trying to do you wrong just so she can have her cake and eat it, too."

Her last words hit him more than her admission that he was a good man. Pushing himself off the couch, he moved around the coffee table, holding on to her attention as he closed the distance between them.

She didn't stop him from taking her beer out of her hands, nor did she back away from him. Jordan placed both bottles on the coffee table and took her damp hands in his.

"Amber," he grumbled, hoping his voice wasn't as obviously laced with his feelings as it sounded to him like it was. "You're more of a princess than Tory is."

She blinked, but kept her expression solemn, straightening a bit although she still had to tilt her head to see his face. "You two are probably accustomed to living in a world of backstabbing and lies. I'm not," she offered simply.

And it hit him at that moment it was that quality right there that made her glow, made him ache for her, and made him crave keeping her with him for as long as possible.

"Don't change," he said simply and let go of her hands, reaching for her hair and easily undoing the clasp that confined it behind her head. "Being accustomed to it doesn't make everyone like it, or agree to be part of it."

"Good," she whispered, her voice cracking.

She wanted him to kiss her. And there wasn't anything he wanted more at the moment. Soon he would figure out his best method of counterattack against the princess. He would prefer doing nothing, but unfortunately, Amber was right. He did live in a world where backstabbing, cheating, and lowlifes came in the most expensive of suits and décor. That didn't mean he would ever condone it or tolerate it. What he would do was get to know this gorgeous creature standing in front of him.

Dragging his fingers through her thick hair, he forced her head back farther. Amber relaxed into his touch, her long lashes fluttering over her dark blue eyes.

"This isn't wrong," he whispered into her mouth before pressing his lips against hers.

She'd told him she was scared to come to him. And he already knew she had intentionally avoided him since the night in the swimming pool. Amber stayed away from him out of fear of being used. Yet the woman his grandfather wanted him to marry would readily use and abuse. Her work ethic was quite possibly as strong as his. He always viewed it a warped irony that his family was upset over his desire to earn his keep, to wake up to an alarm every day and feel the sore muscles by the time the sun went down. Maybe it was money, or something deeper engrained that gave his family such a warped, misconstrued outlook on life.

But Amber was a kindred spirit. Like him, she viewed the quality of her work as what represented her. She believed the world judged her by how well she did whatever task was at her fingertips. That part of her nature alone made her a better person than anyone else on this island or, unfortunately, in his family.

He feasted on her, dragging his mouth from her lips to her neck. Tasting the sweetness of her flesh, enjoying how smooth and soft she was, he knew if he stood here much longer, devouring her like this, his cock would be so hard it would be difficult to move.

Jordan lifted Amber into his arms, ignoring her squeal of surprise, and carried her to his bed. "If you don't want this, you'd better say so right now," he told her.

"And that would stop you?" There was a mischievous grin on her face when he laid her on his bed.

Jordan stared down at how her long hair fanned around her as she stared up at him with beautiful, bright, dark blue eyes. "It would give me a clue to start in on my excellent persuasive arguments."

Her grin shifted to a smirk but she didn't move, and didn't tell him to stop. Yanking his T-shirt from his body, he didn't want a single moment passing when he couldn't gaze down at her. Her strapless dress rode up against her hips and the way she'd bent her legs, he still couldn't tell if she wore underwear or not.

Undoing the top button on his jeans, his cock danced with so much eagerness in his jeans, it hurt to pull down his zipper.

"Spread your legs, Amber," he growled, his voice thick with desire. There wasn't any hiding it from her. She pulled something out of him, something buried so deep inside him he hadn't really acknowledged it before.

"Like this?" she whispered, brushing her fingertips over her knees and up to the edge of her dress as she stretched her legs, bending them so her feet were flat against his bed, and then opened for him.

For a moment he couldn't answer. Amber wasn't wearing a damn thing under that dress.

His expression obviously pleased her very much. She licked her lips, trying to hide her satisfied smile, and moved her hands slowly up her body.

"Or maybe this is better," she teased, moving her fingers over her shaved pussy.

"Damn it, woman." He struggled out of his jeans, visualizing ripping that little dress off her body. "You're asking for trouble."

"Am I?" She played it coy, slowly stroking her smooth flesh until a sheen of moisture made her pussy glisten and her fingers wet. "I don't think that's what I'm asking for."

His cock was so damn heavy, he swore every ounce of blood had drained to that part of his body. Kneeling on the bed, he gripped it, feeling his heart pulse feverishly as he stroked his shaft. Amber's attention shifted to the act, and she licked her lips, leaving no doubt exactly what it was she wanted.

Knowing how badly she wanted him—that possibly prior to coming here and rehearsing what she would say to him, that making love to him dominated her thoughts—made this moment even more special. Something had changed in her line of thinking. Since meeting him, she'd run from him, always been on the defensive. Jordan really liked this submissive, willing side of Amber a lot better.

"Move your hands." He grabbed her legs, spreading them farther as he lowered himself and breathed in her ripe, rich scent.

"Jordan," she whispered, making his name a question and request all at once.

He'd learned this about Amber quickly. She loved him tasting her, feasting on her, and lapping her juices when she came. He held her legs in place when he dragged his tongue over her smooth, wet flesh and kept her where he wanted her when she cried out and bucked against him.

"God yes!" she cried out, and then moaned so beautifully he needed to exert more concentration than usual so as not to come before he could enjoy every inch of her body.

"I love how you taste, sweetheart," he growled against her pussy, easing his tongue inside her and feeling her muscles constrict against him.

Her inner thighs were smooth and warm and he dragged his fingers down them, and then pressed his fingers around her hard, swollen clit. Then, tickling it with his tongue, he watched her face. She'd squeezed her eyes shut, and the intensity of concentration lining her face as she turned her head from side to side showed she also fought to hold on to the moment and not let go too soon.

There was a difference between them, though. Amber would come for him again and again. He wanted to watch her orgasm until she lay limp in his arms, many, many hours from now.

"Don't fight it, darling. Let go and enjoy everything I'm going to do to you."

She opened her eyes, her blue orbs glazed over with such a dark, sultry shade they were breathtaking. "What are you going to do?" she whispered, her voice thick with lust and desire.

"Absolutely everything," he promised. "For as long as you can take it."

"What if I can take it for a very long time?" Again that teasing smile played at her lips.

"Then you're going to be a very happy lady for quite a long time."

He dipped his tongue inside her again and then ran it along the length of her opening, moving lower as he adjusted her legs. When he pressed against her tight, puckered flesh, Amber cried out, grabbing her head and covering her mouth.

He would guess she worried—a moment too late—about anyone else in the castle hearing them. Not that he cared. To hell with Princess Tory. Soon he would plot out his method of recourse. But if Tory wanted her father to know he was more interested in the social planner than her, so be it. Jordan didn't have a problem with her informing her father she didn't make the cut. But it would be Princess Tory offering that information, not Amber. That much Jordan had already decided.

He circled her ass with his tongue again, loving how Amber's cheeks glowed a beautiful rosy shade. What he wouldn't do to take her there. Allowing the thought to take form made him even harder. His balls tightened in anticipation, the pressure inside him mounting with a fever that made it hard for him to focus on anything else. All that mattered at the moment was pleasing the beautiful woman he was so blessed to have met. And as he dwelled on the different ways he might take her this evening, it became clearer to him that letting her go would be damn near impossible. Somehow, they would make this work. Amber wasn't going anywhere. And accepting that fact brought him more peace and happiness than he'd experienced in years.

Moving his tongue back to her pussy, he drank in the rich cream that soaked her flesh and filled his mouth. Amber reached down, digging her nails into his shoulders, and moaned beautifully as she did her best to hold him in place. But he wanted more, needed to push her to consider more, and dipped his tongue back to that tight puckered hole he would have to take.

"Jordan," she cried, her pleading tone bordering on desperation.

He had her so close. She blinked, lifting her head to better look at him. Once again he moved his tongue to her asshole, and this time pressed past the tight muscles that constricted in an effort to prevent his entrance.

"I want all of you, Amber," he warned her, watching her face for any sign of protest.

Instead of answering, she dropped her head back onto the

bed and moaned, moving her fingers over his shoulders and to his neck.

"Please," she cried. "It feels so good."

Her moans were the most beautiful sounds he'd ever heard. Jordan dragged his tongue up her smooth, soaked flesh, knowing that if he lubricated her enough with her own cream he would be able to fuck her pussy and her ass, if she would let him. She didn't tell him no, but the way her body tightened when he rimmed her ass and then dipped inside the tight hole proved to him it wasn't an act she partook of often. Contemplating the possibility that she'd never had anal sex before hardened every inch of him to steel. His blood raced in his veins, creating a ringing in his ears that was as loud as a locomotive, rushing with a mad fever through his body. He would be her first—and her only.

"Let go, Amber," he instructed her, moving to her clit and sucking it into his mouth.

"God!" She spasmed and arched off the bed, her legs tightening against him while she came so hard she screamed.

Jordan knew a warped satisfaction as he prayed he wasn't the only one to hear her cries of pleasure. He continued teasing and taunting her, even as her orgasm ripped through her body. When she let out a long sigh, relaxing her body and moving one hand to push strands of hair from her face, Jordan took his time enjoying the cream that clung to her smooth pussy.

Her face was flushed when she smiled up at him, moving her fingers to his mouth and wiping the moisture from his face as he lowered himself over her.

"You taste so damn good," he told her, but then hissed when she reached between them and wrapped her fingers around his shaft. "Amber, damn it," he growled.

"I need you now," she informed him, tugging slightly as she adjusted him at her entrance.

"What about a condom?" he asked, his mind so feverish he

would thrust inside her right now if she continued torturing him like this.

"I'm on birth control," she whispered. "I want to feel you."

She had no idea how her words moved him. Knowing he could enter her, be one with her without latex, would make her even more his.

"There will be no one else, then," he informed her, pressing into her soaked heat and feeling her muscles drag him deeper into her tight pussy.

"For either one of us," she informed him, spreading her legs and then lifting them, wrapping them around him.

"Agreed."

He tried for gentle, wanting to give her the best there was to seal their verbal agreement. But the fever burned too furiously inside him. Jordan thrust inside her, moving to his knees and dragging her farther underneath him as he impaled her.

It was a view to die for, watching his cock disappear inside her. Feeling so many tight, wet muscles stroke him, caress his shaft, made it worth the hell of pulling out slowly. Her white cream coated his shaft as he watched his swollen cock recede from her pussy.

"Fuck me, Jordan." She reached for him. "Give me everything. Now!"

He shifted his attention to her face. She pressed her lips together, staring at him with dark blue eyes, while her hair tangled around her face and fell past her shoulders. Amber was so petite, so delicate looking and absolutely gorgeous. In spite of giving the appearance that she needed to be sheltered, she wanted to be seen as tough and confident.

"You've already got everything," he informed her, diving deep into her pussy and then increasing the momentum.

Amber stared up at him, her mouth forming a small, perfect circle as she panted, her perfect breasts bouncing while he fucked her. If his words registered with her, she didn't give any indication, which was for the best. Jordan would take his time, ensuring she grew accustomed to the idea he wasn't going to let her go. No matter where she needed to go once they left the island, somehow he would do what it took to keep her in his world. Or hell, he would enter hers. But he would also need to continue taking care of the ranch.

"You're going to give me everything, too," he informed her, his voice gravelly and sounding winded as he plummeted deeper inside her.

"Okay," she whispered, continuing to stare up at him.

"Everything" covered a very large area, and many aspects of their relationship. For now, fighting to not lose himself inside her yet, he felt the strain against every muscle in his body. Amber might be a tiny thing, sweet and adorable and made of what was good and right, but she would pull his will to please her right out of him. Just the way her lashes fluttered over her sultry gaze and the way she moved her hands, cupping her own breasts, gave her more power than he prayed she would ever find out.

"I don't want it slow," she immediately complained when he regained control by easing in and out of her with meticulous care. "Jordan, please," she begged.

"Trust me, sweetheart, you're going to get everything you need and want." He lowered his mouth to hers, tasting her and silencing her pleas.

He wasn't lying about her getting everything she wanted. Telling Amber no to anything seemed to be very hard for him to do. He moved his hand between them, lifting her leg to his shoulder. Immediately the new angle felt so wonderful he ached, plowing deep inside of her again, just to feel so many soaked muscles clinging to him and dragging him deeper into her heat.

Her body was hot, damp, and smooth under his fingertips. She breathed hard into his mouth, panting while he continued his slow and torturous path as he fucked her. When she moaned into his mouth, feeling every inch of him buried deep inside of her, his balls tightened with such ferocity that he held his breath, riding out the intense craving to spill everything he had inside of her.

"Not yet, sweetheart," he growled against her lips, and then pressed his mouth to hers, knowing if he heard her protest he wouldn't last another moment.

Moving his fingers between them, he reached beneath his scrotum and touched her sensitive hole. Amber jumped and damn near bit his lip off. He raised himself off of her, gradually receding from her heat, and focused on their joining.

"I want you here," he informed her, watching for her reaction.

Amber's lashes fluttered until her dazed look faded and she focused on his face. "I know," she whispered, staring into his eyes.

"Let me take your ass, darling."

"I don't know. I'm not really into pain."

"If it hurts I'll stop."

"How could it not hurt?" She wrinkled her brow, truly not understanding how perfect he ached to make her feel.

Amber was an incredible woman, daring and adventurous, and not telling him no even now. But at the same time he saw her fear, her uncertainty, and knew without a doubt he would kill anyone who used her or tried hurting her. As he pulled out of her heat, immediately hating not being inside her, Jordan saw with incredible clarity how Amber was meant for him. She was perfect in every way. And he was going to seal the pact he'd already made in his mind to make her his woman by taking the one part of her he knew she'd never offered to any other man.

Watching her closely while stroking her ass with his finger, lubricating her with her own moisture, he fought the eagerness building in him to simply take what he knew he could have.

This was for Amber at least as much as it was for him. By her consenting, not only to this but to having unprotected sex with him, she'd given him an incredible gift: her trust. He would honor that as he would honor her.

"Relax, darling," he whispered. "Trust me that you're going to love how this feels. I promise you."

Her smile was tight, proof that she doubted him. "I'll try it," she offered, again being nothing more than honest with him. He doubted she would consider lying, to him or to anyone. And whatever her personal world might have been like prior to coming here, he was sure by her reaction to the princess's scandalous offer that Amber wasn't used to dealing with terrible people.

"You're so tight, but so damn wet," he growled, feeling her muscles constrict around his finger when he penetrated her.

"Oh God," she hissed, grabbing the blanket on either side of her and fisting it around her fingers.

"Breathe nice and easy," he coached, easing his finger in and out of her, making her wet as he prepared her for him.

When her eyes again glazed over and he watched her begin breathing easily, he knew he had her where he wanted her. Continuing finger fucking her for a few more minutes, he battled the overwhelming pressure threatening to push him over the edge. More than anything, even after coaxing her tight muscles and making her ass as wet as her pussy, he would have to maintain control when he fucked her. It was imperative he show her that this form of lovemaking could equally pleasure a woman just as it did a man.

"You're ready." He wanted her with him when he took her and waited for her gaze to meet his.

Amber slowly lifted her attention to his face, her tongue darting over her lips. She appeared to be lost in a state of lust, eating up the attention he gave the most sensitive part of her body. He didn't wait for her to respond. She didn't need to say anything. Jordan wanted her eyes on his; he needed to see her pleasure and know everything he would now give her would take her over the edge along with him.

Adjusting himself between her legs, he stroked her thighs while pressing the tip of his cock against her ass. Her muscles tightened, instinct kicking in on her end and fighting to prevent his entrance. His blood boiled, anticipating the suffocating heat and knowing he would die inside her, giving her more than she would ever know. As he pushed past the puckered flesh, he felt her stretch and the smooth skin part and allow him inside. Her satiny skin wrapped around him, spasming and sucking him deeper into her smoldering cavern that would forever be his.

"You're perfect, Amber," he encouraged. "Breathe and relax. Let me make this amazing for you."

"You're huge," she gasped, gulping in a breath and raking her nails down his arms as she spoke.

When she pressed her damp palms against his chest, their warm, gentle touch contrasted with the raging heat suffocating him as his dick sank deeper into her ass. He lowered his mouth to her breast, nibbling at her nipple, and began moving inside her.

Her ass was so tight, her flesh smooth and soft against his cock as he began a swift, fluid motion in and out of her. He loved her soft cries, how she dragged her fingers down his back and then slowly raised her legs, wrapping them around his waist, and held on as he took her more intimately than any man had ever taken her.

"Jordan," she cried, holding on tightly as her breathing came hard, her breasts sliding against his chest and building the fire out of control inside him. "Yes, faster, faster!"

All he could do was oblige. Taking her hard and quick, feeling her suck the life out of him, Jordan emptied everything he had deep inside her ass. And even before he collapsed onto her, something deep inside him told him he poured more into her than his sperm. He'd lost a bit of himself to Amber at that moment. The swelling inside him was no longer from the need to come, but the need to secure his heart, before he lost all of it to her.

10

"What is it?" Amber wrapped her towel around her, holding it with one hand to her breast while balancing her other towel on her head and hurrying to her door.

"I'm so sorry, Miss Amber." Cook wrung her hands and looked worried when Amber opened the door to her room and stared at her.

"What's wrong?" She would have soaked in the hot shower longer, willing the many sore muscles in her body to go away. Every inch of her still tingled, and not from the pounding jets in the shower. Amber wasn't sure how long it would take her to recover from the intense lovemaking with Jordan earlier tonight.

"I'm sorry to get you out of your bath," Cook offered. "Princess Tory insists on seeing you."

Something twisted in Amber's gut. Princess Tory—or anyone else in the castle—didn't hear her and Jordan fucking, did they? Cook looked so distraught about having to interrupt Amber's evening.

"It can't wait until the morning?" She clutched her towel between her breasts, shifting her weight from one foot to the other and feeling the sting in her inner thighs. Other places on her body were incredibly sensitive and the last thing she wanted to do was visit with the princess right now. "I was getting ready for bed."

"Trust me, I suggested it wait for tomorrow. She's rather insistent she meet with you before retiring."

Amber had already retired, but obviously she couldn't deny Princess Tory's request. Sighing, she nodded. "I'll meet her."

"Thank you," Cook said, sighing too, as if she had feared Amber would refuse the request and leave Cook to explain why. "Princess Tory is in the parlor downstairs."

"The parlor?"

"Yes. She asked you to meet her there in ten minutes."

"Good grief. Ten minutes?" Amber gripped her towel, backing into her room. "I'll hurry."

"Yes, Miss Amber." Cook was already heading down the hallway. "I'll let Princess Tory know you'll be right down."

Ever since returning to her room, Amber had mentally replayed the events with Jordan in his room. The incredible and very intimate sexual experience, everything Jordan had said to her, weighed heavily in her mind. Now she worried about what Princess Tory wanted her for.

A new thought hit her as she hurried back to the bathroom, peeling the towel off her head. Jordan wasn't thrilled about her returning to her room. He seemed a little less concerned with anyone else learning they were fooling around. But Amber wouldn't look at it as anything more than that. They were having fun. A hell of a lot of fun.

She'd done something tonight she'd never done before: anal sex. Jordan made an act she'd always believed was something she wouldn't enjoy into the most incredible experience she'd ever had. Granted, she was tender, but it hadn't hurt. What would have hurt, though, was staying with him and then Cook looking for her and Amber not being in her room. Would Cook have thought to look for her in Jordan's room?

"What the hell do you want?" She stared at her reflection as she started brushing out her hair. Then, dropping the towel from her body, she hurried naked into her bedroom to the dresser and closet. It was damn near midnight. She didn't have to dress formally at this hour to see the princess, did she?

"This better be important," she grumbled.

She felt the tightness on her thigh muscles as she pulled black leggings up her thighs. She pulled out a new blouse she hadn't worn yet since arriving here. It was bright blue, a shirt her mother had insisted on, saying it brought out the color in her eyes. The silk material was cut close, showing off her slender figure but loose enough that she didn't feel she needed a bra. It hung past her hips and looked good with a simple pair of black flats.

Once again she dragged her brush through her still-damp hair. Grabbing a hair tie, she pulled her hair back, then bent over and fixed it into a high ponytail.

"It's as good as it's going to get," she decided. She didn't move from the mirror, though, and started feeling a growing ill will toward Princess Tory when she applied some base and powder and brushed on some blush before rushing out of the bathroom.

In the hallway, Amber glanced in the direction of Jordan's room, imagining him stretched out on that large bed of his, sleeping, possibly naked. His warm, muscular body sounded so much better than heading downstairs to Princess Tory.

"Part of the job," she whispered under her breath and then took the stairs, her legs wobbly as she descended them.

Cook wasn't anywhere around when she reached the parlor. Lingering outside the large opened doors for a moment, she strained to hear the soft voices inside. She didn't see anyone.

Possibly Cook had felt her job was done and had headed to bed. Amber didn't blame her. Clearing her throat, she stepped into the parlor.

"There you are." Carlos stood behind Princess Tory, who sat on the couch, her back straight and her hands folded in her lap, looking very stiff and rather uncomfortable, or maybe upset. Carlos moved around the couch to Amber. "Princess Tory has been waiting for you," he added quietly, making it sound like a reprimand.

The older man wouldn't get a rise out of her. "Good evening," she offered, nodding to him and then past him to the princess and Raul, who leaned against the mantel watching her with dark eyes that were hard to read. "I'm sorry you had to wait but I was getting ready for bed when Cook asked me to come visit with you. Is something wrong?"

"Princess Tory wants to see the list."

"The list?" Amber frowned, not having any idea what he was talking about.

"The list!" Princess Tory flew off the couch. "The list Father sent earlier this evening stating whom you will invite to this party of yours."

"I haven't received a list." Amber frowned, shifting her attention from Princess Tory, who now was damn near in her face, to Raul standing behind her. He'd moved from the mantel and hovered around the furniture, possibly concerned his woman would fly into a rage and need him there to console her. He didn't look like a whipping boy but she'd seen better men reduced to spineless yes-men by incredibly nagging women. "If you don't mind, I'm going to head on to bed. As soon as I get it I'll let you know," she added, needing to get away from this bitch of a woman before Amber lost her cool and said something she'd regret.

"He e-mailed it to you and promised to copy me on it and

then forgot." The way Princess Tory said "forgot" implied she didn't believe her father really had.

"Oh," Amber said.

"Have you checked your e-mail?" Carlos frowned, rubbing his cheek as he watched her with dark annoying-looking eyes.

They were all getting on her nerves. "I'll check it in the morning."

"You'll check it right now!" Princess Tory demanded.

"Why are you so worried about this list? It's simply supposed to be friends of yours to invite to the island to party with us." Amber had a strange thought: Princess Tory was too annoying to have friends.

The bitch marched back to the couch, resuming her stiff position when she parked her butt on the edge of it and once again pressed her hands together on her knees.

"Carlos, bring her a laptop," she ordered.

"That isn't necessary," Amber interrupted, turning to leave. "If it matters so much to you I'll head to my room and check it from there. I can print it for you."

"If it matters to *me*?" Princess Tory asked, her voice reaching an unpleasant pitch.

Amber paused in the doorway, looking over her shoulder while taking a deep breath to keep from growing too frustrated. More than anything Princess Tory needed to be put in her place, but Amber reminded herself it wasn't her job to do that.

"This is even more proof she isn't the professional she professes to be." Raul gave Amber a once-over, but it wasn't disgust registering on his face. "I told you I searched for her on Google and very little came up."

"Have you even checked your e-mail?" Carlos attacked from the other side.

"I was busy with phone calls this evening and haven't looked at my e-mail in a few hours." She needed to think quickly. The other day Princess Tory had invited her into her corner. Granted, it was to perform her dirty work. Amber couldn't allow the three of them to belittle her to the point that they had each other convinced she couldn't do her job. "If you'll allow me a few minutes I'll let you know if your father's e-mail is there," she offered, keeping her tone as soft and pleasant as she could muster. She also focused only on Princess Tory. "I will let you know right away if he's sent a list."

"He has," Princess Tory insisted.

Amber hurried out of the parlor. Raul was giving her more than an appraising once-over. She knew very well when a man showed interest. If he were willing to be the lover to a woman who was prepared to marry someone else, he would possibly be willing to have a fling of his own on the side. That was one sordid triangle Amber would steer very, very clear of.

Between Raul's dark, lust-filled gaze, Carlos's condemning attitude, and Princess Tory's pretentious demands, Amber was flustered and a bit put out as she hurried up the stairs. Her muscles screamed in protest as she rushed to her room, half expecting Princess Tory, if not her men, to follow her.

She rushed into her room, closing her door louder than she should have. "I can't handle this!" she hissed, leaning against her door for a moment and fighting to keep her wits about her. Staring at the computer on her desk, online but with the screen saver swirling around the monitor since she hadn't touched it all evening, Amber willed herself to march across the room and pull up her e-mail. She stared for a moment at the A, the Anton Enterprises logo, as it moved around the screen until she touched the mouse and made it go away.

She plopped down in her chair, immediately feeling a sting. The tender parts of her body brought a flash before her eyes, one of Jordan looking down at her, his face flushed and intense with long black strands rimming his face. The image stole her breath. There might be a few sensitive parts of her body for a while, but if every time she felt them she was reminded of what caused them, it would be damn hard to focus on anything else.

"E-mail," she grumbled, proving to herself she'd rather think about Jordan than Princess Tory.

Pulling up her e-mail program and then typing in her password, she waited for mail to load into her in-box and leaned back, deciding that Jordan probably slept soundly after the incredible sex they'd had. If only she were sleeping, too.

Princess Tory's invasion of her evening prevented her from regretting any of her earlier actions, though. She told herself she and Jordan were having fun. He was a wonderful man, intelligent and so incredibly sexy. Outside of this surreal world, though, the chances of them ever having met were slim to nil. And in three weeks, she would return to her world with wonderful memories and hopefully enough money to buy the house she, her mother, and her brother and sister lived in right now. If she accomplished anything with this outrageous experience, getting their piss-poor landlord off their backs would be worth it.

"And then you put Jordan out of your mind," she told herself, leaning forward and looking at the mail in her in-box.

Amber made quick work of deleting all the spam. She honestly didn't expect Pierre Anton or Lord Duke Alixandre to respond to her request so quickly; however, there was one e-mail from Pierre and two from Lord Duke. She clicked on each of them, glancing down lengthy lists of people each man would like invited to the party Amber had told them she was planning. The second e-mail from Lord Duke wasn't a list, though.

She read the e-mail, cursed, and read it again.

Miss Amber Stone,

Please find a separate e-mail with a list of those you will invite to the party for our daughter and Master Jordan Anton. Every person on the list sent to you will be invited. You will not leave anyone out. Princess Tory has no say in this matter. She, of course, shall be the charming hostess, gracious to all her guests and ador- ing to her future husband.

We anxiously await our invitation and look forward to being formally introduced to you, as well as seeing this gorgeous island we've heard so many wonderful things about.

Sincerely Yours,
The Lord and Lady Duke and Donita Alixandre

Amber stared at the e-mail for another minute. Then, telling herself she would get more than a little satisfaction in putting Princess Tory in her place, she printed the e-mail. Watching the paper feed through the printer, she didn't doubt for a moment Princess Tory would throw a fit. Amber would remain neutral and sympathetic, and she would do her job. After printing the list of those to invite and groaning at the number on the list, she grabbed the papers from the printer and left her bedroom.

"Have everything the princess needs?" Raul asked when he reached the top of the stairs and faced Amber.

He didn't move. There was a lingering scent of stale after- shave, pungent and as annoying as the way he seemed to focus on her breasts instead of her face.

"Sure do, and I can take it to her if you'll let me pass," Amber told him.

He grabbed her arm, pulling her against him when she tried moving around him. "I'm going to give you a piece of advice, love," he told her, his accent adding to the cheap, pretentious nature that turned her stomach.

"Get your hand off me," she growled.

"You're the feisty one," he snarled, tugging her arm hard

enough that she lost her balance and slapped her hand against his chest to balance herself. "But if you cross Princess Tory, or me, you'll regret it."

"What makes you think I'm doing anything she doesn't want?" Amber nodded at the printed papers in the hand that he held at her wrist. "I'm doing what she wants when I'd rather be in bed."

"I wouldn't doubt that's where you're at your best," Raul said, lowering his voice. "You are one hot little lady."

"I heard you in Princess Tory's room when you two were all cozy." Amber glared at Raul and then yanked her wrist out of his grip. Her flesh stung and the force it took to get free of him caused her to stagger by the stairs. She grabbed the banister when she jumped out of arm's reach of him. "You're her boyfriend and she's here to become engaged to another man. That doesn't mean you can find something on the side, too."

Raul's black hair was greased back, and his features were already intimidating in a bully-type fashion that he appeared to work hard at pulling off. Amber worried for a minute that she had possibly pushed Raul too far. His black eyes narrowed on her and there wasn't any doubt she'd unleashed a fury that bordered on losing control.

As quickly as she saw blind rage tear across his expression, something masked it, and he straightened, glancing over her shoulder.

Raul tapped her chin with his finger when she would have looked behind her. Her backside tingled, a rush of heat heightening the already-sensitive muscles throughout her body.

"Remember what I said," Raul whispered, his thick, cold finger brushing across her jawbone. "Don't cross Tory and don't cross me. Everyone has a part to play in this little scenario we're enjoying. Your part is very cut and dried: providing social entertainment. And, little one, you *will* entertain."

Raul nodded to the person standing behind her, his silent

presence as obvious as the outrage still simmering inside Raul when he turned and headed toward the princess's wing.

"What was that all about?" Jordan asked before she could turn around.

Amber couldn't stop from shaking. Raul had one hell of a lot of nerve. It only made matters worse that Jordan had overheard any of it.

"What are you doing here?" she asked, still gripping the top of the banister with one hand and the papers for Princess Tory with the other.

Jordan followed Raul with a harsh stare when the man left them. His eyes were a darker gray when he shifted his attention to her, something hardening his expression and causing her insides to quicken as she stared up at him.

"You weren't in your room," he informed her, again looking in the direction where Raul went, but then turning his attention to the papers in her hand. "What were you doing?"

"Princess Tory wanted to see the names of those I'm supposed to invite to the island."

Jordan took the papers out of her hand without asking. He studied them, his expression not changing when he finally handed them back.

"At midnight?"

"I wasn't thrilled about it either. She sent Cook to get me. I was almost in bed asleep." She wasn't sure her legs would hold her going down the stairs. Already they felt way too wobbly just standing facing Jordan. "I need to take these to her."

"You aren't her servant," Jordan growled, taking her arm, although his grip wasn't rough and his touch warmed her insides.

As sore and sated as her muscles had been a moment before, she began throbbing between her legs, her body believing she could take him again. "You're right. I'm not." She moved to the first step, slipping her arm from his grasp. "But I am hired help, Jordan. I have to honor Princess Tory's request just as I would any request you made."

"Does that mean you would honor Raul's request?" Jordan grabbed her shoulder, preventing her from descending the stairs.

Amber turned quickly, but then grabbed the banister so she wouldn't trip. "Of course not! I can't believe you asked me that."

Jordan came down the stairs with her, walking next to her while she used the banister until they reached the first floor.

"I understand that Raul and Princess Tory are lovers," Amber said when they paused in the hallway at the bottom of the stairs. She focused on Jordan's chest, taking in the drawstring sweatpants and plain gray T-shirt he wore. Even dressed as he was now, Jordan was still the best-looking man she'd ever laid eyes on. "Just because they are willing to enter into this arrangement and continue with what they have on the side doesn't mean I want a thing to do with it."

Jordan didn't comment and, when she chanced a glimpse at his face, he stared down the hall, his hard, brooding expression stealing her breath. His ponytail was loose at his nape, leading her to think he might have gone to bed, but for whatever reason got up again. She ached to ask him again what he was doing out of his room. What motivated him to leave there in the first place?

"Go take care of this matter," he said, as if just coming to the decision he would allow her to do so. "I'll wait here for you."

There wasn't any point in arguing with him. It didn't take knowing him for years and years to understand just by watching him that he wouldn't take no for an answer. At the same time, it was clear he didn't like the idea of her doing anything for the princess. Realizing Jordan was displeased with her being hired help left a bitter taste in her mouth. Somehow, Amber needed to make him see they weren't the same social status. Nor would they ever be.

Less than a minute later Amber marched back to the staircase and to Jordan, who stood where she left him, where he promised he would be.

"It would have been nice of Raul to tell me Princess Tory was no longer in the parlor," Amber hissed, bounding up the stairs and leaving Jordan to follow her. "I swear spoiled-rotten rich people seem to think the rest of the world are simply tools for their amusement."

She almost flew off her feet when Jordan took her arm and yanked her in the opposite direction, down the hallway where her room was.

"What are you doing?" she complained, but this time couldn't get him to let go of her.

"You're right. Spoiled-rotten rich people are pains in the ass. And you are not going to chase her around like she owns you," he growled, stopping once they were outside her bedroom door.

"Jordan," she said, sighing and hating that she would probably piss him off even more when she stated the obvious. "This is my job!"

"Your job is to provide entertainment while all of us are on the island—entertainment for *only* myself and Princess Tory. No one else."

"Princess Tory threw a fit to see the names of everyone being invited to the party I'm supposed to organize."

"I'm sure she's very good at throwing fits." He reached for her bedroom-door handle and then pushed the door open. His hand seared the flesh on her back when he escorted her into the room and then closed the door behind them. "Now is as good a time as any for her to learn you aren't going to run every time she decides she wants something."

"You don't get it!" Amber walked over to her computer and tossed the papers she'd been holding next to her keyboard. "When I have a job to do, I'm going to do it to the best of my abilities."

"I'm quite possibly the only person on this island, let alone in her family or mine, who does get that," he growled, standing in the middle of her room with his arms crossed over his broad chest. "I've lived my entire life with servants. I didn't like it then. And I won't live that way today. Every single one of us on this island, and everywhere for that matter, is equal. We each have a job to do. But because of what you do, or what I do, doesn't make either one of us outrank the other. Do you understand that?"

"Then quit yelling at me." Her insides turned numb as she stared at him, his words slowly hitting her as they sunk in. If he did view her as someone so far out of reach from his social status, and didn't care, where did that leave them now? She didn't dare allow her mind to go there, or even contemplate what possibilities might exist for them if what he claimed just now was true.

He cleared the distance between them and then took a strand of her hair from her shoulder, rubbing it between his fingers while studying her face. His eyes were still a very dark gray, but a hint of blue contrasted around his pupils, leading her to believe he wasn't as angry as he'd been a moment before. She stood her ground, her heart pounding in her chest, and refused to touch him. It meant she had to clasp her hands in front of her just to keep them off all that perfectly sculpted muscle that bulged against the soft gray T-shirt stretching across his chest.

"When Princess Tory wants you, she can come to you," he offered, his voice now a husky whisper.

Her insides flip-flopped. Before Cook came to her room, Amber had been going nuts wondering what Jordan was doing.

Now here he was, in her room, touching her. His penetrating gaze burrowed deep inside her, while her heart continued pounding against her chest so hard she was sure he must be able to hear it. Forcing the breath out of her lungs, she looked away first, although lowering her attention to eye level simply gave her a mouthwatering view of his broad shoulders and muscular chest apparent through his shirt.

"You told me you run a ranch," she murmured, suddenly acutely aware of the throbbing, moist heat building between her legs, even with the burning from their intense lovemaking still more than apparent.

"That's right."

"And that you have ranch hands you've hired."

"Yup."

"A ranch probably doesn't shut down at five o'clock."

"Nope."

"If you ask one of those ranch hands to do something for you during the night, they will do it."

"We work as a team. I don't ask anyone to do something I wouldn't do myself."

She nodded, seeing that he would be a very fair employer. But nonetheless, he was the employer. "I can see that about you. If some task needs tending to and you ask one of your men to take care of part of it, they would do it."

"If I need help with something and ask for it, then yes, they would."

Her eyes burned when she leaned her head back to stare into his eyes, the brush of his knuckles against her shoulder more of a distraction than she should allow it to be. It would be too simple to let him believe things without trying to show him her side. A glimmer of hope sparked inside her that something could develop between the two of them. But being anything other than a realist would only bring her pain. There was too much to gain from this month. And she would gain it. She would do her job right, honor all reasonable requests made of her, and return home satisfied she'd done what was asked of her to the best of her abilities. That was all she could ask for, and dreaming about anything beyond that was a fool's mission.

"Jordan, I am that ranch hand," she whispered. "I'm not the employer, the boss, or the owner. More than likely I won't ever be. Something is asked of me and I'm doing it. I won't ever do anything that isn't honorable." But being with him pushed the limits of honor, and the moment the last sentence left her mouth and a small spark lightened the shade of his eyes, she guessed he thought the same thing. The two of them being together wasn't exactly how things were supposed to be. She walked away from him, planting her butt in the office chair at her computer, and gathered the papers she'd tossed on the desk. "You should go now, Jordan. I'll talk to you tomorrow."

It surprised her, and immediately disappointed her, that he didn't argue. When he reached the door, he paused before opening it, his black ponytail curling around itself at his nape and reminding her how silky-smooth it was.

"Amber," he said, breathing her name with such a soft baritone it sent chills over her body. He gripped the door handle but looked at her over his shoulder. "You could be that owner, or the employer, or the boss, if you wanted to be."

She couldn't answer him. Her heart lodged in her throat as he opened the door, stepped out of her room, and closed it silently behind him. She stared at the white, high-gloss paint that covered the heavy wooden door, her eyes still dry and burning. If he only knew how far from her world a position of that rank was.

11

"This is the list?" Princess Tory sat at the formal dining table beside Jordan. She leaned back in her chair, stretching her bare legs underneath the table so her feet brushed against Jordan's.

Amber moved closer to the table so she couldn't see under it anymore. So far, she'd managed to not be around the two of them when they were together. When Princess Tory called her to their breakfast table, Amber knew why she was wanted. She automatically brought the list with her, but held the second e-mail from the princess's father folded, behind her back.

"Yes, it is," she told her, keeping her attention on Princess Tory and not watching Jordan, who sat at the head of the table, appearing to ignore both of them while he focused on his breakfast.

"I waited for you to bring this to me last night." She sounded unusually pleasant and even smiled, her dark brown eyes full and round and offsetting her smooth complexion. Thick black hair was pulled back tightly from her face, glowing against the morning sun streaming through the long windows. The tight curls behind her head fell in ringlets over her bare shoulders.

"It's imperative you and I go over this before you proceed further with invitations."

"Are you concerned some of the addresses might be wrong?" Amber asked, unsure why she waited to show Princess Tory the second e-mail but deciding she had a right to a small amount of pleasure from goading the princess once she learned she couldn't tamper with the party list.

"Oh, I'm sure they're all right." Princess Tory had a melodic laugh that was as erotic as her smooth-flowing accent. It was disgusting how beautiful she looked this morning. "Jordan, darling, do you want to go over the list with me?"

When she placed her hand on top of Jordan's, it was almost impossible not to dive over the table and attack. Amber held her ground, fighting not to wrinkle the second e-mail in her hands and rip it to shreds in her effort to not show any reaction to Princess Tory speaking and acting so affectionately around Jordan.

"I really don't care who comes," Jordan informed her, putting down his fork and reaching for his coffee. He made no attempt to make her take her hand off his.

"Darling, you really should care." Princess Tory moved her hand, but instead of leaving him alone, reached over and ran her fingers over his hair, as if attempting to keep it neatly arranged in his ponytail holder, which it already was. "This will be the first announcement to the world that you and I are here together. You know it will hit all the society pages and every magazine."

"There is another list I've received from Jordan's father," Amber offered, wanting Princess Tory to give her the attention and not Jordan. Her blood boiled and her mind raced while she thought of something to do to get the princess's hands off him. Then, damn near biting her tongue, she clenched her teeth, trying to get herself to accept that it didn't matter to her what Princess Tory did.

"Did you bring it, too?" Princess Tory didn't look at her, but instead appeared to be adoring Jordan, as if she were helplessly in love.

"No, I didn't."

Princess Tory did look at her then, her smile in place and her dark eyes glowing with amusement. Somehow, she knew her actions were pissing Amber off, and she was loving the hell out of it. That pissed Amber off even more. There were no indications, no proof that Amber cared at all for Jordan. She exhaled, returning the easy smile even when it made her face hurt. No way would she give the princess the satisfaction of knowing how much she got under Amber's skin.

"Goodness. What are we going to do with you?" Princess Tory's tone was still pleasant, but something changed in her expression, hardening enough to show she would now insult and chastise Amber in front of Jordan. "Are you sure you can handle organizing a party of this magnitude?"

Jordan shifted in his chair, putting distance between himself and Princess Tory, finally. "You aren't suggesting my grandfather doesn't know how to hire a social organizer, are you?"

"Of course not." Princess Tory waved her hand in the air, dismissing the comment. "But we must go over this list," she continued, this time running her nicely manicured fingernails down Jordan's arm. "It's apparent right now there are some names on it that are not acceptable. I won't have paparazzi at my party."

"Everyone on the list will be invited to the party." Amber straightened, enjoying the hateful look Princess Tory gave her. It was clear the woman wasn't capable of being nice and friendly for long periods of time. "I will prepare the invitations to mail out today. Would you like to see them?"

"Apparently I will have to see them," Princess Tory snapped. "If you're too incompetent to follow simple instructions I might have to put one of my servants on the task of mailing them out. Everyone on this list will *not* be invited."

"I have my instructions," Amber offered, proud of herself for maintaining her calm tone and even smiling into the princess's hateful glare. "There are two hundred invitations being made, one for each person on that list and the list sent by Pierre Anton."

"How do you manage to hold down a job?" Princess Tory leaned back in her chair, crossing her arms over her chest and displaying way too much cleavage. The bra she wore did a fine job of pushing her breasts up on their own, not that a young lady her age needed any help looking firm and in place. But her button-down shirt was unbuttoned to the middle of her bra, allowing an even better glimpse of what she had and apparently wished to show off. "You're not hearing a word I'm saying."

"There is no reason to talk to her like that," Jordan informed her, not shifting from where he leaned to the side in his chair or even looking at Princess Tory when he spoke. "Talking down to people seldom helps you get your way."

"I don't have to worry about getting my way," Princess Tory said, twisting her torso just enough to enhance the view of her cleavage for him. "She's just a . . ."

"She's just a what!" Jordan snapped, and when he did look at her, his expression hardened even further.

Or Amber couldn't help hoping it did. Princess Tory was beautiful, young, and had a perfect body. But he had to see how coldhearted she was. Even though he hadn't flinched when the princess caressed and fondled him, it had to be apparent how much of a bitch she was.

"She is most definitely not your servant," Jordan continued. "Furthermore, she doesn't answer to you at all."

"She is the social organizer, right?" Princess Tory's tone turned as cold as his. "And she is organizing my party. Therefore she most definitely will do as I say." As quickly as her expression grew lined with determination, it softened, once again showing off her youth when she smiled and reached for Jordan. "Leave the planning of the party up to me, my dear. Weren't we talking about spending the day with each other? Why don't you go change into your riding clothes and we'll meet at the stables."

"Your father told me this wouldn't be necessary," Amber interrupted, more than anything not wanting to hear about how the two of them were discussing hanging out together all day long. "He assured me you would be cooperative," she added for good measure and smiled when Princess Tory slowly shifted gears again, glaring at Amber as if she had a lot of nerve to interrupt. Amber really didn't care what Princess Tory thought. "I brought this e-mail down, just in case. And I'm sorry I have to show it to you now."

Amber moved closer to the table and intentionally stepped on Jordan's foot—which he'd moved out of the way so Princess Tory couldn't play footsie with him under the table—hoping she could inflict just enough pain to let him know she wouldn't be played with behind closed doors and then have him run off and spend the day with this vixen.

She dropped the folded piece of paper she'd held behind her back onto the table and then turned, glancing at Jordan in time to see him raise one eyebrow. Immediately her face burned. Damn him for thinking she might be jealous of the little brat.

But she was. And God, she hated it more than she hated admitting she was falling for Jordan. She turned to leave, damned if she would wait to be dismissed.

"What?" Princess Tory screeched, and then shoved her chair back from the table, forcing it to make a very unpleasant sound over the floor. "We'll see about this!" she announced, marching past Amber without a word and storming out of the room.

"You could have told her right away that she didn't have any say over the people being invited to the party," Jordan said, sounding way too calm.

Amber fought like hell not to grin when she faced him. "What? And ruin all the fun?" she asked, batting her eyes at him in a mock show of innocence.

"I really should make you pay for disrupting my breakfast like this," he growled, his mouth twitching at the corner when he pressed his lips together and stared at her with raw desire apparent in his eyes.

The room got so hot she couldn't breathe. Amber's pussy swelled with no notice, the throbbing and moisture such an intense distraction that for a moment she couldn't move. All she could do was imagine what he might think of as a way to make her pay. Every image that came to mind just got her hotter.

Over the next few days, Amber spent most of her time in her bedroom, learning quickly there was a hell of a lot more involved with throwing a party for Jordan and Princess Tory than she originally thought. After learning from Cook how many rooms were available in the castle, and shocked to find out the huge, old structure could successfully hold a few hundred people, she then ran into the issue of who could be put in each wing with whom.

"This is ridiculous," she complained, throwing the stack of three-by-five cards that she'd written the names of each guest on down on her table. She'd had Jesse help her bring the small table into her room and set it up close to her balcony, which she realized now allowed her plenty of time to daydream instead of work. "The guests are going to have to be happy with wherever I put them," she decided, repulsed with the knowledge that certain families in the world of the rich and famous didn't speak to other families and therefore couldn't be asked to stay in the castle anywhere near each other. "The lot of you will get along, or else," she ordered, glaring at the scattered cards on the table.

Her cell phone rang, again. "I haven't gotten this many calls all month," she moaned, pushing herself out of her chair and lifting her phone from next to her computer. Amber was getting used to not recognizing the caller, or the country number. "Oh wow, an American caller." She accepted the call. "Hello?"

"Amber, my dear, how are you doing?" Pierre Anton's deep, raspy voice sounded nothing like his grandson's.

"Great," she said, brushing her hair from her face as she glared at the three-by-five cards on the table by the balcony. "And I'm having fun," she added for good measure.

"That's my girl." Anton jumped right in to the reason for his call, something she'd learned he was very good at. "Have you been propositioned yet by our potential groom?"

Amber decided Anton learned more with surprise attacks and on more than one occasion felt she'd be wise to learn to use the tactic. "No, I haven't. Do you anticipate him doing that?"

"I know it will happen." He didn't sound excited or disappointed with this revelation. "And in the meantime, you're getting out the invitations?"

"You'll get yours in the mail next week. I'm going to need to hire more staff." If he told her no she'd scream.

"My dear, you have an unlimited budget. Money is no object. You'll spare no expense on making this party the event of the season. But you'll earn your paycheck when I hear the announcement that my grandson is marrying at the end of the month, if not sooner."

"I understand." She stared at her fingernails, noting they could stand to be painted. Being reminded she was working her ass off just so Jordan could marry another woman sucked almost as much as not seeing him for several days.

"There is a reason for my call."

"I figured there was."

Anton laughed and she cringed, doubting she'd ever master learning how to speak to a man who had enough power to make or break a person's life depending just on his mood at that moment.

"I want you to be honest with me."

Amber blinked, standing slowly and frowning. "I've always been honest with you."

"You might not be this time."

She swallowed, her mouth suddenly too dry. There were dark clouds over the ocean and she stared at the odd formation, wondering if a storm would prevent the plane from delivering everything she'd ordered to arrive today.

"I guess if the question is too personal," she offered, hating how Pierre could make her nervous from the other side of the world. She tried for a light edge to her tone and made herself busy straightening the cards she'd scattered over the table as a hard breeze came through her open balcony doors, sending half of them to the floor.

"Have you had sex with my grandson?"

"What?" she gasped, dropping the cards she'd just gathered and watching more of them slip off the table.

"Are you sleeping with Jordan?" he asked, his voice taking a harder edge. "The signs are all there, Amber. He's defensive of you. My grandson is way too righteous and optimistic for his own good."

"You and Jordan have talked about me?" The question slipped out as she gave up on the cards and hurried to close the balcony doors. "Why were you talking about me? I mean, in a not-so-professional manner?"

"You're a delightful breath of fresh air. I can see why he's attracted." Pierre continued as if she'd already answered his question. "Of course, he denied all of it."

Amber was positive she hadn't said anything to suggest Pierre's speculation was accurate. But hearing Jordan had denied being with her hurt more than it should. She blinked, then rubbed her suddenly moist eyes, hating Pierre Anton for successfully pulling emotions out of her he probably intended to trigger all along.

"Of course he would," she said, staring at the cards all over her floor. "So why are you bringing this up to me?"

"Simply to see if I got the same reaction from you that I did from him," he offered. "Amber, my dear, don't forget where you came from, and where you're returning when this month is over. You'll leave my grandson alone, and do what you're hired to do, or you're fired."

The line went dead before she could think of a decent response.

Amber had always loved storms. It felt different outside from anything she'd ever experienced before, which was perfect. She was living a life she'd never known before. And it was temporary. Pierre Anton did a good job reminding her of that. She was here to do a job, nothing else.

There were phone calls to make and no one said she had to make them in her room. One thing she enjoyed about this job—well, okay, there was more than one thing—was that while on the island, no one told her what to do. Princess Tory didn't count. Amber loved how the princess had avoided her ever since Amber had shown her the e-mail from her father. It had been worth ruining Jordan's breakfast just to watch Princess Tory storm out of the room.

Heading along the path toward the cliff and ocean, she held her cell in her hand, checking for a signal. The bars were strong, another amazing thing about this remote island. The service they used almost always had a signal.

No matter how far she walked from the castle, her thoughts still tortured her. Every bit of her focus needed to be on this party if she were going to pull it off. More than one person had already suggested she couldn't do it. That was all the incentive she needed to make it the best party any of these rich snobs had ever been to. Amber continually tried to put all her effort into organizing this thing, but she couldn't quit thinking about Jordan.

Pierre wasn't the only one who wanted Amber to quit thinking about Jordan. Princess Tory had behaved the way she did at breakfast the other morning to get under her skin. Amber knew competition when she saw it. The princess didn't give a rat's ass about Jordan. But somehow she'd figured out that Amber cared about him. And that was all the fuel the princess needed to try to get under her skin.

And damn it, she did care about him. It had taken less than a week for her to see in him a man she would kill to know better. His perfect sex appeal, the way he thought about things, his determination to make her see him as honorable when no one else in this world seemed to care at all about that quality, made him unique. But it was more than that. The way he looked at her, touched her, made love to her—the entire package showed her he felt the same way about her.

But he couldn't care enough to throw everything he knew away just to be with her. She wouldn't ask that of anyone. And she wouldn't expect to do it herself. Pierre Anton had made it clear in his phone call. And Amber didn't doubt he meant it. He would fire her if she didn't leave Jordan alone.

She'd hiked to the rugged cliffs lining the ocean and finally paused to take in her surroundings, realizing she'd walked farther from the castle than she had since she'd been on the island. Finding a perch, she got comfortable, sitting cross-legged on a smooth, flat rock that offered an incredible view of the ocean on one side and a high, flat meadow on the other. The island was possibly one of the most beautiful spots on earth, and she should be thrilled to have some time here to enjoy it.

Thunder rumbled overhead, at the same time bringing a chilly breeze off the ocean when Amber placed her call. She needed more help, administrative assistants who could assist in organizing this party. Pierre had told her she could hire whomever she wanted. Why not offer others like her, in dead-end jobs, the experience she was having?

"Anton Business Solutions." Angie Wilcox, who'd been the main receptionist for the office where Amber had worked for the past three years, answered with her usual stiff, cheerful tone.

"Angie, it's Amber," she said when another rumble interrupted her overhead. "Can you hear me?"

"Amber, good grief, woman. You sound like you're on the other side of the world."

It didn't surprise her that their supervisor hadn't enlightened the women in her department as to where she'd gone. He was a worse gossip than the women there. "I *am* on the other side of the world," Amber said, laughing, the sensation of being pulled back into her old life, her real life, causing a bittersweet sensation in her. "Is Olive or Barney working?"

"Both of them are. But sweetheart, what happened to you? You know all of us are speculating."

Amber didn't doubt that for a minute. "I took a temporary job," she offered, remembering how the man who hired her for this job told her not to tell anyone where she was going. He'd been from Anton Enterprises, the parent company of Anton Business Solutions, and made her feel so important at the time. "But I'll be back at my desk at the beginning of next month." Which seemed like a lifetime away.

"Oh really? But they've already put someone else at your desk. Now who did you say you wanted to speak with?" she asked, her tone turning professional. More than likely, Ralph, their supervisor and the old geezer who'd pulled her away from her desk just a week ago to inform her someone wanted to speak with her—a meeting that changed her life—was now leaning against Angie's desk.

"Put me through to Barney, please." Amber wouldn't worry right now as to why someone else was at her desk. When she'd met with Pierre Anton's personal secretary, a young man who'd proposed she take the job as social planner for a month, Ralph had been brought in at the end of the meeting and assured her that her job would be there when she returned.

"Anton Business Solutions. May I help you?" Barney Holden spoke in his usual nasally tone.

"Barney, it's Amber."

"Amber! Girlfriend!" he squealed, but then quickly lowered his voice. "What happened to you?"

"I'm working as a social planner, organizing a party. And I sure could use help!"

"You left here to get a job as a party organizer?" he asked in disbelief. "Well, you go, girl!"

Amber smiled, holding the phone to her ear with one hand and pushing herself off the rock when she felt a raindrop splatter on her arm. "I'm in charge of party organizing for some of the richest people in the world. There's a lot to fill you in on, but would you consider coming to work for me for a few weeks if I could guarantee you got your job back at Anton Business Solutions when we were done?"

"Girlfriend, if the money is good then I'm out of here. But temporary? You know that word scares me."

"It is temporary, but the experience of a lifetime. Right now, I'm on the most beautiful island in the world, off of New Zealand." She didn't bother to mention it was starting to rain and she might have been a fool to climb on rocks that were quickly growing slippery. "Think about it and I'll get back with you on how much you'll get paid. Is it okay to call you tonight?"

"Sure thing," he agreed, then gave her his number.

After hanging up, she added his number to her phone. She'd

forgotten to confirm with Pierre how much she could offer to pay anyone she hired. The thought of calling him back turned her stomach with trepidation.

Concentrating on the rocks and not falling on her ass, she hurried back to the shelter of the trees as thunder, and now lightning, created one hell of a light show above her. More than once she paused, glancing at the sky and enjoying the heavy black clouds and the lightning racing across them. Something caught her attention across the meadow, and she shaded her eyes with her hand, squinting to see better as large raindrops began soaking her shirt.

"You don't care what they're doing," she told herself as her stomach twisted in a knot that rose to her throat fast enough to make it hard to finish muttering to herself.

She was lying to herself anyway. Standing there, unable to move as she watched Jordan and Princess Tory race across the meadow on horses, was proof enough how much she cared. It didn't matter to her anymore that she was becoming soaked. There wasn't any turning away from watching Jordan's tall, muscular frame on top of Lord, who moved with the superiority and confidence of his rider.

Jordan's black hair flew behind him, which meant he didn't have it in his ponytail. Had he taken it down for Princess Tory? She didn't strike Amber as the type of lady who would like a man with long hair. For that matter, she didn't appear to like anyone but herself and what it would take to accomplish her personal goals.

What if the affection she had displayed at the breakfast table the other morning wasn't fake? Maybe as she spent more time with Jordan she learned how good of a man he was and now liked him.

"Good God, girl," she grumbled, forcing herself to start walking again.

The rain was coming down steadily now, and suddenly it

seemed dark enough to be nighttime instead of the afternoon. Amber tucked her cell phone into her pocket to keep it from getting soaked, and worked her way off the rocks and to the nearest tree. She ducked her head, refusing to look in their direction, and forced herself to pay attention to her footing so she wouldn't slip and be forced to return to the castle soaked and dirty. As it was, her hair clung to her shoulders and back, feeling like a wet blanket stuck to her body. If she were lucky, she wouldn't see either of them and could slip away to her room unnoticed.

The trees didn't do a lot to keep her from getting soaked, and there were open areas where she continued to see Jordan and Princess Tory galloping across the meadow. They would be heading to the barn, which meant if she headed to the front of the castle, no one would see her.

"And you can run like a coward to your room." This was ridiculous. She'd never run from anyone in her entire life. "You're the fighter, girl," she told herself.

She was, too. Jordan might have done something to her, touched her in a way no other man had touched her. Which he had, both literally and metaphorically. For some reason, Jordan made her angrier, more nervous, and hotter than any man she'd ever had even a slight interest in before. There had to be a reason for that.

As soon as she figured out what that reason was, then she could figure out what to do about it.

12

Amber made it across the rocky ground, through the water-laden trees, and then slipped on her ass when she reached the beautifully manicured gardens. She fell hard, her feet flying into the air and her rear end and head conking against the stone-paved path simultaneously.

"Damn it!" she howled, and then lay there on the ground, staring at dark clouds that seemed to swell and rotate overhead into the oddest patterns.

Maybe hitting her head did her some good. All at once it seemed everything made perfect sense. She knew why she couldn't get Jordan out of her head. In barely a week, she'd fallen in love with him. He was, after all, every woman's dream come true. Funny, though, that the one thing most women would probably love about him the most—all the money he came from—was the one part of him she despised. But she couldn't exactly ask him to disown his family just for her.

It was a truth she'd battled for the past few days. She thought of the last time they'd made love, the way he held her, fucked her, and the things he said.

"And you said you didn't want anything to do with that princess," she growled, still lying flat on the ground while the rain splattered against her cheeks and her neck, and soaked through her clothes.

So if she loved him, and he acted as if there was something special between them, there must be something she could do with this knowledge. Rolling to her side, the world kept moving even when she leaned on her elbow. It made it harder for her to decide how to handle this situation.

Crap. She'd hit her head hard. Amber stared at a plant, dripping with water, that she didn't recognize. Some tropical, odd-shaped leaf thing. The longer she stared at it, the more her head started hurting.

"No, no. Not a concussion." She pushed herself up, making it to her knees and once again feeling the world topple to the side.

As soon as she got to her feet, she would march to the back of the castle. Maybe stop in and see how Cook and Jesse were doing. She wouldn't hide from Jordan and Princess Tory, even if she looked like crap. She'd never hidden from anyone, or run from anyone.

"I'm not a coward." She groaned, managing to get to her feet, and then stood, letting the rain hit her and imagining it washed all the dirt from her backside off her body.

Her hair weighed half a ton. She would swear to it. It also seemed to hang sideways off her head. But when she touched her head, running her fingers over her soaked hair, she cringed from the pain when she felt the goose egg on the back of her head. She gingerly fingered it while forcing herself to walk to the castle.

"Amber!"

She looked up at the sound of her name. Then, focusing on the tall, dark image as he moved away from the castle and started in her direction, she continued staring as he moved closer.

"Amber!" He called her name again, this time his voice more distinct.

"What?" she asked, seeing Jordan near her and straining against raindrops as she blinked and looked into his face.

"Crap. What happened to you?" He didn't wait for an explanation but wrapped his arm around her, pulling her against his warmth.

"I fell." Apparently the way she touched her head clued him in.

"Oh my God! You're hurt." The concern in his voice raked over her senses, attacking her reserve and stealing her ability to defend herself.

"I think I'm fine," she mumbled, but wasn't able to stop him when he moved his fingers over her head and then touched the spot she'd found with her fingers. "Ouch!" she cried out.

"Crap," he said again, scooping her into his arms and then bounding toward the castle. "You're going to be fine, sweetheart. Talk to me. Tell me what happened."

He wanted to make sure she was coherent. She understood what he was doing. "I slipped on the rocks," she began, pretty sure that was what happened. It all seemed a blur now. She wanted to tell him she was arguing to herself and ordering herself to be strong.

"You are strong, darling," he whispered, lowering his mouth to her forehead and brushing his lips over her wet skin.

Had she said her thoughts out loud? Jordan wasn't a mind reader so she must have. Which wasn't a good sign. It would be best not to say anything else for fear of incriminating herself. Besides, being nestled in his arms, while he moved swiftly through the gardens, bringing them to the castle and out of the rain a hell of a lot faster than she would have been able to do on her own, was a treat in itself.

But when they reached the kitchen, and suddenly Cook and Jesse were swarming around her, she found herself more coherent—if anything, just out of defense so they would all quit touching her.

"I'm fine," she assured all of them, able to focus a lot better now that she wasn't blinking raindrops out of her eyes every few seconds. "I promise. I'm a klutz, but I'm fine."

"I'll be the judge of that," Cook decided, sounding firm, and setting her jaw with a determined look when she turned from Amber and marched to the refrigerator.

"I found her standing in the rain, soaked to the bone," Jordan explained, his arms crossed over his massive chest, and his cotton shirt clinging to roped muscle that bulged and stretched underneath it. He looked better than she'd ever seen him before. "She could barely stand. And that bump on the back of her head. Sweetheart, you took quite a fall."

"I slipped. The rocks were wet." She eyeballed the pack of ice Cook was now rolling in a dish towel. "I've always loved storms. I guess I stayed out in this one a bit too long."

"And you'll regret the hell out of it if you catch pneumonia for being a fool," Cook snapped, and then pressed the loaded dish towel none too carefully against the bump on Amber's head. "Hold still or the ice won't take down the swelling. Quit moving or we'll strap you down. I swear it."

"I'm fine," Amber stressed again, but was simply outnumbered.

"Will she be okay?" Jordan asked, ignoring her when she glared at him, and instead frowned at where Cook pressed the ice to her head. "We could call in a doctor but I doubt we can get one here before tomorrow."

"I don't need a doctor. I've lived this long without one and I'm sure I'll make it through this as well. I'll take the pack of ice to my room and lie down for a bit," Amber suggested, doubting her attempt to be free of the three of them hovering around her would work.

"You aren't lying down," Jordan said, suddenly stern. "You could have a concussion and you can't fall asleep if that's the case. Sit right there and keep that ice where it is for a while."

He moved around her while Cook brushed soaked strands of hair away from Amber's face with her free hand. "He cares for you, girl," she whispered. "You let him fret or he'll get a temper. I guarantee it."

As strange as Cook's words sounded, not to mention as much as Amber wanted to dispute them publicly, she knew Cook was right.

"Maybe I should do that." Jordan was right behind her, his chest pressed against her back, creating a rest for her to lean against while sitting on her stool. "You get her some strong, hot tea going. She's shaking like a leaf."

Amber hadn't even noticed she was shaking. And she didn't have any problem trying to rob Jordan of his body heat. He took over holding the ice pack to her head and if she leaned back against him more than she probably should have, no one commented on it.

"What were you doing out there?" he whispered over her head, using his free hand to stroke her damp shoulder and move her hair so it hung straight down her back. "Why didn't you come in when you realized it was going to rain?"

"I was too far from the castle," she admitted, unable to see Cook and Jesse with the wrapped towel on one side of her head and his arm blocking her view in the other direction. "I'd just gotten off the phone with your grandfather," she added, remembering Pierre mentioning he'd spoken to Jordan before calling her.

"The son of a bitch," Jordan growled, apparently not caring that Cook and Jesse had to be within earshot. "He upset you, didn't he?"

"I wasn't thrilled by everything he had to say," she confirmed, her guard too low at the moment from the dull throb in her head and Jordan's body continually stroking her damp flesh to keep her thoughts to herself. "I hate it when an employer threatens to fire me if I don't do as he wishes. I swear, if I had a dollar for every time . . ."

"Threatened to fire you?" Jordan roared. His entire body seemed to grow behind her, his outrage so apparent Amber tried hopping off the stool. "You aren't going anywhere," he bellowed, his hands clamping down on her shoulders and putting her right back where she'd been.

"Then quit yelling right now!" Her authoritative voice usually only got results with her younger cousins and coworkers.

She was therefore surprised when Jordan's firm grip on her shoulders suddenly became a very distracting massage.

"I promise you." His deep, soft baritone caressed her with a soothing sensation almost as much as his fingertips did. "You will not lose your job here. I won't allow it. You're the only scrupulous person my grandfather has hired in years."

At the same time Jesse cleared his throat and Cook appeared in front of her, moving surprisingly fast for a woman her size. "I beg your pardon," she clipped, sounding more like she scolded than complained.

"You know I didn't mean either of you." Jordan continued using that deep tone that obviously had an impact on more than Amber. "Grandfather has gone too far this time, and Cook, you know what I mean."

"That I do," she said, sighing. Her cheeks flushed and she smiled, showing off the dark hole where a tooth once was. "And I also know it might be best for the two of you to continue this discussion in a room not quite so public."

She held a thick mug, steaming with the strong smell of chamomile. Handing it to Amber, she then pulled the ice pack from Jordan's grip. Her thick, rough-looking hands were as gentle as a mother's could be. Amber closed her eyes, still feeling a dull ache but not minding so much when Cook's strong fingers worked her way through Amber's head, inspecting the area of her scalp around the bump.

"The swelling is already going down. A bit longer with the ice pack and she'll be good as new," Cook announced. "It might be better if Jesse were to help her to her room, Master Jordan."

"Cook, you're a gem. But I'll take her to her room. I'm not cowering before either my grandfather or an impetuous princess."

Cook made a very unladylike snorting sound, but then pressed the ice pack again in place and backed away from Amber.

"I think it would be best for Amber to dine in her room tonight," Jordan said, making the decision as he walked around her.

"Should she be alone? I agree she's more coherent now," Cook determined, stroking her chin with her thick fingers and studying Amber's face. "But maybe it would be best if I brought up dinner for two."

Amber knew she must still not be thinking clearly. She swore Cook winked at her.

"Very good idea. And if, by chance, my grandfather were to call either of you this evening, you will make it very clear I decided to have dinner with Amber instead of Princess Tory."

"Jordan," Amber protested, scooting off her chair and then standing and moving to face him. "That isn't a good idea."

Jordan moved the stool out of the way instead of trying to walk around it. Placing it next to him, he walked into her, and then pulled her into a hug that felt at least as good as when he'd cradled her earlier.

"You won't hesitate with that information," Jordan continued as if she hadn't spoken. "I want both of your words on it, right now."

Jesse grunted and Cook mumbled her agreement. The stout woman crossed her arms over her ample chest, standing to the side when Jordan once again scooped Amber into his arms.

"I'm pretty sure I can walk." She knew she didn't sound very upset once again being nestled against all that powerful, roped muscle.

Jordan took the hot tea, which Amber hadn't even sipped yet, out of her hand and handed it to Cook. "Follow us up with her tea, and please bring something to snack on to hold us over until dinner."

He carried her from the kitchen and up the stairs as if she weighed nothing and didn't say another word until he closed the door to her room behind them with his foot.

"Now tell me exactly what Grandfather said to you when you talked to him on the phone earlier." He placed her on the edge of her bed, letting her go as he took in the cards scattered across the floor.

"He accused me of sleeping with you and told me if it didn't stop I was fired." She stood, feeling somewhat queasy, and headed to the bathroom. As much as she didn't want to see how bad she probably looked right now, she wouldn't sit and discuss anything with Jordan until she did something about her appearance.

"If he fires you, I'll be leaving on the same plane you do," Jordan growled, turning from where he surveyed everything at her computer and following her into the bathroom.

"You don't get it!" She cringed at her reflection in the mirror and dropped the towel with ice into her sink while steadying herself and deciding whether to shower or bathe. It would be impossible to do either with Jordan leaning in the bathroom doorway. "Already my mother doesn't believe I'll be able to buy the home we live in and rid her of an annoying slumlord. I can't lose this job."

"What were you doing before you agreed to be my social planner?" he asked, crossing his still slightly damp arms across his clinging shirt.

It was hard enough to think with her head throbbing. The

upper part of her hip was tender. But staring into Jordan's blue-gray eyes made her forget the bump on her head, or the bruise that was probably spreading across her hip. There was no way she could talk about anything other than wanting him to fuck her.

She looked away from him first, facing her shower curtain and focusing on the only things she could allow herself to think about. "I worked for Pierre Anton prior to coming here," she told him, giving the rehearsed answer Anton told her to offer if Jordan asked about her work history.

"What did you do?"

"I worked for Anton Business Solutions." Amber remembered Anton telling her offering that information would mean nothing to Jordan, that he didn't keep up with his Grandfather's businesses. "Granted, I never organized a party of this magnitude," she said, refusing to look at him.

"Have you ever organized parties before?" he asked, his voice soft and soothing.

With his tone he suggested he wouldn't be upset if she confessed to a truth he had already guessed. And God, she didn't want to lie to him. Amber didn't want anything between them based on falsehoods. There was no way she could allow a foundation to a relationship form with anything other than honesty and trust.

"I know what I'm doing," she told him, making an effort to give him a pleasant smile when she faced him. "And I look like hell. You need to leave, Jordan, so I can bathe."

He raised one eyebrow as if shocked she would suggest bathing without him. When she didn't say anything, he continued studying her face and then finally gripped the doorknob and backed out of the bathroom.

"I'll be right out here if you need anything." He sounded displeased that she'd asked him to leave the bathroom, but also determined. There wasn't any point in suggesting he leave entirely.

Primarily because she didn't want him to leave. Jordan didn't offer her much, but she hung on to the comments he made, the most recent one being if she were fired he would leave the island with her.

Amber opened the bathroom door when he closed it. "I need clothes," she announced, moving to her closet and aware of him watching her like a hawk.

Someone knocked on her bedroom door and she jumped, showing how on edge she was. Jordan reached the door in several long strides and opened it, allowing Cook to enter.

She pushed a cart in front of her and parked it next to the table, careful to wheel it around the cards still on the floor. "How are you feeling, Miss Amber?" she asked.

"Foolish," she admitted, managing a small smile for Cook and then Jordan when he shifted his attention to her quickly, again cocking an eyebrow with an unspoken question. Amber sighed, gesturing to her closet. "I need to get out of these clothes and take a hot bath."

"You shouldn't do that alone." Cook let go of the cart and took a step toward Amber.

"I'm staying in here with her," Jordan announced before anyone else could say anything.

"Oh," Cook said, turning quickly, and busied herself with the items on the cart. It was the first time she'd entered the room without instigating a conversation, instead arranging the tea cups and laying out several plates with a variety of cheeses and crackers on them. "Shall I still bring dinner to your room as well?" she asked, facing Amber, her expression relaxed, if not peaceful looking. When she offered a small smile, her fingers fluttered around her apron, as if she weren't sure what to do with them.

Amber opened her mouth to tell Cook she'd eat in her room, although since she usually ate here, she wasn't sure why Cook had asked.

"Bring both our meals up here," Jordan informed her before Amber could say a word.

"Very good." Cook flew out of the room faster than she'd ever moved before.

"She doesn't like Princess Tory," Jordan told Amber, as if he guessed her curiosity was piqued.

"That doesn't make it okay for you to have dinner with me," Amber protested. "Do you want me to get fired?"

"You aren't going to get fired," he promised, moving closer and then wrapping his arms around her waist. "And if owning a home for your mother is your dream, I swear to you, you'll have it."

He was gentle when he kissed her. It took a moment to realize he dipped his head, enabling her to kiss him without tilting her head back. The bump on the back of her skull throbbed, but so did her pussy, need rushing through her with a savage intensity she couldn't control.

Grabbing his shoulders, she went up on tiptoes, leaning into him as he deepened the kiss. His hands moved down her back, then slowly peeled her shirt up her body.

"Will you trust me, Amber?" he whispered into her mouth and then straightened, pulling her shirt carefully over her head.

"Trust you about what?" she asked, her lips tingling from his kiss.

She was immediately cold without her shirt. Wrapping her arms around her waist, she fought the urge to cuddle into him, demand his body heat keep her warm. Instead, she turned away from him, knowing if she didn't head for her bath now, she wouldn't get one. And she needed to clean up. He might look sexy as hell with his hair tousled, still damp but drying into small curls at his nape. His clothes still clung to him, showing off every rippled muscle as his cotton shirt hugged his chest and arms. The view made the torturous craving to have him inside her even worse.

"Trust me and know you can be with me. I will prevent Grandfather from making your life hell."

"Oh." She opened her dresser drawers, pulling out clean leggings and a simple blouse that she knew hung to her hips and was as comfortable as it was sexy. "You know your family better than I do," she told him, heading to the bathroom.

Amber expected Jordan to join her in the bathroom. From the point where she stripped out of her clothes, surveying her naked body in the mirror and noting the pale green discoloration on her hip and part of her rear, to the time while she soaked in a steamy hot bath, every inch of her tingled in anticipation. The bathroom door never opened, though. She decided to put her hair up and wash it later when the goose egg on her head went down a bit. She relaxed her neck on the edge of the tub, taking her time soaping her body. No matter how much she enjoyed the hot water caressing her flesh, her attention continually darted to the closed door. Amber sighed, sinking deeper into the water, hating herself for how much she craved him entering the room and joining her.

Jordan didn't say much when she joined him half an hour later, her body still rosy and warm from bathing. He sat at her computer, the cards that had been scattered across the floor now stacked neatly on the corner of the desk. His back was to her, his hair still tousled and his ponytail twisting in small ringlets from having dried after being in the rain.

"I took the liberty of helping you arrange sleeping quarters for all your guests," he informed her, not turning around. His large hands worked the keyboard with surprising ease and he didn't appear to be on a page she recognized.

Amber walked over to the table and poured hot tea from the carafe. Adding a thin slice of lemon, she brought the cup to her lips, watching Jordan warily. Part of her wanted to tell him he had no right to be on her computer while another part of her simply ached to know what he was doing. She inched closer, determining he was on some kind of stock-market page.

"Thank you. I was in the middle of doing that when your grandfather called."

Jordan grunted, possibly not hearing her. He clicked from one page to another and then used one of her small notepads and jotted something down on it. Odd, she hadn't noticed he was left-handed before.

"I hope you don't mind my taking care of some business while you bathed." This time he did glance over his shoulder, taking her in with a quick swoop and then returning to whatever it was he was doing. "I respect your desire for discretion and to be viewed as honorable more than you believe," he informed her. "You took a good blow to the head, though. If you'd needed me when you were in the tub I would have been right there. And if you'd stayed in there much longer, I would have come in to check on you."

"Damn," she mumbled, instantly aggravated knowing if she'd soaked just a bit longer he would have come to her. But then immediately regretting voicing her frustration out loud, she tried for a quick coverup to avoid embarrassment. "You didn't clear out the work I had open on the computer, did you?" she asked, still feeling the heat on her cheeks and praying he wouldn't look at her again until it faded.

"There wasn't anything open on it," he said, frowning and turning the office chair.

Amber tried jumping out of the way of his long legs when he shifted his large body and faced her. Jordan took her wrists, pulling her closer while he continued sitting, and stretched his muscular legs on either side of her. His callused fingertips pressed against the inside of her wrists, intensifying her pulse.

She was certain he felt as strongly as she did. His blue-gray eyes faded to a deep sensual gray as she watched.

"How are you feeling?" he asked, searching her face and looking so concerned she damn near melted while her gaze remained locked on his. "Are you sure you're okay?"

"I'm fine." Unless he wanted to take into consideration that every inch of her burned with the need to be in his arms, feel his body caressing hers, and have him buried deep inside her. She shifted her focus to his long straight nose, and noted as well how broad his cheekbones were and the firm set of his jawbone. At the same time she searched for some thought that would distract her from wanting him so desperately. Amber had never begged a man for anything in her life, and she'd be damned if she would start now. "What are you working on?"

The corner of his mouth twitched. Was it because he took pleasure in her interest in what he was doing? Or did he see right through her, knowing she was completely infatuated with him and finding it amusing?

Jordan pulled her to him, then let go of her wrists and turned her, bringing her down to his lap as he swiveled the chair to once again face the computer.

"My Aunt Penelope owns Big Sky Ranch. It was owned by her great grandfather and has remained in her family over the years. With the economy sucking, many ranches are going under. The ones run by smart, business-savvy people are managing, but our ranch is in danger." He situated her on one leg and reached around her, switching to a different Web site while talking. "I've taken some of the profits from the ranch over the years and invested it, lining up stock to try to help keep my aunt from losing all she has."

"So the ranch isn't yours at all?" Amber was in even more trouble when his muscular arm wrapped around her.

He relaxed his hand over her leg, sitting comfortably underneath her as if talking with her like this was nothing to him at all. "Aunt Penelope was married to Uncle Jorge, my father's twin. When they divorced, the family wasn't very supportive in helping her hold on to the ranch."

"Pierre Anton impresses me as a man very interested in making money. Is the ranch not capable of making a profit? You would think if it were he would be all about keeping it thriving."

Jordan's body grew harder underneath and around her. "You're right about Grandfather in that he loves his money. He loves the feeling of power and control he believes it gives him."

"That's hardly a compliment," she said, learning daily how much he appeared to dislike his grandfather.

"It wasn't meant to be. Grandfather takes any divorce in the family very personally. No one leaves an Anton. We're perfect, don't you know?" He gave her a slight squeeze, trying to make light of it but the dark, forbidding tone he held on to showed his anger outweighed any humor he saw in the situation. "Grandfather would rather destroy Aunt Penelope and see the ranch go on the auction block than lift a finger to help, or keep the ranch intact."

"That doesn't make sense. He obviously feels strongly about family values. You just said the ranch has been in her family for generations."

"He cares about *his* family, no one else's. And even that is being generous. Grandfather only concerns himself with those who kiss his ass. You need to remember always: Grandfather only cares about himself. He will be nice and generous to you as long as you do exactly what he says."

"Well, he was very clear about me staying away from you." Even as she spoke she couldn't bring herself to try to get off his lap. His body was so warm, so hard and masculine. "And he told me that he told you the same thing."

"Yup." He tightened his grip on her, forcing her to lean into him more. "Grandfather doesn't own me. He wants to. And he believes this month will be a nice lesson for me. Grandfather wants to show me that without him, I'm nothing."

"Pretty loving grandfather," she mumbled, liking Pierre Anton less and less the more Jordan enlightened her as to his nature.

"Grandfather doesn't have a clue about love. And it's not my duty to teach him its value. What he will learn is that I can, and will, live without him." Jordan moved the mouse, clicking on a page that showed Jordan's personal investments. "These are investments that Grandfather didn't know about."

Amber's jaw dropped at the figures he showed her. She wasn't sure why Jordan took the time to show her what he was worth but the figures were staggering. "Looks like the ranch is doing pretty damn good if you've been able to invest money like this."

"I admit some of it came from personal investments that I've transferred over the years."

"But wait. You said investments your grandfather didn't know about. Have you told him about all this money now?" Amber doubted it would be in Jordan's favor to enlighten Pierre about any secret weapons he might have.

"Sweetheart. Grandfather lives to control everyone around him. This is his island, his castle, and these are his computers. How much do you want to wager that he's got these computers programmed to tell him where everyone who uses them surfs?"

Amber stiffened. Turning so she stared into Jordan's eyes, she wasn't sure how to react to the dark, intense predatory look she saw there. "If what you're saying is true, not only are you letting your grandfather know you're worth millions on your own accord, you're letting him know that you're sharing that information with me."

Jordan searched her face, that predatory look on his face hardening and sending chills rushing over her flesh. "That's right. He will know that I'm not going to be bullied. And even more so, if he threatens you again, he'll regret it more than he can guess."

13

Jordan headed out of his room, worried that Aunt Penelope might not be able to make it a month without him on the ranch. Maybe consenting to Grandfather's wishes had been a stupid move. It had taken Jordan two years to put that ranch in order. He'd be damned if in less than two weeks without him it would go to hell in a handbasket.

Aunt Penelope complained about two of his ranch hands, two young punks still wet behind the ears he'd thought showed potential. There were tools coming up missing and a couple of cattle were unaccounted for. His aunt confirmed that yesterday the fence on the southern end of the property hadn't been repaired as instructed. Jordan listened to Aunt Penelope rant and heard what she didn't say. His men weren't listening to her. Jordan headed to Amber's room, as he'd done every morning since she'd fallen and hurt her head, grinding his teeth in frustration. He should have hired someone to run his men while he was gone instead of allowing his aunt to convince him she could handle it. Obviously she now decided he'd been right since she asked him several times during their conversation when he'd be home.

He was a good businessman. Two years of turning the ranch around and keeping it from going under proved that. But the difference between Jordan and his grandfather was that Jordan had a heart. Running Big Sky Ranch wouldn't make him rich. That wasn't what it was about. It was about family, the true meaning of family. Aunt Penelope was part of that land, but so were a lot of her ranch hands. More than a few had worked that land all their lives, and their sons now worked it, too. They lived in town or in the bunkhouses on the property, and sweated and bled to keep the place from going under. There were a few stragglers who would show up from time to time, predominantly drifters needing work. Jordan gave them a chance as long as their records were clean. Keeping Big Sky Ranch from going under was about all of those men, women, and children who relied on the ranch to survive. He wouldn't put them out of a job.

Jordan hadn't ever taken Grandfather on to this magnitude, but then again Grandfather had never pushed his way so far into Jordan's life before. It was bad enough when he insisted Jordan walk away from his life for a month to get to know a woman his grandfather viewed as a good candidate for a wife. The ultimatum of marrying Princess Tory or working in one of Grandfather's corporate offices pushed the entire matter too far. Then Grandfather had threatened Amber, which obviously upset her enough to send her running into a rainstorm.

Grandfather made this matter personal. Jordan shook his head, realizing that to any stranger he would be dubbed as out of his mind to think the matter of marriage didn't qualify as personal. It was probably that Jordan never thought of this marriage thing as anything real. One way or another he would have managed his way out of the ultimatum of marrying for money or working the corporate life. But when Grandfather had contacted Aunt Penelope in Jordan's absence, demanding to see her books, he pissed Jordan off. And when he threatened Amber, Jordan knew it was time to attack.

Princess Tory's wing appeared to be an active place when Jordan reached the double doors, which were open today. Her two servant ladies were hauling bedding out of one of the bedrooms. Apparently it was laundry day, if the piles of sheets outside each bedroom door was any indication. The servants chattered amiably in Italian, not bothering to keep their voices down.

Jordan wouldn't call himself bilingual. He was proud of his Harvard education, even if that pride differed from what his mother and Grandfather believed it should be for. At this moment, he managed to pick up a few phrases and keywords that he remembered from introductory classes.

The word for "pregnant" and phrases "early enough" and "married soon" froze him in his tracks. Jordan stepped out of view, pressing himself against the wall as he glanced hastily up and down the hallway. Then he strained to catch as much as he could from the two wound-up young ladies.

As if there wasn't already enough crap going on in his life! Jordan pulled his phone out of his pocket, placed a call to himself, and then held it flat in his palm, concealing it and at the same time pointing it toward the long hallway. The servant girls were working their way closer to Jordan.

His Italian sucked at best and he wasn't sure how well his phone would record their conversation to voice mail. But if he could interpret any more phrases to help him understand what he was overhearing, it would help.

The two young ladies repeated the same word—*incinta*—over and over again until Jordan started feeling sick to his stomach.

He pressed his back against the wall, but knew if anyone saw him they'd either think he was sick or grow suspicious.

Jordan needed time to digest this information. There was a slim chance his phone had picked up their conversation, but if it had, he needed a translator. Someone he could trust.

The ladies spotted him when he continued down the hall, both stopping what they were doing and offering shy smiles. They were flighty, ridiculous females. Not incredibly intelligent, very submissive, and by the look they both offered him, interested in doing anything with any man who might help them have a bit more comfort in their lives. They tripped over the bedding and each other making him wonder why the princess kept either of them on staff.

He nodded when they grinned at him, his expression probably darker than it would have been if he'd passed them without overhearing their gossipy chatter. More than likely the ladies believed he didn't know Italian. Princess Tory had asked him if he did and he'd told her no. Which wasn't a lie. He didn't know enough to carry on a conversation with her in the language. And telling her no had made her relax around him and speak openly to her lover when she believed he couldn't follow a word of what she said. Now it appeared she would willingly enter into a sacramental marriage with him, prepared to commit adultery the first chance she could, as well as carry another man's child. He was fuming by the time he reached the wing where Amber stayed. Princess Tory would lead him to believe he would be a father when in truth the child couldn't be his.

He reached Amber's door, then forced himself to take a deep, calming breath. It was early in the morning. He liked the routine of coming to her before either of their days started.

A week had passed since she'd fallen, their second week on the island coming to a close, and it had become more routine. He tapped on her door, realizing he still held his cell phone in his hand and fingering it while waiting for her to answer.

"You almost missed me," she offered in greeting when she pulled open the door but then turned back into her room and hurried to her desk. "I want to be down at the runway when the plane gets here."

"That's right," he said, following her inside and closing the door behind him. "Your hired help arrives this morning."

Amber was beaming when she faced him. Her long, thick brown hair was held back in a bright green headband that matched the color of the sundress she wore. He knew she'd ordered more dresses after arriving here, having caught her drooling over women's clothing magazines, and had even offered a few suggestions of his own.

"That's the dress I told you to buy, isn't it?"

Her blush answered his question for him. "I don't want them to land without me there," she said, changing the subject and tapping her painted fingernails over the clipboard she held in her small hands.

"It looks better on you than it did on the model in the magazine." He liked the way the black belt showed off her slender figure. The dress was simple, casual business attire. Amber made it look classier than he was sure it was designed to look.

Amber glanced down at herself, and a strand of long brown hair fell over her shoulder. "I admit it makes me feel more important when I'm dressed in all these fancy clothes all the time."

"What did you wear at your old job?" He had heard the comments she'd made from time to time, implying her usual life was anything but glamorous. He imagined that a party organizer would be more used to a life of glitter and festivities.

"Dresses," she offered, but then waved off the question as if it didn't matter. "Planning parties is the dirty work," she added, giving him a shrewd look. "Going to them is the easy job."

"You'll be at this party."

She blinked, as if the thought hadn't crossed her mind. "There will be a lot to do . . ."

"Which is why you're hiring more help: to delegate," he informed her, taking the clipboard from her hands and placing it on the desk, then holding her hands in his. "You're going to be at that party, and we need to take time soon to find you the perfect dress to wear to it."

"Jordan, you'll be there with Princess Tory."

Just the mention of the princess's name made his blood boil. And the way her eyes opened wider proved she noticed it, too.

"That's the reason all of us are here," she whispered, emphasizing the fact to him.

"Do you know Italian?" He didn't want to talk about Princess Tory, or to even think about having her on his arm at a party where everyone who was anyone in the world would be present to watch.

"What?" Amber blinked, staring at him as if the question didn't make sense.

"Do you know Italian?" he asked again, rubbing her hands and then moving his fingertips up her bare arms. She didn't back away from him and continued watching him with wide, dark blue eyes that didn't blink as she stared at his face. "I took it while at Harvard, along with a few of the other Romance languages, but I'm not sure I could translate. Did you ever take it?"

Something dulled in her eyes when she pressed her lips together. She dropped her attention to his chest, still not trying to move away from his touch. "No. I never took Italian. Why do you ask?"

He didn't want to discuss what he thought he overheard until he was sure he'd heard right. There was nothing worse than bad gossip, which often got started when someone eavesdropped when they shouldn't have and then took the information out of context.

"Let's just say I want to confirm something."

Amber nodded. "One of the people arriving this morning is Italian. His family always speaks it at home."

"Really? Do you trust him?"

She returned her attention to his face. "With my life," she said, and pressed her glossy lips into a straight line, showing she wouldn't suggest such a thing about just anyone.

Jordan wondered if she would say she trusted him with her life. He already knew she would in the physical sense. But what about really trust him? They went through the motions of having a relationship of sorts, in spite of her continually reminding him about Princess Tory. Jordan figured she was scared he would start falling for the princess, since they were required to spend time together daily, all their activities arranged by Amber and chaperoned by Carlos. Jordan was more certain every day that he couldn't wait until he didn't have to see Princess Tory ever again.

"Bring him to me once he arrives. I want him to listen to something for me and interpret it."

"Okay," Amber said slowly, acting as if she ached to know more.

"Do you want me to ride with you to the runway to meet the plane?"

She shook her head. "You need to have breakfast with Princess Tory and I do believe today the two of you are taking a walk along the beach."

"It's going to be a very short walk." Jordan pulled her into his arms, loving how she fit so perfectly against him. Her petite body, with her full round breasts, snuggled against him as her long, thick hair fell like raw silk over his arms and down her back. "I'd rather be with you," he confessed.

"Seriously, Jordan, I don't see why you keep torturing me. What is the point?" she demanded, suddenly exasperated.

"What is the point?" he growled, not liking her tone at all. Keeping her in his arms, he tilted her head and stared into midnight blue eyes that were slowly taking on a violet hue. Her emotions were running strong. "I just said what the point was. I want to be with you."

"And in two weeks you'll go back to your life and I'll go back to mine. I'm sorry, but quick affairs aren't my style." Her eyes were suddenly violet as she glared at him.

"I wouldn't care so much about you if they were," he informed her, not hurt by her insulting comment and knowing she had said it to put her defenses in place, not because she believed that was what existed between them. "If all I wanted from you was sex, I would have pushed harder for more from you before now," he added, hearing the harshness in his voice but noting that he had her attention when she didn't try pulling away from him or diverting it elsewhere. "Sweetheart, I want the entire package."

"Jordan, I need to go," she said, her voice flat. She brought her hand up between them and pressed her palm against his chest. "The plane will be landing in half an hour."

"You want me, too."

"That isn't the point," she wailed, struggling now to get out of his arms. "We live on opposite sides of the country. And right now neither of us is even in our normal element. This isn't how you build a relationship, and any levelheaded person knows long-distance relationships don't work."

He wasn't ready to let her go. And he didn't have answers as to what to expect two weeks from now. He was building his ammunition and just because he hadn't heard from Grandfather didn't lead him to believe the old man wasn't preparing for Jordan's attack. Grandfather hadn't gotten where he was by being foolish.

"We're together right now," he said, knowing he couldn't speculate yet on where they would be after leaving the island. He needed assurance that Grandfather would leave him alone when he left here before he asked Amber to come to the ranch. But once he forced Grandfather's hand, then he would take

Amber. "And you need to trust me," he added, but he could tell by the look in her eyes that it wasn't enough.

"I've got to go." This time when she pushed he let her go, letting his hands drop to his sides when she headed to her door. She opened it but then leaned on the handle, waiting for him to walk out ahead of her. "I've got a busy morning."

"Bring the man you mentioned to me," he ordered, pausing in the doorway with half a mind to kiss her silly and be damned if anyone were to see them.

"I'm assigning them rooms in this wing alongside mine," she told him, encouraging him out of her room and pulling the door closed behind her. "We'll spend the morning training so each one of them understands what they'll be doing here. But I'll let you know when we take a break and you can meet all of them if you wish."

"Bring the one you mentioned to my room," he insisted, placing his hand on her shoulder and leading her down the hallway. He kept a slightly firm grip, silently daring her to brush him away in case anyone might see.

Jordan had time to shower after walking along the beach with Princess Tory and Carlos. He wanted the musky smell of her perfume off of him before Amber brought over the man she'd hired. The princess seemed to be a lot more affectionate the past few days. She suggested more than once they would make a better show at the party if they were convincing in their relationship. Her implication that they should have sex made his stomach roll.

He dried off after his shower and slipped into shorts and a T-shirt when there was a soft knock on his door. Jordan opened the door barefoot and with tousled hair and enjoyed the hell out of Amber's sudden flush that spread over her cheeks. Knowing she wanted him as badly as he wanted her helped him through this otherwise hell of a month.

"Jordan Anton, may I present Barney Holden," she said, waving her small hand from one man to the other as she made introductions. "Barney is my lifesaver," she bragged.

The small man puffed out his almost atrophied chest and beamed, but then extended his hand seriously. "It's an honor to meet you, sir," he offered.

"Call me Jordan." Grandfather would have pointed out that anyone in a servant position should never offer to shake hands with the head of the household. Jordan didn't know where Amber found Barney, or exactly what his position was on the island now that he was here, but he didn't care. Shaking the small man's hand, he then stepped aside for them to enter. "I appreciate you making time for me."

"I told Barney you had something in Italian you wanted him to translate," Amber said, pausing in the middle of his bedroom and then clasping her hands in front of her, still wearing the bright green dress and looking hot as hell.

"I'm not as good at translating written Italian," Barney warned him. "Nonna wouldn't speak English in the house and our parents were strict about us honoring her wishes."

Barney stood at possibly five feet six inches, maybe an inch or two more. Jordan bet he was one hundred fifty pounds dripping wet at the most. He was a sharp dresser, and moved with a feminine air about him, as if he were proud to have mastered his movements.

"This isn't written." Jordan reached for his cell phone and then gestured the two of them to the couch. "My request is an odd one. Amber swore to me you could be trusted with a very incriminating situation."

He took a moment to register Barney's reaction. Jordan was a good judge of character and knew making a blunt statement and noting a stranger's initial reaction was all he needed to determine whether the man could be trusted.

Amber looked up at him wide eyed, straightening where she

sat on the edge of the couch. Barney didn't flinch. Instead he nodded solemnly.

"Amber doesn't say anything about anyone that isn't true, Jordan." The small man was loyal to a fault to Amber, which was a good sign. "If you have a delicate situation and she believes I can help, I'll do my best to."

"Good enough." Jordan held out his cell phone in his palm and then pushed the buttons to pull up his voice mail. Putting it on speakerphone, he played back what he'd recorded earlier.

Parts were hard to hear, but at other times, the two servant girls' voices were recorded with incredible clarity. Barney frowned at the phone but then his eyes grew round as quarters and his jaw dropped. When the recording ended, he cleared his throat, looking to Amber as he frowned and almost appeared nervous.

"What did they say?" Jordan barked.

Barney jumped noticeably. "I'm . . . umm . . . would you mind playing it again one more time?"

"What is it?" Amber asked, noticeably confused.

"A conversation I wasn't supposed to hear and recorded between Princess Tory's two servant women."

The way Barney shook like a leaf and started rubbing his hands together nervously made Jordan even more certain he'd picked up on possibly the most damning evidence against the princess yet. And quite possibly he had just assured his way out of this mess without having to expose his relationship with Amber. He forced himself to remain calm as he replayed the recording.

"Well?" Amber demanded before he could say anything. "What are they saying?"

"This is most embarrassing, Jordan." Barney rung his hands and looked very apologetic. "Here we are just now meeting and you ask a very uncomfortable favor of me."

"Tell me what they are saying," Jordan demanded.

"Barney, it's okay." Amber reached across the couch and covered Barney's hands with hers. "If the women are saying something bad, we should know about it, right?" Her tone was so soft, her touch comforting.

For a moment Jordan thought he felt a twinge of jealousy. He watched Amber reassure Barney and noted a bond between the two of them that had reached a comfort level she hadn't reached with him. Barney looked like a lost soul, though, his pleading expression locking with Amber's but then relaxing after she spoke.

"It's nothing bad about you, girlfriend," Barney offered, almost whispering. He continued watching Amber, even shifting on the couch so he faced her. "They're talking about a princess being pregnant. Apparently she just found out. The two women are making jokes about it. This princess is going to marry a man and tell him the child is his but in truth it is her boyfriend's. And the princess and boyfriend know this. The poor sap, or *sciocco* as they called him, also known as a fool." Barney blushed terribly and pulled his hands out from Amber's and covered his face. He did whisper, leaning into Amber, as he continued. "They are calling Jordan a *sciocco*."

Amber drew in a deep breath, pulling her hand back and continuing to sit on the edge of the couch, her back perfectly straight as she pressed her hands together in her lap.

"Barney, I appreciate your translation. Would you swear under oath that what you just translated is accurate?" Jordan asked.

Both Amber and Barney shot their attention to him, both looking surprised. Jordan wouldn't be the fool when all was said and done here. But for now, he kept his composure and watched Barney watch him. The man was trembling and would probably collapse if put on a stand. But knowing the man would swear to the accuracy of his translation was good enough.

"The women are obviously Sicilian by their dialect," Barney began. "Which I know because my grandmother, my *nonna*, was born in Sicily. I know what I heard," he finished, nodding at the phone Jordan still held. "I really don't want to have to say that in court. My God, just the thought of it is bringing on a panic attack."

"Breathe slowly," Amber ordered, reaching for him again and this time rubbing his thin shoulder.

"But I'll swear that is what they are saying." Barney shifted uncomfortably on his side of the couch. "Hell of a thing to say to a man when you first meet him," he added, laughing nervously. "And girlfriend," he added, turning and grinning at Amber although he still looked grossly pale and his cheeks were feverish with his embarrassment. "You were right. He is quite the looker."

Jordan blinked. Amber's laugh was melodic even as she scowled at Barney. "We're getting you out of here before you make me blush," she scolded, grabbing Barney's hand and pulling him to his feet.

"Where are you going?" Jordan demanded.

"I was going to escort him back to his room."

Barney patted Amber's hands, giving them an affectionate squeeze. "Don't you worry about me, honey. I can find my way around. Besides, you said we could explore and I'd love to check this ancient shack out."

"At the end of the hall are the stairs." Jordan reached the door first and then held it open for Barney, this time extending his hand first to shake Barney's. "At the bottom of the stairs turn left and you'll find the kitchen. You tell Cook I said to treat you right. You'll love her cooking."

"Pure vegetarian, here," Barney told him, patting his belly but then eagerly shaking Jordan's hand. "I'll give her a shout out, though. And it was a pleasure meeting you. Don't let those bitches make a fool out of you. You tell that princess chick to take her swollen belly elsewhere."

"Sounds like a good plan." Jordan decided he liked Barney. The guy was as odd as they came, almost fragile in his manner-isms, but honest. Jordan liked a man who made eye contact and didn't appear to have some hidden agenda. He prayed Princess Tory never got her hands on the guy. Barney wouldn't stand a chance. He closed the door, then turned to find Amber already pacing behind him. "Keep the princess away from him."

"It's already crossed my mind," she said, waving her hand in the air. "Not that we really have anything to worry about. I have half a mind to go kick her royal ass right now."

"You would fight for my honor?" He grabbed her, pulling her into his arms.

If he was a bit too aggressive she didn't seem to mind. "How am I supposed to go through with planning this party when I hate her more and more every day?"

His heart damn near exploded in his chest. He doubted Amber realized how much her complaints professed her feel-ings for him.

"We'll make it through this together." He grabbed her chin, tilted her head back, and then pounced on her mouth. He'd waited long enough after Amber banged her head, and he needed her now.

14

Amber fought to ignore the stabbing pain that shot right through her heart when Jordan spoke. They would get through this together. He needed her to maintain stability through this horrific ordeal. And it was a despicable arrangement, growing uglier and more absurd by the day.

She hated accepting the knowledge that she appealed to him because she was a rock in very unstable water. If they weren't on this island, if he were on his ranch, in his world where he controlled everything, Amber wasn't sure she would appeal to him. Possibly she would as she did now—physically. But being a piece of ass was a raw deal. And not a deal she wanted to be a part of.

Her world was filled with bills, leaky roofs, and bad plumbing. Trying to make it to the train on time, or carrying work clothes in a grocery store bag so the twenty-block walk to her job wouldn't mess them up. Life was about sipping coffee at the kitchen table before it got light out and listening to her uncle share prospects of possible jobs. She and her mother would set their alarms, get up early enough so both could shower and have hot water and pray the hot water heater didn't screw up. It was about helping her mother with her teenage half brother and half sister. It was about coming home at night to the smell of homemade soup or bread and sitting with her family in the living room, watching DVDs since they couldn't afford cable. Her life was full, and as she felt Jordan's powerful arms around her, she knew this could only be temporary.

This was a fantasy, a seduction. And in two weeks it would be over. If she was smart, right now she'd push away from him and tell him no. Amber admitted she wasn't the most intelligent person on the planet.

His hands moving over her body felt too damn good. There weren't men in her life. Hell, who had time? Those who did come around once in a while didn't appeal to her. Or they were men who would hit on her and her mother at the same time. Her mom might find it amusing, but Amber wasn't into players.

Jordan had struck her as a player when she had first met him. But she saw him now as just about the most perfect man she'd ever known. His strong, dominating nature, his drive to do right, and his compelling good looks created a package that surpassed anything she'd ever fantasized about.

While devouring her mouth, he somehow managed to unhook her belt. It fell to the floor and then his knuckles rubbed down her back when he unzipped her dress. Jordan groaned, moving his hands to her shoulders and pushing aside her dress, then planting moist kisses over her bare skin.

She would never be part of his world, where staying one step ahead of the enemy and planning surprise attacks were what life was all about. But for now, for this moment, Amber couldn't deny herself the pleasure he offered. His lips seared her flesh and his fingers caressed her, stroking her until the pressure inside her threatened to explode and send her over the edge.

"I've waited a week for this," he informed her, then lowered his mouth to her breast, pushing her strapless bra out of the way and pouncing on her nipple.

Amber swore her toes curled up as he tugged and nibbled, creating electric sparks that shot straight through her to her pussy.

"If I was smart I'd tell you no," she groaned, tangling her fingers in his hair and then pulling his ponytail holder out and freeing his long, silky, black strands of soft hair.

"If you were smart you would *never* tell me no," he growled, moving from one nipple to the other and latching down hard enough that he zapped all of her senses at once.

"I don't know how smart I am." She cried out, almost laughing, when he lifted her into his arms and pushed her dress off her body, letting it fall to the floor as he carried her to his bed.

"You're one of the most intelligent ladies I've ever met," he informed her.

Amber bit her lip, knowing if she told him she'd never finished high school it would ruin the moment. She was being selfish, and wrong. Maybe if she enlightened Jordan, told him who and what she really was, he would back off and slow down the seduction. But damn it, all of this attention was too much to pass up. All she needed to do was keep her heart wrapped up securely, enjoy the incredible sex, and let it go at that.

Which made her no better than the players she continually complained about.

"Don't confuse common sense with education," she whispered, stretching out on his bed and running her hands down her body. When all was said and done she could point out she never tried misleading him. Maybe it would help her save face.

It grew harder worrying about parting ways with Jordan when he stripped out of his clothes. She hummed her approval when he stood at the side of the bed, naked and harder than steel. Her mouth watered as she stared at his cock, which reached for her.

"I see honor and integrity," he told her, crawling over her onto the bed. "And I see a gorgeous woman with work ethics that are as intact as mine. Amber, you're one hell of a lady. Don't ever let anyone tell you otherwise."

He lowered his mouth to hers, nibbling at her lower lip and sending goose bumps racing over her flesh. There was a slim chance he might like her for who she was. Everything he said just now was true. If he saw her as gorgeous she wouldn't argue the point. She knew she wasn't ugly. But she was honor bound, and she did have integrity. Otherwise it wouldn't bother her so much that they were from different worlds.

"Jordan," she hissed, his lips still against hers when his cock pressed against her pussy.

"You need me," he growled.

She brought her legs up, wrapping them around him, and lifted her hips off the bed instead of answering him. He was so damn hard. He needed her, too. And that knowledge pushed all worries out of her head. Later she would decide the best thing to do, whether to tell him the truth about where she came from or leave well enough alone and simply enjoy what they had right now.

"Tell me how badly you want this," he ordered, pressing the swollen tip of his cock against her soaked entrance but not penetrating, no matter how hard she tried drawing him inside her. He lowered his mouth to her neck, scraping her tender flesh with his teeth and then sucking and licking her skin until she swore she'd fly off the bed. "I want to hear that you need me as badly as I need you," he told her.

"Please," she begged, unable to form words when he was making her insane with his cruel inflictions. "You aren't the only one who's waited for this."

Apparently that confession worked for Jordan. He thrust

into her heat, separating her and filling her as he pushed deep inside her pussy.

"God! Yes," she cried out, arching into him and tightening her grip on him with her legs.

"Do you feel how perfect we are together?" he asked, lifting his head and staring down at her.

He began moving inside her, forcing the pressure to build while he stroked her pussy walls. She opened her eyes, doing her best to focus on him and to stay grounded. Her fingers moved over his bare shoulders, feeling all that roped muscle twitch against her touch while she caressed his smooth, warm flesh.

"It feels so good," she whispered, lifting her legs higher and encouraging him deeper.

"Better than good, sweetheart. Your pussy was made for my dick, like a personal glove. It's exactly what I need." He drew out his last sentence as he plunged again and again into her heat.

Jordan picked up the momentum, fucking her hard. She wasn't surprised he didn't go for gentle. Not with the news he'd just had. Reminding herself of his predicament made her feel a bit selfish for worrying about how a relationship would thrive and survive between the two of them. There was enough to worry about right now to keep her from dwelling too much on the future.

He dove deep into her pussy, gritting his teeth while staring down at her. His intense look, those gorgeous deep-gray eyes that didn't hold a bit of blue to them at the moment, helped take her over the edge.

"Fuck me," he growled.

At first she didn't understand, didn't follow what it was he wanted from her. But as she held on, unable to look away, while slipping over the edge, her fogged brain slowly grasped his meaning. Her orgasm ripped through her, causing her to tremble underneath him. Which was what he wanted.

Jordan might have a Harvard education. He might have been raised among the rich and powerful, but incredible insight came from taking time to really see people. He guessed her thoughts were drifting from their lovemaking.

"Fuck me more," she whispered, barely able to form the words, but unable to let him believe he'd guessed right. If he thought her mind was elsewhere as soon as they finished he would demand to know what worried her.

Jordan chuckled and a warm sensation, aside from the heat pouring over her insides from his cock throbbing deep inside her, spread over her body. The way he pinned her with his dark, brooding gaze led her to believe she hadn't been as coy as she'd hoped just now. The sensation that he might know her that well already, and was strong enough to keep them going while reading her thoughts, caused her heart to do a triple beat. For a moment she couldn't catch her breath.

He was perfect—perfect for her. Nothing turned her on more than knowing a man was truly strong enough for her. Not in the physical sense, although all that rock-hard muscle was definitely to her liking. He was strong enough emotionally. A terrible scenario had just played itself out before him and now he fucked her, knew her mind, and carried them together to ultimate bliss. That was raw, untamed carnal control and power. And it turned her on more than anything else about him.

She felt the waves from her need smash against the dam of her resistance and didn't try fighting it. "That's it," she hissed, realizing when she spoke that her teeth were clenched together but she was unable to loosen her jaw. Every inch of her was too close to the edge, too tight and throbbing for her to even attempt relaxing. She clung to his shoulders, pinning him with her thighs, and rose off the bed, meeting his final thrust and taking all he could give her with a howl.

Amber tossed her head from side to side, sparks igniting before her eyes as the world she'd known up until this moment exploded in an array of color, from bright reds and oranges to deep, warm purples and radiant blues. She swore he'd hit a part of her never before touched by anyone. It released the need she'd pent up all these years, forced it to come crashing all around her.

"Amber, sweetheart!" His voice sounded so far away.

But then his lips were on hers, hot and searing his brand deep into her soul. She managed to move her mouth, accept his kiss, and slide with him into a space so much warmer, so much more comfortable, and so incredibly perfect.

"I'm falling in love with you, darling."

Amber's heart pounded so hard in her chest, and the ringing in her head made it impossible for her to know for sure if she'd actually heard Jordan say he loved her or if she imagined it. Sparks of energy singed her flesh. Every inch of her was one huge, throbbing nerve ending. When he moved his fingers over her bare, damp shoulder, she jumped, and tried opening her eyes.

For a moment she thought her world would remain blissfully dark forever. Jordan was still inside her, his orgasm as intense as hers. She knew it had to have been. He throbbed and twitched against her still-too-sensitive pussy and she shivered, feeling firm muscle brush over her body as he slowly lowered some of his weight onto her.

"You are so beautiful." If he kept singing her praises like this she would never overcome the intensity of what they had just experienced.

Amber blinked a few more times, bringing him into focus, and then stared at his gorgeous face. Thick, straight black hair fell around his perfectly chiseled facial features. His broad cheekbones and straight, regal nose gave him a rugged, he-man look. But the way his lips curved into a smile softened the edges. She noticed how clear his gray eyes were, with small flecks of blue around his pupils that weren't there a moment before.

"You aren't so bad yourself," she answered him, her voice scratchy. She hadn't screamed that much, had she?

"I'm good because of you." He wasn't smiling anymore. He meant what he said.

Amber understood Jordan enough today to know he wouldn't say sweet nothings to a woman after fucking her just to make her feel good. He'd credited her as being an intelligent woman. She didn't need false praise as a thank-you for letting him use her body to get off.

Because that wasn't what this was all about. He wasn't using her. And she knew she wasn't using him. Their lovemaking was off the charts. There weren't words to describe it. But Amber knew in her heart and her soul she could make it through this month just fine without sex. She allowed him to fuck her because she wanted *him*. And hell, Jordan probably could have taken either of those servant ladies, possibly both of them if he wanted to. He could have gotten off using them, and inflicted a bit of revenge with the act, too.

That wasn't his nature, though. No more than it was hers. He'd made love to her because he wanted her. And he'd said what he said to her right now because he meant it. Did he tell her he was falling in love with her?

She searched his face, looking deep into his eyes, trying to learn the truth. Jordan lowered his mouth to hers, his cock once again dancing inside her from the aftermath of wonderful sex.

15

_____

Amber led her small group into the very large ballroom. She paused when she stood almost in the middle of the grand room, glancing at the domed ceiling and then at the incredible statues on display along the walls and the beautiful stained glass windows that added mystique and elegance to the room. It was like walking into another time, pausing and seeing a glimpse of how life once was. How many parties were thrown in this room to honor the announcement of marriage by two people who barely knew each other? Or worse yet, who hated each other's guts?

"This is just too cool!" When Olive Crain clapped her hands together, the sound echoed off the walls. "Oh my, we're going to have too much fun. I still can't believe this is real, Amber." Olive hadn't stopped grinning from ear to ear in the two days that she'd been here.

"It's real." Amber wished she shared half of Olive's excitement.

But Olive needed the money she'd make here as desperately as Amber did, if not more. Amber remembered how devastated

Olive had been the day the father of her two-year-old strolled back into her life with papers from the courts announcing he'd managed full custody of the boy. Olive didn't have a dime to fight him. And her son, her reason for living, was yanked out of her life by a sperm donor who now believed he could financially care for the boy and give him a better life than Olive could.

"It's all so romantic," Olive said, sighing deeply as she turned around slowly and took in the large room.

"It's business, girlfriend. Pull your head out of the clouds." Barney kept his promise to not say a word about what had happened the other day when he translated the recorded conversation for Jordan. Amber could tell it pissed him off, though, that all of them were part of this sordid ordeal. She didn't blame him a bit and gave him a knowing look to show him as much.

"My head isn't in the clouds." Olive pouted, crossed her arms, and scowled at Barney. "Allow me a moment to imagine a life like this, would you?"

"You can imagine on your own time," Amber told her, but kept her tone friendly, in spite of the overwhelming surge of panic that had hit her when she woke up this morning and realized the party was the following weekend. "We have a week to pull this off."

"Not a problem." Barney strutted around the two of them, holding his elbow in one hand and pointing with the other at the room around them. "Picture this. And you said money was no problem, right?" he asked before continuing.

"Right." Amber had known that bringing Barney on board would be a wise choice. He loved throwing parties and oftentimes when anyone in the office wanted to organize any kind of event, he was the one they turned to. "Tell me what you have in mind."

"Well, first of all, the room is way too open. It's large enough for all the people who will be here. But we need to break it up."

He walked away from them and stopped, doing a full circle before facing them. "This is probably the middle of the room. Imagine a fountain right here. Something to break the room into sections. Then we put a band over there, and a dance floor in front of them. We want tables on one side of the fountain, but then leave it open on the other side, a place for everyone to mingle or watch the dancing."

"I've seen fountains you can rent online for parties." Olive was the Internet junkie. If anyone wanted to know where to find anything online, Olive was the lady to ask. "But I don't know about shipping anything like that to this island. Have you explored all the rooms around this ballroom? There might be party supplies already here."

"It's a thought." Amber glanced at the many closed doors around the ballroom. "Honestly I haven't checked to see where any of them go."

A couple of hours passed while the three of them explored the rooms off the ballroom. Cook showed up more than once, with comments or questions about the ten additional servants Amber had hired. They weren't supposed to arrive until later that week but somehow communication broke down and the service Amber went through had put them all on a plane and flown them to the island that morning. Cook was a lifesaver and eagerly accepted the role of head of the household.

"You're in charge of the entire staff," Amber told her, making a quick delegating decision. "Assign them rooms on my wing. Bunk them together if you have to. Give them a tour, and you decide what chores each of them will do."

"I ran a staff of thirty servants before." Cook stood taller, puffing out her ample bosom as she proudly accepted the responsibility. "You keep going with your work here, Miss. Don't you worry about a thing with the servants."

"I'm not worried." Amber grinned at Cook. "But I'm going to be starved when we get done here."

Cook was already heading out the door. "Lunch will be ready for the three of you in an hour."

It was actually fun exploring the different rooms, of which several were in fact storage rooms.

"This isn't a fountain," Amber announced after helping pull huge, canvaslike sheets off of the items in a large room where they all stood. She brushed dust off herself and grinned at her friends, who looked as dirty as she felt. "But it's pretty cool."

"Whatever it is," Olive added, tapping her finger against her lips as she walked around the large, odd-shaped statue. Her short, cropped dark blond hair was tousled and she had a smudge of something dark gray on her cheek. "If I didn't know better I would say it's a huge dick."

"Don't get your panties in a ruffle," Barney snapped but then tilted his head, clucking his tongue in his mouth as he surveyed their latest discovery. "You've got a point, though."

"It would make an interesting conversation piece." Amber wasn't sure if the people attending this party would appreciate the statue, though.

"Maybe I should search online and make sure it's not some kind of bad-luck charm." Olive wasn't joking and told Barney as much with a hard look when he snickered. "Who knows how old this thing is? It could have been used at some dance hundreds of years ago to curse some unknowing groom."

"In a way, you're right." The three of them jumped when Sara Bird spoke from the doorway. She tossed her long, thick braid over her shoulder and entered the room, ignoring Barney and Olive's curious stares at her intrusion. She walked up to the incredibly tall, uniquely shaped figure and then reached for it, gently stroking it with the palm of her hand. "I'd almost forgotten it was here. I think it was my grandmother who covered it up and put it in storage. But it was once out in the ballroom with the rest of the statues."

"What is it?" Amber asked, moving next to Sara. She'd

meant to seek out the older woman when she'd had time to learn more about the island.

"Well, it would have been her grandmother, or maybe great grandmother, who last held a ball here at the castle." Sara got a faraway look in her soft green eyes as she stared at her hand, which no longer moved, but was pressed flat against the smooth surface of the statue. "You must understand it was a different time back then. Carvings like this weren't done to pass the time, but were done on demand, and to meet the needs of the kingdom. During that time, the women in our family were having a run of bad luck. Every man they married seemed to be weakening our family line. I'm sure some of the ladies in my family tree would be surprised to know I carry on the name," she added, chuckling.

"What are you saying?" Barney asked. "Were they not fertile?"

"The Bird family tree was headed by women. For generations the firstborn was a daughter, and the rulers of this castle were women, not men. It gave them a bit of an edge, the power to search for and find a mate that they believed was compatible instead of some dominating male relative marrying the women off to whom he saw fit. But there were many things they took into consideration that today you and I might not view as important."

"You mean they wanted them to have a big . . ." Olive didn't finish her sentence, but instead suppressed a giggle as she looked up at the giant statue.

The more Amber studied it, the more she decided it could be someone's interpretation, albeit somewhat malformed, of what a dick might look like, complete with balls, and facing upward toward the sky, as if the rest of the man were lying down, hard as stone—no pun intended—or clay, or whatever it's made out of.

"A man was viewed as fertile if all of his parts were in very good working order." Sara took her hand off the statue and backed away a step or two, still studying it. "If he were able to get hard, and remain hard as stone, then he must be able to produce healthy, strong off-spring."

"Did it work?" Barney asked, walking around the huge statue and studying it from different angles.

"I'm standing here, aren't I?" Sara offered, and then laughed along with the rest of them. "Are you considering putting it back in the ballroom?"

Amber had already decided she wouldn't do anything to the castle that Sara didn't approve of. Regardless of whether she no longer owned the land she lived on, this was her heritage.

"Would you mind?" she asked.

"You want to use this?" Olive asked, her jaw dropping.

"I like the idea, too," Barney announced, appearing from the other side of the statue and grinning.

"Well, not if Sara has a problem with it."

Her comment must have meant as much to Sara as Amber guessed it would. Her smile softened, and she took Amber's arm, guiding her out of the room. The others followed, curious, when she led them to another room off the ballroom.

"You can use what you want. If you want to put that giant dick in the ballroom for your party, by all means, have at it," Sara told her. "Let me show you a few other statuettes," she added, and began pulling the white cloths off of other objects in a room the three of them hadn't explored yet. "I come from a superstitious people, and I admit, I buy into a lot of it. I've seen the right combination of charms and good-luck pieces pull off amazing feats." She paused after revealing a small figure. "You should put this out at your party, too, possibly by the entrance to the party."

"What is it?" Amber studied the figure, which was on a marble stand and stood maybe two feet high. It looked like a fairy, although the stone carving was slightly worn and dusty, even though it had been covered by the cloth.

"She is a love fairy." Sara spoke with enough reverence to prove she believed in the fairy, who appeared to be a child, kneeling and reaching her hand out toward something.

"A love fairy? What is she reaching for?" Amber touched the cold stone, brushing dust away from the figure's shoulder. It seemed for a moment the coolness from the smooth carved stone surged through her, giving her a chill. Amber wasn't sure she liked the sensation.

"She is reaching for her lover."

"She looks like a small child," Olive pointed out, frowning and shifting her attention from the statuette to Sara. From her serious expression, it appeared she wasn't about to dispute anything Sara told them.

"A long time ago, children knew who their future betrothed would be. It wasn't until more recent times we've moved into the ritual of dating and finding our own spouse."

"And divorce rates are a lot higher," Amber muttered, although the thought of someone else deciding who she would live out her days with didn't sound very appealing.

"It's said that if this fairy is placed at the entrance of the ballroom, she will allow each person who enters to immediately spot his or her one true love," Sara told her, smiling at the statuette in appreciation.

"We should definitely put her out on the floor," Olive decided, rubbing her hands with excitement.

"This island is so much a part of you," Amber mused, standing next to Sara and watching Olive and Barney discuss which door to put the statuette by. "Why did you sell it?"

"I didn't." Sara held her fingers out in front of her, studying them as if they were of great interest. "My grandparents put a mortgage on it, which I inherited when they died. At the time I figured if I had to pay for the island all over again, I would live here. I rented out the castle and stayed in the servants' quarters, which are actually really nice and plenty of home for me."

"I don't blame you. You could get lost in this castle," Amber said, grinning although Sara wasn't.

"I didn't make enough money renting out the castle. Tenants would move in and then not pay. I started losing money trying to evict them and then advertising to find new tenants. The mortgage payments fell behind until the bank foreclosed." Sara frowned, staring across the ballroom.

Amber didn't say anything as she guessed the ending.

"The bank tried evicting me. I didn't fight them. But I didn't really have anywhere to go. When Pierre Anton paid cash for the island, buying it outright and making it so once again there was no mortgage on this land, he agreed to let me live here." When Sara laughed, there was a bitter edge to it. "I remember his letter saying I was the selling edge to this place. It made me feel as if he bought me right along with the castle. But in a way I guess I am part of this place. And it's very much a part of me. I was smart enough to get in writing that I may live here without worry of ever being turned out."

Olive and Barney were still chattering, both enthused about organizing the party and arguing over each other as ideas popped into their heads. Amber begged off lunch, although her stomach growled, and told them if she didn't get a shower she wouldn't be able to form another thought.

If only that were true. Thoughts were spilling over each other in her brain. But every one of them concerned Jordan. Although she'd seen him every day, he hadn't enlightened her as to what he planned on doing with the knowledge of Princess Tory's pregnancy. Amber knew what she wanted to do. She ached to expose the fraud for who she was.

After showering all the dust and grime off, and making note

that the ballroom would need to be seriously cleaned, she met with Cook and was introduced to the new staff members. Cook had already informed her that her part in this introduction was simple. The staff lined up military style, each of them facing her in their simple black dresses or suits, while Cook went down the line, announcing each by name and then stating what their duties would be during their time on the island. When introductions were done, Amber nodded, informed Cook that it all sounded perfect, which was what Cook had told her to say, and then dismissed the servants to begin their duties.

Barney and Olive were long since through with lunch, but Amber was forced back to her room when several phone calls came through. Anxious guests to the party wanted to speak with her personally, concerned their rooms would meet their specifications, and then after announcing sternly what they would and would not tolerate, softened their tones and thanked her for the outstanding job she was doing. Amber was sure she'd never met a stranger lot of people. Everyone behaved according to protocol. Olive had done even more extensive research online about these kinds of parties than Amber had and told her to expect such calls. After the guests berated Amber, Olive swore that each of them would then sing her praises.

"It's how it's done," she offered nonchalantly.

Amber shook her head, hanging up after finishing her third call. It was amazing how accurate Olive had been in predicting the behavior of their guests. Amber went over her growing stack of notes, still paranoid as hell she would somehow goof this up and be shunned by proper society for the rest of her life. In spite of Barney suggesting she view this as a huge birthday party with a bunch of spoiled rotten, abrasive eight-year-olds attending, Amber couldn't relax. She knew that she wouldn't be able to exhale and enjoy life again until all of this was over.

And then she would return to her world, without Jordan.

Maybe she'd see if she could find him. That thought created a quickening inside her that damn near stole her breath. She was out her bedroom door and headed toward his room before she gave it another thought. It wasn't until she reached the main hallway that she hesitated. Today was the first day since everyone arrived on the island that she hadn't created a strict schedule for Jordan and Princess Tory. Usually they spent half of the day together, parting ways midafternoon, and then meeting again at dinner. Today, however, they weren't together after breakfast, so that both could prepare for the first onslaught of guests scheduled to arrive tomorrow.

Jordan might be in his room, or possibly in the barn. He seemed to spend a lot of his free time with the horses. It was something Amber found rather intriguing about him but she'd overheard Princess Tory comment more than once that he smelled like a stable boy. She glanced in the direction of his wing, but then heard people coming up the stairs.

Carlos Rodriguez, Princess Tory's chaperone, appeared at the top of the stairs first, saying something over his shoulder Amber didn't catch. Princess Tory followed and Raul, her lover, moved easily at her side.

Raul spotted Amber first, his smile fading instantly although he caught himself from scowling and immediately gave her a slight nod while mumbling under his breath to the other two.

"Amber, my dear," Carlos said, his smooth accent sounding relaxed and pleasant. "We're very impressed with the efforts for the princess's party so far."

"Thank you," she said, straightening and feeling a wash of relief that she'd showered and that they timed arriving at the top of the stairs perfectly. A moment later and they would have caught her heading to Jordan's room. "I hope you're just as pleased with the party."

"We wish to speak with you about that," Princess Tory said,

offering an incredibly sweet smile that almost made her look young and innocent.

The princess definitely had youth on her side, but Amber doubted she'd ever been innocent. Immediately her guard went up. Raul frowned, scowling at Princess Tory's backside when she stepped forward, leaving her companions at the top of the stairs, and wrapped her cold, bony fingers around Amber's forearm. Patting her hand with her other hand, Princess Tory began guiding the two of them in the direction of the princess's room.

"There are several things we need to be perfectly clear on," she continued, still using her soft, amiable tone as if she and Amber were the best of friends. "I know you didn't have anything to do with who was invited to the party. And I see now how awkward you must have felt that morning when you interrupted our breakfast to break the news to me. Looking back now, the way you hesitated and hated showing me the e-mail from my father ordering you to invite everyone on his list shows me you had my best interests at heart."

Princess Tory smiled at Amber, turning her head while not one hair piled on top of her head moved. Her large brown eyes didn't appear to show a hidden agenda. If anything, she seemed sincere as she spoke, which scared Amber even more. She'd known her fair share of women of all ages, who didn't bat an eye at manipulating a man into marriage for all the wrong reasons. These women didn't view love as a useful tool so had no reason to believe in it. They were one hundred percent motivated by greed and the drive for success and control. Princess Tory was no different, in spite of the fact that she'd probably never been poor, and more than likely never would be.

Amber chose her words carefully. "I'm doing my best to make this party as wonderful for the two of you as I can."

"Of course you are." Princess Tory patted Amber's arm

again while continuing to hold on to her until they reached her wing, and then her bedroom door.

Carlos stepped in front of them to open the door, then hold it as if it would slam shut on them of its own will if he didn't. Raul remained directly behind Princess Tory, the ever loyal boy toy, when Princess Tory guided Amber into her room.

"I know how hard you've been working," she said, still smiling as if they were best friends. "Carlos, send for Marie and Leona. We need refreshments while we visit."

Carlos nodded, moving stiffly as if she were the Queen of England or something. When he left the room, Raul closed the door and moved across the room, a little less concerned with formalities as he helped himself to a cigar from a box on top of the mantel. Amber had already assumed that the fireplaces in each room were once the only heat the castle had to offer. She could only guess how many years had gone by since each had last had a fire in them and wondered if they even worked anymore.

Princess Tory slipped out of her high heels and walked in her stocking feet to the couch, gesturing for Amber to follow. "We're all very informal here," she announced, acting anything but that as she sat on the edge of the couch in a straight-backed pose with her head held high and her breasts pressing against the V-neck cut of the silky-looking pale yellow dress she wore. It probably really was silk, Amber decided, believing Princess Tory wouldn't wear anything that wasn't a top brand name and incredibly expensive.

"What did you want from me?" Amber asked, relaxing on the opposite end of the couch but not getting too comfortable. The entire setting had her wary as hell.

"First of all to thank you for everything you're doing," Princess Tory told her, leaning forward and patting Amber's bare knee. She ignored Leona and Marie when they hurried silently into the room and kept her focus on Amber. "The Anton family definitely knows how to hire the best of social organizers. I most definitely plan on using you for all of my events in the future."

Princess Tory beamed, obviously believing she'd just paid Amber the highest of compliments. It would be in Amber's favor to play along and show the gratitude the princess anticipated seeing. The bomb would be dropped soon enough. When it landed, Amber needed to have her appreciative, nonconcerned expression well in place. It was best to make a show of feeling that way all along.

"I'm more than flattered, Princess Tory. You really honor me." Amber brought her hand to her heart, hoping her show of giddiness didn't come across as completely disgusting and sickening as it felt. At the same time, she gave silent thanks that Barney and Olive weren't with her. She would never live this down if they saw her behaving like this. And she never wanted Jordan to see her playing the idiot that she was positive she appeared to be at that moment. "I just know you'll love everything we've planned so far."

"We're already more than impressed." When Princess Tory glanced at Raul, who leaned against the mantel, obviously his favorite place to pose in the room, the look of affection she offered him wasn't missed by Amber. "We took the liberty of giving ourselves a small tour. The ballroom is grand. You must see to it that the entire party is recorded. You plan on doing that, don't you?"

That hadn't even occurred to Amber, who honestly believed that once it was over no one would want to give it a second thought. Again she thought on her toes, positive she'd leave this room with a raging headache, but doubting seriously that Jordan would want any of it recorded. Especially if he had some scheme up his sleeve. He wouldn't want any kind of permanent record.

"I hope I don't disappoint you," Amber began, allowing her expression to fall for a moment and then giving Princess Tory a shrewd look. She'd noticed security cameras in several of the rooms, very discreetly placed, but although she'd investigated hadn't found monitors anywhere that would show someone what was recorded. She wouldn't tell the princess this though. "I already noticed your grave disappointment with paparazzi being invited. I've made an announcement, and plan on doing it again, that no recording devices of any kind will be allowed in the ballroom. Now, if you wish, I can arrange for a professional photographer. If anyone wishes to purchase pictures of the event, you and Jordan can have a say in which photos go public."

Princess Tory was incredibly attentive as she nodded slowly. "You definitely do think on your toes, Amber. We're impressed," she added, and began tapping a perfectly manicured, thin finger against her lips, which were plastered with shiny pink lip gloss.

Amber imagined her finger getting sticky with the small act. "Thank you," she said, hoping her sincerity rang true.

"We can record the event discreetly. There will be quite a profit in selling copies of it afterward and we can arrange for you to have a cut."

It was obvious Princess Tory wanted every moment of the event documented. What Amber wanted to know was why.

"I'll take care of it," she decided, knowing if she were in charge of any recording, she would at least have the master copy. Although Jordan hadn't confided in her about any plan since discovering Princess Tory was pregnant, Amber guessed that he plotted to expose the princess and make a show of her true nature. Maybe she could say she was recording the party and then claim the camera malfunctioned.

"We have another request."

"What?"

"We just know you're going to have fun with this," Princess Tory said, looking as if she were ready to explode with an exciting piece of juicy gossip. "We believe you're a modern woman, obviously self-employed and assertive."

Amber didn't say anything when Princess Tory paused. Even though she wasn't really self-employed, she'd always viewed herself as willing to go after what she needed to be happy in life. An unwanted thought crept forward at that moment. If she were that assertive woman, wouldn't she fight to pursue a relationship with Jordan once this month ended? She shoved the thought out of her head, not wanting anything in her expression to give Princess Tory a clue to her actual thoughts.

"We've decided . . ." Princess Tory began, her grin spreading across her face as she made a show of building the dramatics. "Oh, this is so exciting," she added, once again ignoring Leona and Marie when they approached them and placed two silver platters on the table, one with coffee and tea, and one with an assortment of cookies, cheese and crackers, and something gooey Amber didn't recognize. "We've decided that during the ball we're going to make an announcement."

Princess Tory snapped her finger and then held her hand out to Raul, who approached silently, his brooding expression impossible to read. He pulled a small velvet box from inside his suit jacket and handed it to Princess Tory. The princess in turn snapped the box open and held it out for Amber to see.

"We're going to propose to Jordan during the ball!"

16

Jordan leaned forward, patting Lord's neck, as he watched the figure approach from around the large rock formation that blocked his view of the castle.

Matt Ramon, a man he'd called friend for over ten years now, huffed and puffed, then scowled at Jordan when he came into view.

"What happened to the days of meeting in a bar and buying me a drink?" Matt immediately complained and then kicked his hiking boots against a rock when he stopped in front of Lord. "Nice Thoroughbred you have here," he added, putting little validity into his previous complaint as he greeted the horse with his palm under Lord's nose.

"Lord comes with the castle, and we've quickly become good friends." Jordan wouldn't risk meeting Matt anywhere other than far from the crowds that were quickly assembling in the castle. With three days until the party, he'd admitted to himself more than once that Amber was doing one hell of a job. The couple of times he'd managed to make it to her room without being noticed, she'd been so exhausted he hadn't pushed having sex. His balls were tight with need for her, but he hadn't made it this far in his crazy life without mastering some level of patience. Taking his time to meet with Matt, when his friend knew he hadn't been invited to a happy reunion of college friends, was proof in itself that Jordan was being careful as hell. "What do you think of the place?" he asked, not surprised when Matt gave him an incredulous look.

"Why? Planning on celebrating all your wedding anniversaries on this isolated rock?"

Jordan snorted, not surprised that Matt was up-to-date on all the gossip flying around the busy castle.

"You should have seen it when I first got here. There were just a few of us on the island and it really could be a tropical paradise."

"Under different circumstances," Matt grumbled.

"Definitely under different circumstances," Jordan agreed.

"Are you going to marry that princess? She's not much more than a girl, Anton."

"Have you met her?" Jordan was pretty sure Matt's first question was rhetorical.

Matt shook his head. "I've heard enough talk. Sounds like she's just a gem."

Jordan snorted. "She's a bitch," he said, knowing he didn't need to mince words with Matt, and that if he were to try to do so, he'd be called on it in a second.

"So what do you want me to do?" Matt cut to the chase, squinting up at Jordan. "And would you get off that horse before you give me a neck ache?"

Jordan slid off Lord, letting go of the horse's reins so he could enjoy some of the fresh grass in the isolated meadow. "How good is your Italian?" he asked.

Matt shrugged. "Probably as good as yours," he said pointedly. "What gives, man?"

Jordan didn't bother pulling out his phone but explained the conversation he'd recorded.

"Crap," Matt hissed. "And this Barney will testify if needed that what he translated is accurate?"

"A deposition would work. He'd get torn to shreds on the stand. But I seriously doubt we're going to need to take it that far."

"Okay," Matt said, but Jordan knew his brain already was wrapping around the situation and he would formulate a plan and share it when he was ready.

Jordan had seen his friend in action many times over the years. "I need you to help me expose her for what she is."

"I can do that." Matt Ramon had helped more than one police department, as well as the FBI, crack cases that were a hell of a lot more dangerous than dealing with one spoiled-rotten princess. "My usual fees?" he asked, cocking an eyebrow as he gave Jordan a level stare.

"I'm going to pay you in cash this time," Jordan said, having already decided he wouldn't incriminate his longtime friend when this mess blew to hell. "I want more proof, pictures of her being intimate with her lover."

"Let me guess: the stocky young Italian stud who is always by her side. Not the older gentleman." Matt grinned, although there was a cold glare in his eyes.

"Yup. His name is Raul."

"Of course it is."

"And he's Sicilian."

"Whatever." Matt waved his hand in the air, dismissing the trivial information. "So, pictures. Want me to bug her room?"

"Think you can do that?"

Matt just stared at him, apparently unwilling to honor Jordan with an answer to a stupid question. "The big bash is Saturday night. By the time you're making sure you got your tails on right, I'll have enough dirt on your Princess Tory to give you all the ammunition you need to blow her clear back to her home country."

"Good enough." Even though Jordan was positive there wasn't anyone else anywhere around them, he glanced at the quiet meadow before pulling out his wallet and offering Matt a few bills.

"One more thing." Matt said, pocketing the money. "Stay away from that hot little brunette until all of this is over. It's going to make my job a hell of a lot easier proving your proposed fiancée is a slut if you aren't banging the party organizer every night."

Jordan almost denied it, but Matt had been cracking cases even before he had a license to do so. There wasn't much that got past the man, which was one of many reasons why he was an incredible asset to have around.

"Is it that obvious?"

"Nope. Your discretion should be applauded. And for what it's worth, I have met her and she's a sweetheart." Matt didn't compliment people very often.

Jordan nodded. He didn't plan on leaving Amber alone regardless of what his friend thought of her. But it didn't surprise him that Matt would have met Amber, and that he would approve. Any man would approve of Amber.

"I don't want her knowing what you're doing," Jordan told him. "She's already got enough on her plate dealing with all the guests and organizing this party. I don't want her worrying about anything else."

"You know I don't talk." Matt sounded offended. He kicked his boot against the rock once again and then turned in the direction of the castle. "And you owe me for all this exercise you're inflicting on me today."

Jordan took Lord's reins and climbed onto the horse. Laughing, he started in a different direction from the way Matt would return to the castle. "It's good for you, man. But if you like, I'll buy you that drink tonight at the castle."

"Big of you," Matt yelled at him. "Considering the drinks here are free."

Jordan laughed, encouraging Lord into a run. His smile faded quickly, though. The plan was in motion. He didn't doubt that long before Saturday Matt would have more dirt on Princess Tory than Jordan would want to see.

Jordan hated leaving Lord in the barn once they'd finished their run. He swore the horse gave him a remorseful look. Jordan eyed the handful of guests who loitered near the barn door to see what castle stables looked like.

He took his time, bringing Lord fresh hay himself, and then grooming the horse until his coat shined. Matt didn't have to present a good argument on why keeping clear of Amber would be to Jordan's benefit, especially since he wanted to prove Princess Tory was not a good candidate to be a wife. The news of her pregnancy might be enough, but women these days didn't bat an eye at abortions. It wasn't something Jordan approved of, but he could see Princess Tory agreeing to terminate the pregnancy to see the marriage through. She'd made it very clear to him that marrying an American was very in vogue these days. Not once, though, had she indicated her feelings for him. Suggesting to him that they have sex hardly qualified.

Jordan had Amber's phone number, although it was a cell phone she'd been given by his grandfather. Amber told him Grandfather had insisted she use the phone since the particular service Grandfather contracted guaranteed hardly any dead spots on the island. It also assured that his grandfather would be able to keep track of all of her incoming and outgoing calls. Jordan could justify calling her once, maybe twice, since she was his social planner. But with Grandfather already threatening Amber that he'd fire her if she didn't steer clear of him, he didn't want to make her nervous.

Somehow, though, he needed to figure out a way to spend time with her. He didn't want to exert the level of control necessary to leave her alone.

Heading out of the barn, he patted Sara on the shoulder, not missing the frustrated scowl she aimed in the direction of the curious guests. "Make sure no one enters this barn other than you and me," he told her.

Sara nodded, and although he would always view this place as her castle, he knew she understood she no longer owned it and looked grateful that he authorized her doing exactly what she wanted to do.

He put on his professional smile, nodding to people he'd never met before in his life, as he headed to the castle. It would be like this if he talked Aunt Penelope into opening her ranch up to guests. Many of the ranches in Montana were already offering "reality vacations" where families or tour groups could come live on the ranch, work or relax, and get a feel for a different way of life. For some ranchers, it allowed them to keep land in the family without the banks foreclosing.

Deciding to take one of the side service doors, Jordan entered the castle through a back hallway that wasn't very far from the ballroom. Loud noises and lots of laughter greeted him. It didn't surprise him that any crew Amber would have working for her would be happy and enjoy their work. She showed all the signs of being fair and honest with everyone she worked with. He wondered what she would think of working on a ranch. There wasn't any doubt in his mind Aunt Penelope would love her.

A ray of hope lifted his spirits when he thought he might see her if he stopped in to see how the party preparations were going. It would be something any party host would do. If anything, Jordan might want to survey their progress and approve or disapprove anything they were doing.

He stopped at the first set of open doors and then gawked at the view playing out before him. It looked like four men were guiding a giant stone cock across the marble floor on flat ramps with wheels. Jordan watched, amazed, as Amber walked backward, looking beyond beautiful in tight-fitting blue jeans and a tank top that didn't quite cover her flat stomach.

"Not too much farther, guys," she yelled, laughing at the same time. "Just a bit more to the left." She backed up farther and looked down.

Jordan noticed an *X* created by duct tape. She used her hands, continuing to guide them, until they moved the huge sculpture over the *X*.

"You've got it. Good job!" She grinned broadly when the men dropped their ropes. "Now unleash him, men."

"Him?" Barney appeared from behind the group, strutting around like a male peacock on the prowl. "Do you think he doesn't like the rope around him?"

Amber giggled, but then looked over her shoulder at Jordan when Barney spotted him and blew his cover. Jordan would have stood and inconspicuously watched her in action for as long as he could. But he didn't mind watching her come to him, her smile not fading as she approached.

"What do you think of it?" she asked, brushing her long braid over her shoulder. She was more dressed down today than he'd seen her since she arrived, probably because she planned on getting dirty and jumping in with her hired help to get the work done.

"What is it?" he asked, tilting his head and trying to imagine it from a different angle. "Don't you dare start a rumor that it's the sculpture of anyone attending the party."

Amber broke into a fit of laughter, bending over and trying to catch her breath as she looked up at him, her bright blue eyes glowing in amusement. "Now there's an idea. I hadn't thought of that."

"Does Princess Tory know about it?" he asked.

They were alone in the doorway and Amber didn't mind showing her true feelings when she faced him, her back to everyone in the ballroom.

"Would she know if that sculpture resembled anyone who might be at the party?" she demanded, her smile gone as she searched his face.

Amber was jealous of Princess Tory, and her wave of possessiveness stirred his cock to life. "I don't have a clue whom she can identify and whom she can't."

Amber didn't say anything but continued watching him.

"She doesn't know what I look like," he told her, giving her what she wanted to hear.

"Good," she muttered under her breath, returning her attention to her crew before he could see her facial expression.

"Once you have the rope off it, we'll move the small statuette out here," she yelled at the guys. "It won't weigh as much but it's very, very old and we'll need to be very careful with it."

"You're going to make this ballroom come to life in a way it probably hasn't in centuries," he told her, meaning it.

"That's the idea." She was chewing her lip when she stared into his eyes, looking like she wanted to say more. "Jordan," she began, almost whispering. "I need to talk to you about something."

"Oh?" A strange sensation washed over him, something carnal and incredibly predatory. He didn't like the worried expression that suddenly replaced Amber's smile and felt an overwhelming urgency to remove the burden of whatever bothered her. "Tell me. I'll take care of it for you."

"It's not as easy as that. And I can't tell you right now." She continued searching his face as if she might be able to read his thoughts.

"I'll tell you what. Take Bess out to the meadow by the base of the mountain later tonight."

"I can't ride a horse," she hissed, keeping her voice low.

"Neither could Princess Tory, but she managed." It didn't surprise him that that was all it took.

"Fine. But if I break my neck it's your fault."

"I would never suggest you do anything that would harm you," he told her, aching to reach out and touch her. He would be so glad when this month was over and he could make sure the entire world knew she belonged to him. "I'll let Sara know to meet you at the barn at eleven. She will help you saddle Bess and set the horse in the right direction. All you have to do is hold onto the reins. Bess knows what to do and she'll bring you to me and Lord."

Jordan didn't have to encourage Lord out of the shadows when Amber and Bess appeared halfway across the meadow.

"Hold easy, boy," Jordan whispered, knowing the horse sensed Amber's tension and uneasiness from this distance.

Jordan couldn't pick up what the horse could, but just watching her silhouette in the darkness, the way she sat stiffly in the saddle, he knew without any doubt she was terrified. Deciding finally to put her out of her misery, and at the same time feeling his heart swell painfully in his chest, he headed out to meet her. Amber had gotten on that horse, a creature that scared her to death, to come see him. My God! She was the woman for him and he would do whatever it took to keep her by his side once they left the island.

Before he reached her, he was able to see her expression in spite of the darkness. He hid his grin when he realized her eyes were squeezed closed. Her long brown hair was in a clasp at her nape and fanned down her back. She no longer wore the tank top, but instead had on a button-down flannel shirt that was tucked into her snug-fitting jeans. She wore boots and this Western image looked as hot on her as elegant dresses.

"Hey there, sexy," he growled in a slow, lazy drawl but then had an even harder time not cracking a smile when she jumped. "It's okay. You're fine," he assured her, reaching over and putting his hands over hers.

"It wasn't so bad," she said in a soft, almost terrified voice.

Jordan didn't press the issue that he had to pry her hands from the reins. He patted the old quarter horse. Bess was a good horse to bring his woman to him.

"I can see that. Do you want to get down?" he asked.

Amber didn't seem to notice that she now clung to his hand with both of hers. "Oh. Well, I guess we can sit like this. They won't run off, will they?"

"No," he said, squeezing her hands. "You must really have something to say to me to take on your fear of the horse and come out here."

"I do. I wasn't going to tell you at first, but it's bugging the crap out of me." Amber noticed her hands in his and stared at them a moment, then down at her horse. "Maybe I do want to get down."

"Okay." Jordan edged away from her, watching her when she let go of his hands. But he didn't grab her reins and instead held on to the saddle. "I'll help you."

"No. No. I can do it." She waved him off when he slid off Lord and approached her. Amber shook her head at him. "Sara made me mount and dismount Bess a couple times. She said if anything I would need to know how to get on and off of her, just in case."

Jordan watched her take her time before swinging her leg over the horse and then jumping free. She still had her foot in the stirrup, though, and would have fallen on her butt if he hadn't moved in and wrapped his arms around her. Amber slid her foot out, collapsing against him.

"That didn't happen the couple of times I tried it at the barn." She sounded embarrassed.

Jordan couldn't be more proud of her. "Learning to ride

takes time. For someone who knows nothing about horses, you're doing better than most."

"Liar," she accused, turning in his arms.

He wasn't ready to let her go, though. Matt had warned him about being seen with her, but they were alone out here and no one could sneak up on them without them seeing any intruders first.

Jordan pinned her against him, then cupped her chin, tilting her head and devouring her mouth. She tasted sweet, like a breath mint, and was warm and soft. His hands were all over her before he could stop himself, and in seconds his cock grew harder than stone. More than he needed his next breath, he needed to be inside her.

"Jordan." She lowered her head and breathed heavily as she pressed her small hands against his chest. She didn't try escaping from him though, but kept her head down when she continued speaking. "Princess Tory asked me to her room the other day. I thought of telling you but each time you came to my room, I admit I was selfish and didn't want to ruin the moment. I figured there would be an opportunity, and I knew it would seriously piss you off."

"What?" Instantly, every muscle in his body stiffened, the blood slowly recirculating through his brain when she looked into his eyes and he saw worry—and fear—swarming in her dark blue eyes.

"Well, I think it will upset you," she added. "Maybe," she continued, lowering her voice.

"Tell me and I'll let you know." Again the incredible protective urge he'd felt earlier ransacked him as he kept her in his arms.

"Princess Tory is going to propose to you at the party in front of everyone. She showed me the rings." She said the words quickly and then watched him, as if his first reaction was very important to her.

"Son of a bitch," he hissed, dropping his arms and then combing his hair back, catching his fingers and yanking a few strands loose from his ponytail holder when he pulled his hand free. "Does she think I wouldn't humiliate her in front of all those people?" he demanded, glaring at Amber.

She didn't answer him, but watched him, her expression guarded. He hated the look, hated the realization that she wasn't sure. And as the words came out of his mouth he knew, under normal circumstances, he would never humiliate any woman. Princess Tory believed she'd pushed him into a corner.

It wasn't his outrage over the princess's coldhearted nature that upset him as much as Amber's way of looking at him. She wanted a reaction, for him to say something. But she should know already what he would do. Somehow he would get out of it. He needed time to think.

"Jordan!" Amber yelled behind him when he marched across the meadow. "Hey, are you just going to leave me here?"

He didn't answer but headed for the rocks, knowing it wasn't the smartest move to climb them in the dark but at the moment not giving a rat's ass. Amber called out to him again, but he ignored her, taking on the rocks with a vengeance and practically running up them.

The humid night air held just a slight chill. But he broke a sweat anyway, and forced himself to keep going. He wanted the burn in his muscles, the strain on his body. It would help him feel, keep him grounded. And then he could think this through.

He didn't turn around, didn't stop, and ignored the burning in his palms when he scraped them over sharp rocks. Finally, winded and almost feeling light-headed, he stopped, parking his butt on a flat rock. Jordan didn't look over his shoulder toward Amber. He stared into the black night, letting his thoughts ransack his brain and fought to deal with them as they hit.

It was enough that his grandfather had approached him with this absurd ultimatum. Jordan's initial reaction had been to tell him to take a flying leap. No one would uproot him like that and decide for him that his life wasn't going in the direction it should. Maybe he'd made mistakes but he'd also done a lot to be proud of. Turning Big Sky Ranch around, getting it heading in the right direction, was one hell of an accomplishment.

Family meant something to him, or it had before coming to the island. While here, his opinion of Grandfather had sunk to an all-time low. He didn't appreciate learning Princess Tory believed he stalked her. She arrived on the island believing he was superficial about appearances and chasing after her. She wasn't impressed with him, although she did one hell of a turnaround in a two-week time period.

Then there was Amber. An unexpected surprise. The last thing he would have believed no matter who told him it was true was that he'd find his soul mate once he arrived here. Amber was everything he'd always imagined, so hard working, driven, absolutely gorgeous, and the best lover he'd ever had in his life.

Her only fault would be her disbelief that anything would become of the two of them in the long run. It might be she didn't want to pursue a relationship with him after leaving here, but he seriously doubted it. Maybe her line of work required she travel around the world. No matter how many times he'd tried searching for information about Amber online, he'd come up with nothing to enlighten him about her past.

Then, to make matters worse, she came to him, throwing a piece of information at him, and stood waiting for his reaction. It was the look on her face, as if she'd expected something in him to come forward and reveal what she'd feared all along.

God. Amber might be one of those women who needed it spelled out to her. Until they returned to America, Jordan didn't want to propose they continue seeing each other. Apparently, Amber craved that knowledge now. That had to be why she studied his face, not speaking, once she'd informed him of Princess Tory's plan.

Jordan stood, stretching, and finally faced the direction where Amber waited. He couldn't see her in the dark. The horses would have made enough noise to warn him if anyone approached. There were a lot of things the two of them didn't know about each other yet, but that was what time was for.

Jordan did know she was terrified of horses, though. He grinned for the first time since coming out here. Her fear had been his insurance she'd stay where he left her when he headed up the rocks.

"Where the hell did you go?" Amber yelled at him the moment he came into sight.

She'd been sitting cross-legged in between the two horses, holding their reins and jumped up, marching to him. As she neared him her fist came up, ready to attack.

Jordan wasn't ready for an onslaught of her temper, but he reacted in time. Grabbing her fist, he prevented her from giving him a black eye. She attacked just as quickly with her left hand.

"Stop it," he growled, grabbing that hand, too.

"Don't you ever leave me alone in the dark out in the middle of nowhere again. Do you understand me?" she hissed, her eyes a passionate shade of violet as outrage made her cheeks flush a beautiful crimson.

"I don't ever plan on leaving you," he whispered, pinning her hands behind her back and then devouring her mouth.

Her growls turned into murmurs when she relaxed against him, opening for him and allowing him to deepen the kiss. When he let go of her hands, she reached for his shoulders, leaning into him as their tongues danced around each other.

Jordan ended the kiss, staring down at her while still tasting her on his lips. "You did the right thing in telling me this."

"And you acted just like a man when I did tell you," she informed him dryly, pressing her lips together and lowering herself when she relaxed from being on tiptoe. "You threw a fit."

"We do that sometimes," he growled, but knew right now she needed to see his strength. She had come to him with outrageous news and wanted him to put order to it. "I don't want you to worry about this."

"What are you going to do?"

"I've got a plan."

17

Amber stood with Barney on one side of her and Olive on the other. Her evening dress made her feel sexy, but she knew no eyes would be on her tonight. The melancholy sensation flooding her insides only seemed to increase as the evening went on.

"Looks like we pulled it off, girlfriend," Barney said, nudging her with his elbow. "And don't we look fabulous?"

"We really need to take pictures or no one will ever believe us when we get back home." Olive giggled but then glanced past her at Barney.

The two of them gave each other knowing looks, which Amber knew best to ignore. "The staff seems to be doing a good job of keeping the food and alcohol going."

Amber quit listening when she spotted Jordan appear at one of the sets of doors to the ballroom. It wasn't the first time he'd entered, but the first time he'd come in through those doors. It was the set of doors where they'd decided to place the love fairy. He stared at it, as if noticing it for the first time, which possibly he was. Then, following the fairy's extended arm, he searched in the direction the statuette pointed and locked gazes with her.

Something shot through her system, the oddest sensation, as if she'd just been shocked. She gasped, her lips parting, and stared at Jordan, wondering if he felt it, too. He didn't know what the statuette was and, even if he did, he didn't strike her as the kind of man who would buy into such a thing. A few seconds ago Amber might have claimed she didn't believe in fairies either. But something hit her, and it left her feeling tingly from head to toe.

"Are you okay?" Olive asked, giving her a funny look.

Amber glanced at her and then back at the doors, but Jordan was now working his way to the table where Princess Tory sat. So much for fairies.

"I'm fine, just ready for the evening to be over," she admitted.

Pierre Anton walked along the edge of the dance floor where couples spun each other around, doing a dance Amber had never learned how to do. She seriously doubted anyone here even knew the two-step. Waltzing wasn't her forte but it wasn't like anyone would ask her to dance. Pierre walked with a cane, his long tails and the white ruffles on his shirt echoing how every man here was dressed. Something about Pierre's suit made him stand out though: a silver-haired, elegant man, who moved as if he ruled every inch of the world, and everyone around him knew it.

"Amber, my dear. There you are." He extended a gloved hand, which she accepted, and brought her fingers to his cool, dry lips. It was hard seeing any family resemblance between Jordan and his grandfather, in mannerism or appearance. "You have surpassed even my expectations of what you were capable of doing," he said quietly, his voice offering a chill calm when he stood too close and stared deep into her eyes. "Honestly, I didn't think someone like you would be able to pull off the event of the year."

"Someone like me?"

"Yes. I chose you so my grandson would be able to compare rich with poor and see where he properly belonged."

Amber was stunned; she didn't know what to say. For a moment she panicked, fearing Barney or Olive would get mouthy with the old man, running to her defense.

"Walk with me," he instructed, releasing her hand but offering his arm. "Allow me to show you off. It's a shame Jordan's mother couldn't make it. She refuses to fly but is already planning an event to compete with yours and show off the happy couple."

Amber didn't glance at her friends, not wanting to see their expressions, but wrapped her arm around his and tried to get the lump out of her throat. It wasn't that she ever craved being wealthy, and she sure wasn't ashamed of the life she led now. Pierre's words cut deeply, though, especially since it was obvious he believed that her presence allowed Jordan to see that wealth was the road he was born to head down.

It wasn't hard to ignore the dance floor when Pierre escorted her across the ballroom, not saying a word about the large sculpture in the middle of the room, and leading her to the other side, where guests sat at tables, visiting and enjoying all the free food and drinks. Even though she never glanced at the many couples spinning in unison like wind-up dolls or the orchestra she'd hired to play during the dance, she was acutely aware when Jordan and Princess Tory began moving with the other couples on the floor.

I don't ever plan on leaving you.

"The Alixandres will want to meet you," Pierre informed her, patting her hand on his arm as they started moving through the tables. He paused at more than one table, expressing his ap-

258 / Lorie O'Clare

preciation that whomever he spoke to was able to attend his party. Not once did Pierre attempt introducing her, and she got the impression more than once that he enjoyed having a young woman on his arm while mingling among people he'd obviously known for years. "They don't speak very good English, so you won't be required to say a lot. You're doing wonderfully, by the way. Beautiful and elegant. I'm sure if you wanted to pursue a new career it could be arranged. I might be encouraged to help you finance it if you wish," he added, squeezing her hand with his cool, bony fingers.

Amber's stomach turned. She didn't care how rich Pierre Anton was. He was a pig. She assumed he meant a career as a social planner and wondered if it was intentional that he didn't say what kind of career he would finance.

"You're very generous, Pierre," she offered, speaking in as soft of a tone as she could pull off, and was sure she sounded rather sultry to him. In truth, she wanted to scream, smack him as hard as she could, and march out of the party. Her work here was done, anyway. The party was a success, and the staff would see to it that everyone was tended to well into the night. "I'll admit I'm anxious to return home. That's where I belong, after all. You said it yourself. I'm a poor woman and this is pretending for me. We do better when we are who we are. Wouldn't you agree?"

Pierre paused, meeting her gaze with watery gray eyes that might be a family trait. Where Jordan's eyes were full of life and glowed with honesty and integrity and a craving to live life by a strict code, his grandfather's eyes were dead, soulless. Staring into them gave Amber the creeps.

"You are a very wise woman, my dear," he practically purred, pulling his attention from her eyes first and allowing his gaze to drop to the fair amount of cleavage her dress offered. Even in her high heels, she stood a few inches shorter than he did. Either way, he was the lowest of lowlifes and his actions proved that all the money in the world wouldn't make him a better person. "When I was just a bit younger than you are now, I was also very poor. If you were driven just a bit more, you could move forward in life. But many stay right where they are all their lives, where their parents and grandparents were. It takes a special type of person to make something of himself the way I have."

She wanted to puke from his self-righteous attitude. Amber would make something of herself in life, but not with his help.

"Where are the Alixandres?" she asked, aching to be done with Pierre Anton.

The orchestra finished the piece they were playing and everyone on the dance floor applauded, then began mingling. Barney had been smart in splitting the room in two. There was plenty of space on the other side of the monstrous dick for those who cared to socialize while others remained in their seats, talking quietly and almost undisturbed by everyone else.

A few made their way to tables, though, and for a moment Pierre held onto her arm a bit tighter as he navigated them around tables until they reached the edge of the room. They could have walked around all the tables and made it here a lot faster, but Amber realized Pierre enjoyed walking through the crowd, saying hello to everyone and feeling his self-importance while all those who greeted him sang his praises as if he were some kind of god. And in the world of the filthy rich, where bank accounts and prestige mattered more to everyone than the integrity of someone, Amber imagined Pierre was a god. She also would bet good, hard-earned money on the fact that probably very few people in the room liked Pierre. What made it worse was how he seemed to be proud of that fact.

She knew they'd reached the Alixandres' table when a tall, silver-haired man who sat with two women on either side of him stood, grinning and showing off large, very white teeth. He said something in Italian and Pierre answered, speaking his language.

In a way, Amber was glad not to have to be part of the conversation. She would be introduced, would nod and smile, and then hopefully would be dismissed. More than anything she wanted to sneak out of the party. Although she'd been contracted to be here for a month, and technically there was one week left, she wasn't sure she wanted to experience the aftermath of this party. She couldn't imagine what other social activities she might be asked to prepare in the coming days.

"Miss Amber Stone," Pierre announced, switching to English. "May I present Lord Duke Alixandre and his lovely wife, Lady Donita Alixandre."

Amber nodded, unsure if she was expected to shake hands, or curtsy, or what. Lord Duke moved around the table, reaching for her hand, which she offered, and then barely brushed his lips over her knuckles.

"You have made my daughter a very happy woman. We are thrilled to make your acquaintance," he murmured in a deep voice with an accent so strong it was almost appealing.

"I'm sure I'm not the one making her happy," she told him.

She worried she'd said the wrong thing when Lord Duke straightened, looking seriously at her. But then he broke into a large, toothy grin and rocked as he laughed loudly. Obviously he didn't mind drawing attention to himself; those at nearby tables looked on curiously. He then grabbed her by her arms and yanked her to him, damn near knocking her off her feet as he planted a kiss on both of her cheeks.

"You are quite right," he told her, still laughing.

When he released her, Amber was able to stand alone for the first time without Pierre holding on to her with his tight, controlling grip. The Alixandres then continued their conversation with Pierre and ignored her. More than likely it wasn't polite, but Amber mumbled under her breath that they excuse her and moved around the next table until she was able to skirt along the wall toward the door. She knew she couldn't escape the entire evening and run and hide in her room for a really good pity party, but if she could at least have some down time, maybe she could stomach hanging around for the rest of the party.

"Please, everyone. If I could have your attention!"

Amber froze, so near the door but unable to leave, when she heard Jordan's voice over the microphone. The large sculpture didn't block her view of him, looking so damn good in his tuxedo that she immediately felt a quickening in her gut when she stared at him. He didn't focus on her, though, but the people in that half of the room as he stood in front of the orchestra and repeated his request one more time. The room grew unnervingly quiet as all eyes turned to Jordan.

"Thank you. And thank you all for attending our party," he added, which immediately resulted in the room turning into a buzz of chatter as everyone simultaneously voiced their appreciation for being here. "I won't take much of your time from this magnificent party, but I want to make an announcement before it gets too late."

He paused, waiting again for the room to grow quiet. "Thank you. Thank you," he repeated, offering his roguish grin that would certainly have more than one woman in the room praying he would give her a moment of attention, if not more. "As all of you know, I've been spending time with Princess Tory Alixandre." He gestured, extending his arm, and then beckoned the princess forward out of the crowd.

From across the room, Amber noticed Princess Tory watching Jordan warily. Obviously his deciding to make this announcement was news to her, and more than likely was putting a crimp in her plans to ask him to marry her tonight in front of everyone. Amber's heart picked up a beat, a raw excitement building inside her that allowed her a bit of hope. Maybe tonight wouldn't be the worst night of her life after all.

When the princess stood by his side, Jordan held the microphone in his hand and put his arm around the princess, keeping her by his side and angling her so she faced the crowd with him.

"I will admit to all of you that our families encouraged me and the princess to meet on this island and spend a month together, in hopes that the two of us would fall in love and announce an engagement. Doing so would unite two very old and very prestigious families into the ever-growing small circle of the incredibly wealthy and dominating families in our world."

The room grew even quieter. His words didn't set well with more than one person. Amber dared glance at Pierre Anton, who stood next to the Alixandres, his expression so cold it could have been chiseled in ice as he watched his grandson expose him in front of everyone here.

"Fortunately for Princess Tory and myself, we no longer live in the Dark Ages." He smiled, appearing indifferent to the growing air of discomfort that spread across the dance floor. "The princess and I have spent every day together since arriving here. We quickly became good friends and were able to confide in each other our feelings about how our families wished to unite us."

It was a bald-faced lie. Amber watched him, not daring to breathe, as he continued singing Princess Tory's praises as if she was privy to everything he said beforehand. One look at her face, though, and Amber knew she fought the urge to throw a serious tantrum.

"The princess and I have decided not to announce our engagement this evening," he added.

A hum of speculation spread across the room. Amber forced herself to stay put when she watched Pierre reach for a chair in front of him, as if this news was enough to send him into cardiac arrest. Her own heart raced so hard in her chest it was hard to breathe. She didn't grab on to anything for support, but instead continued watching Jordan, afraid to blink in case she might miss something.

"Princess Tory does have news for all of you, though. And it is news I'm more than honored to announce on her behalf." Jordan ignored Princess Tory's bewildered look when he removed his arm and then gestured to someone else in the crowd. "Raul, please come up here where you belong."

Jordan moved to the side when a very wary Raul appeared and didn't fight Jordan when he took the man's arm and placed him next to Princess Tory.

"Folks, we're in the twenty-first century. We fall in love with whom we want to fall in love, and weigh the value of happiness and true love over money and capitalism. Princess Tory and Raul would like to announce their engagement this evening." He turned his back to Amber and blocked her view of the princess. "My dear, if I remember right, you said you were bringing rings tonight. And folks," he announced louder, turning again to face the stunned crowd. "This will be a quick engagement because these two are expecting a child together. And I wish the two of them a happy and prosperous life."

Princess Tory screamed, unable to control herself any longer. Jordan placed the microphone back in the microphone stand and walked away from the couple, leaving them gaping at the crowd, who all gasped in astonishment at the incredible announcement. Amber couldn't see Jordan anymore, but the mood of the crowd ranged from hostile to incredibly amused.

"Miss Amber Stone!" Pierre Anton smacked his cane on the ground when he marched over to her and didn't stop until he glared at her.

Amber backed up, too stunned from Jordan's announcement to even guess at what Pierre might have to say to her. He pinned her just outside of the ballroom, looking for a moment as if he might strike her with his cane.

"I blame you one hundred percent for this fiasco! Pack your bags. You are out of here. And don't think you will get one damn dime out of me. You are fired!" Before she could defend herself, Pierre gestured to two men who seemed to have appeared out of nowhere. "Escort Miss Stone to her room. Stand guard until she is packed and then take her to the landing pad. She is flying out of here tonight."

Amber finished jotting down the few job openings available in Brooklyn that she qualified for and then headed out of the unemployment office, a building she'd prayed she would never have to set foot inside again. It had been as much of a shock coming home to learn she'd been fired for insubordination, which made it impossible to collect unemployment, as it had been being herded off the island so quickly she wasn't able to tell anyone good-bye. Amber no longer had the cell phone that Pierre had given her while on the island. And she could only imagine what lies Jordan's grandfather might have told him after she left.

Worse yet, she brooded, holding her head down as she ran to the bus stop, Jordan didn't know anything about her real life. He would never be able to find her. More than once over the past few weeks she'd thought about searching for an address and phone number to the Big Sky Ranch in Montana. The thought hit her again now, and as it did every time she considered the bold move, her stomach flipped so aggressively bile filled her mouth.

Stories didn't end like this. Prince Charming was supposed to sweep into her town, taking her into his arms while everyone around applauded. Or he was supposed to climb a fire escape with flowers in his mouth when he was afraid of heights. She wasn't supposed to be the one to search and go crazy until she paraded into his world and demanded he be with her for the rest of their lives.

Why did the real world have to suck so much?

Amber reached the match box housing section almost an hour later and paused to get the mail from the group of mail boxes. She then headed down the street, acutely aware of the few houses that weren't a drab gray, proof they owned their own home. Her mom would be at her night job tonight and it was her responsibility to get supper ready for her half brother and sister. At least her uncle had found work. Entering their home, she glanced at Bobby, whose seventeen-year-old lanky body was longer than the couch he was sprawled out on.

"Have you done your chores?" she asked, knowing the answer already.

"Amber, what is a working-ranch vacation?" he asked instead of answering her question.

"Bobby, it's your job to run a vacuum and I can tell you haven't done it yet."

"This brochure says I can work at this ranch when I graduate," he continued, not moving except to take his hand off the remote, which was on the coffee table, and poke at a brochure laying next to it. "It says I can do chores and help those who are vacationing at the working ranch. Do you think Mom would care if I went to Montana?"

"You don't do your chores here. Wait . . . Montana? What?" Amber collapsed into the chair next to him and snagged the brochure from underneath his finger. Flipping it open, she stared at the pictures, read every word on it, then turned it over and read it again. "It says bring your family," she murmured. "We could all work there."

"Like Mom would leave Brooklyn," he grunted. "Besides, it's for me."

He tried grabbing the brochure but Amber kept it out of his

reach. "Where did you get this?" She stared at the small print on the bottom of the backside. *Big Sky Ranch.* There was an address, but no phone number.

"It came in the mail yesterday. I graduate soon and it sounds like a lot of fun. And it's a job."

There was nothing personal written on the brochure. All it did was explain what a working ranch entailed. A small paragraph on the backside announced there were a few job openings and anyone interested could send their resume and work history to the address given.

Her heart pounded so hard in her chest she couldn't stand it. She wanted to scream, jump up from the chair and prance around the living room. Ever since coming home, though, she'd refused to talk about her experience on the island and had lived with her mother telling her, "I told you so," when she didn't get a dime.

She didn't understand the vague invitation, but she would learn what Jordan was about soon enough. It was time to say to hell with traditional fairy tales and go get her man.

"I think you should fill out an application, Bobby," she announced, looking up at him and grinning broadly. "In fact, I'm going to create a resume, too."

"It says you have to have a high school degree, not a GED," Bobby pointed out. "And I'm going to graduate next month."

"Yes, you are," she grinned, undaunted by his accusation. "Now run that vacuum and then we'll sit down and write out our resumes after supper."

She strolled into the kitchen, feeling lighter than air, while studying the brochure. When the phone rang, she didn't give a thought as to whom it might be when she answered it.

"I've decided to forgive you for costing all of us our jobs," Olive announced on the other end of the line.

"Did you find work?" Amber had felt bad enough after her ordeal on the island. But then finding out Olive and Barney were both terminated, too, for excessive absences after being gone for the weeks they were on the island, had been a crushing blow she didn't know how to handle. Neither one of them had talked to her since.

"I start next week at the Grand Café," Olive announced.

"Hey, I hear the tips there are really good."

"Yeah, one of the waitresses working when I was there confirmed that. It sounds like it will be a step up for me pay wise. And I have you to thank for that. I never would have applied there if I still had my job at Anton Business Solutions."

"I still feel lower than dirt for costing both of you your jobs," Amber admitted, more than relieved that her friend was finally talking to her. It had made everything worse going through such hell and then having no one to share her misery with.

"Is Barney talking to you yet?"

"No. He called when he returned to Brooklyn to tell me to go to hell, but that was it." Amber hadn't had a chance to tell him she was already in hell. He'd hung up on her as soon as he spit out the cruel words. "I really couldn't blame either one of you. And I am sorry. I had no idea everything would turn out so disastrously."

"I'll talk to Barney, but honestly, I don't think we got the worst end of it. You never got to see Princess Tory's father disown her in front of everyone at the ball. She left the island pregnant, engaged to a servant, and penniless."

"That would have been worth seeing." Amber glanced at the pamphlet in her hand, feeling a surge of excitement when she brushed her finger over the smooth paper. For a moment, she swore it was the same tingling sensation she'd experienced when Jordan stood next to the fairy statuette in the ballroom. "When you talk to Barney, please let him know how terribly sorry I am."

* * *

The only way Amber could make her mom understand her excitement over Big Sky Ranch was to finally share with her family what happened to her while on the island. It wasn't an easy story to tell. When she caught herself aching to adjust the story just a bit, to try to gain their sympathy instead of laughing at her, Amber paused, knowing the only way to build a relationship was with truth. That truth had to start with her family.

"Montana is so far away." It was almost midnight but her mother sat at the card table in their kitchen, fingering the brochure and then giving her daughter an exhausted look.

"Mom, I couldn't buy our home for you. But I can do this. It's where we're supposed to be. You can't keep working so hard and not even make our rent. And I can't find a job when I was fired for insubordination. We should do this."

"We?"

"Yes." Amber was so excited she could barely stop the tears. "Let's take the family and go to Montana. It's a new start, and one we all deserve."

"Sweetheart, you're asking all of us to give up the only life we've ever known over a man you've known for three weeks." Jennifer Stone had more gray hair than a woman who was only forty-three years old should have. Her long brown hair was wrapped tightly in a bun behind her head and she still wore her waitress's uniform and smelled like a variety of food. There were more lines around her eyes than there used to be, and she looked exhausted. "If I've raised you to know anything it's that chasing dreams only wears you out."

Amber picked up the brochure and held it up between them. "Mom, working fifteen hours a day wears you out. Our life is killing us." She shook the brochure until her mother focused on it. "This isn't a dream. It's real. There's no harm in creating resumes, now, is there? Let's take a chance, see where it takes us. If we move, we'd be leaving for new jobs, a new life. People do that all the time."

"Do you love him?"

Amber blinked, wondering if her mother had heard a word she just said. She was trying so hard to show her mother she wasn't chasing a dream but seeking out new realities for them. Her mother saw right through her.

"Very much so," she admitted, and stared at the picture of the ranch house in the picture.

Five weeks later, Amber leaned against the van window, staring at the endless pale blue sky and rolling meadows that stretched out forever from the road. She didn't know there was so much open land in the United States before. Brooklyn was so crammed full of people, and Montana had all this land with no one living on it.

Ever since receiving the typed letter in the mail, offering her and her mother and half brother employment at Big Sky Ranch, Amber wasn't sure she'd slept a full night from anticipation and nervousness. The letter stated that jobs would await them if they arrived by May first. A check was included to pay for their travel expenses. Directions were included. And that was it.

Amber didn't understand why the letter was so businesslike. She knew it came from Jordan. And the overwhelming sensation that she was coming home sank deeper and deeper into her gut as the van continued down the two-lane highway.

"Is that it?" Karma pointed out the windows on Amber's left.

"Welcome to Big Sky Ranch," the driver announced as he slowed the van and then turned onto a narrow paved road.

"Oh God," Amber whispered, her mouth dry and her heart in her throat as she took in the sprawling ranch house. It looked just like the picture on the brochure that she'd stared at a hundred times since it had arrived over a month ago.

The van came to a stop and Bobby and Karma were out of their seats before she could take off her seat belt. Suddenly her fingers didn't want to work. She stared out the front of the van as a man walked toward them, his long, confident steps that of a man who ruled his land. His black hair reflected the sunlight and his regal expression and broad shoulders, as well as his incredible, muscular body, made Amber's insides swell with need.

"That's him, isn't it?" Her mother nudged Amber's shoulder.

Which enabled Amber to move. "Yes, that's him," she said, her voice cracking.

"Quite the looker," her mother whispered.

"He's sexy as hell," Karma sighed.

"Quit it, both of you," Amber snapped.

There were three other people in the van with the four of them. Karma and Bobby rushed to get out but her mother waited with Amber, allowing the three men who were sitting toward the front to get out. Amber didn't have to wonder if her mother might be as nervous as she was. Jennifer had lived in Brooklyn all her life. Amber knew her mother agreed to this to make her happy, and her mom was scared to death of the thought of changing their lives so drastically.

"Do you think that's where we're going to live?" her mother whispered from behind her when they scooted to the edge of the rear bench seats and met in the aisle.

Amber reached for their suitcases under the seat, and looked where her mother pointed at a row of plain-looking, older mobile homes. She'd seen worse in her life.

"I guess we'll find out," she said, hoping she would be able to get out of the van without her legs giving out. She was shaking like a leaf.

Her mother led the way, carrying a suitcase on either side of her with Amber bringing up the rear. A warm breeze hit her as she stepped out of the side doors to the van and straightened. She stared into Jordan's gray eyes and worried she might cry in front of everyone.

"Hello," she said, her voice cracking. Her palms were so wet she put the luggage down before it slipped out of her hands.

"It's about damn time," Jordan growled, clearing the distance between them as if no one else was around.

Without another word he scooped her into his arms. All the fear, the apprehension, the confusion and pain that had filled her since leaving the island dissipated as if it had never been real and hadn't plagued her over the past weeks.

"Jordan," she cried, wrapping her arms around his neck and her legs around his waist as her mouth met his.

She didn't know who instigated the kiss, and didn't care. She was coming home. There wasn't a doubt in her mind. It would be a new life, a new adventure. But unlike the island, this was where she belonged and where she would stay.

Jordan tasted so good and smelled even better. His strong arms were warm and comforting as he pinned her against his muscular body. And if anyone said anything or laughed or commented that he might let her up for air, Amber didn't care, and Jordan didn't show any indication of listening to them.

She wasn't sure if he kissed her for seconds or minutes or hours. When he finally raised his head and stared into her eyes, still holding her, Amber's lips were swollen and tingly. She clung to him and he didn't loosen his grip.

"I knew I would find you," he whispered.

"You were searching for me?" There were so many questions. At the same time, she didn't want to talk. All Amber wanted was to disappear with Jordan, be alone with him and make love to him for hours. They could talk later.

"I sent those brochures to every Stone family in Brooklyn," he informed her.

Someone cleared her voice loudly behind him. It wasn't Amber's mother, but another woman. Jordan shifted his weight, allowing her a better view of her family, who watched with a mixture of confusion and amusement on their faces, and of an older woman, whose expression was about the same.

Jordan seemed reluctant to let her down, but did. And she was really glad her knees didn't go out underneath her and she was able to stand next to him. She didn't have a clue how ridiculous her expression might be as she stared at all of them.

"Jordan, this is my mom, Jennifer. And my brother and sister, Bobby and Karma." She gestured to her family, feeling her muscles stretch as she grinned broadly, possibly for the first time in weeks.

"And Aunt Penelope," Jordan began, reaching for the older woman, who uncrossed her arms as her strict expression relaxed and a friendly smile spread across her face as she approached them.

Instead of trying to shake hands, the woman, who possibly was the same age as Amber's mother, pulled Amber into her arms and gave her a warm hug. "I never knew there were so many Stones in Brooklyn, New York," Aunt Penelope offered, her laughter contagious and her blue eyes as deep and beautiful as the endless sky above them. "And we actually got quite a few resumes in the mail, too. Jordan tossed every one of them into the trash until yours arrived."

"Too cool!" Bobby piped up. "We were shoo-ins for the job."

"And you'll work, too," Amber informed him, wagging her finger in his direction but unable to sound authoritative, especially with the stupid smile she was sure was plastered on her face.

"He wasn't going to stop until he brought you here," Aunt Penelope whispered into Amber's ear. "Welcome home, my dear."

Jordan clapped his hands together, grabbing everyone's attention. "Let's get all of you settled in. We can get a tour of the ranch after a bit."

"How much of this land is yours?" Amber scrunched her nose as she looked around them.

"As far as the eye can see," Aunt Penelope told her, grinning at her and then offering a warm smile to Amber's mother. "I'm sure you'll want to see where you're staying. I'm sorry it isn't much. But Jordan is already talking about building on and making other arrangements to improve the ranch."

It would work out, Amber wanted to say. She let Jordan take her by the hand, remaining quiet although she wouldn't be surprised if her family already knew she had no intentions of leaving, ever. He led the way to the older-looking mobile homes, which did in fact look pretty rough. Amber prayed her mother wouldn't be disappointed. Their house in Brooklyn wasn't much, but had been their home for years. If the mobile home was more of a dump than their home it would be harder to convince her to stay. Amber might be selfish but she didn't want her mom going back to Brooklyn and Uncle John, who refused to come since he now worked full time.

"Oh wow," her mother gasped, entering the mobile home last and allowing Jordan to take her luggage from her when she walked into the small living room. "This is a lot nicer inside than on the outside."

"I know it doesn't look like much." Jordan apologized anyway, in spite of her praise. "But it is well insulated, I promise. And you'll live here rent free."

"I always pay my way," Jennifer announced, sticking her chin out stubbornly.

Aunt Penelope laughed. "Hon, I have tons of work to give you. You'll be more than earning what this trailer is worth. But it is rent free. We insist. You'll have your own kitchen, although we really would love for you to have meals with us. Now, there are only two bedrooms."

"I'm not sharing a room," Bobby announced, reflecting his mother's expression with the same stubborn look.

"Wouldn't ask any man to do that," Jordan said, slapping the boy on the back. "Let me get everyone's suitcases in their bedrooms and then we'll head over to the house."

Amber noticed he didn't grab her bags and gave her mother a side glance. Jennifer's smile was warm. She approved of Jordan, and first impressions did count. Jordan reappeared, taking her two suitcases in either hand and heading out the door.

"Go on ahead, if you don't mind," Amber's mother called after her when Amber stepped down the two stairs leaving the trailer and reached Jordan's side. "It was a long trip here and I wouldn't mind settling in and showering. Karma and Bobby will stay here, too. Karma and I will share a room and Bobby will have his own room."

"But Mom," Bobby complained. "I'd rather explore."

Amber met her mother's knowing gaze, happiness spreading throughout her until she was sure she would burst. After all the misery she'd known the past few weeks, feeling like this now seemed like a dream. If so, she prayed she would never wake up.

"I'm going to show your sister the house. I'm afraid we don't have anything exciting like X-box or Play Station games. But feel free to explore around outside all you want. If you hurt yourself, though, it's not my fault," Jordan told Bobby, his expression stern although Amber saw the glow in his eyes. He was as happy as she was and not even willful teenagers would sway their mood.

Later that evening, Amber discovered that Montana had more stars in its sky than anywhere else in the world. She walked hand in hand with Jordan onto the back porch after enjoying a tour of the ranch. Every inch of her tingled when they entered the quiet ranch house and walked without speaking through the quiet rooms, up the stairs and into his large bedroom.

"Your bedroom is almost the size of our entire house," she told him, feeling giddy as if she'd had a few drinks. They hadn't had a drop of alcohol, though.

"This is our room," he informed her without ceremony and didn't let go of her when he approached the bed and turned on a small lamp next to it. "I don't have a lot to offer you, Amber. The money I've invested will help keep the ranch going. It's a lot of hard work, but it's rewarding. I'll teach you how to run a ranch and Aunt Penelope will help. I know you'll love it."

"*You're* here," she said, the words slipping out before she could stop herself.

Jordan pulled her onto the bed with him, immediately working to get her out of her clothes. "So that's a yes?"

"There was a question in there?" she asked, laughing and feeling more at ease than she thought she would when they were finally bare flesh against bare flesh.

"There was supposed to be." He began nibbling at her neck while his large, callused hand pressed against her belly, and then began moving lower until he cupped her pussy.

Amber arched into him, groaning. Her fingertips tingled when she ran them over his muscular shoulders and arms. "Maybe you should ask again," she suggested, her voice scratchy as she stretched out underneath him, spreading her legs as she ached to feel him where she needed him most, deep inside her.

"I'm cut off, disowned by Grandfather. It might have had something to do with the way I told him off after learning how he shipped you off the island without letting me see you first." There wasn't an ounce of regret in his voice.

Amber didn't like the idea that she'd created such a terrible rift between him and his family, even if his grandfather was a cruel bastard. "I don't want to be the reason you aren't speaking with your grandfather," she admitted.

"You're the reason why I finally stood up to him and told him what I should have told him years ago," he informed her, stroking the side of her face with his callused thumb and sending shivers over her flesh. "I went nuts over the past month trying to figure out how to find you. It didn't help when I found out Grandfather fired you and your friends. If either of them wants work, we'll take them on."

"Olive found a job and is talking to me again, and I can't imagine Barney on a ranch," she said, unable to keep her hands off him even as they shared a serious conversation. "I'll do my best to get the message to him, though."

"Can you imagine yourself on a ranch?"

She nodded once, her emotions peaking at that moment. His corded muscles twitched under her fingertips when she ran her hands down his arms and then moved them to his powerful-looking bare chest.

"Marry me, Amber. Be my wife."

"Oh my God, Jordan!" she squealed, positive she sounded like an excited schoolgirl who just got asked out by the most popular boy. But this wasn't high school, and he wasn't asking her out. "There are some things you should know about me before you ask me that," she told him, her heart swelling painfully. She would die if anything she said ruined this moment, but they needed to form their relationship on honesty and trust. "I never finished high school," she confessed, feeling her heart move to her throat as panic hit her, making it impossible to raise her gaze to his face.

"I've got a degree from Harvard," he said. "Does that bother you?"

She was searching for his meaning in his eyes before she could stop herself. "But . . ."

"Amber, I don't care what road you took to get where you

are today. What I care about is who you are right now. You're my soul mate, my lover, and you're going to be my wife. Now say yes, damn it."

She laughed, grinning with her eyes closed, and then moved her hand between them, encouraging him to enter her.

He continued teasing her, his fingers caressing her entrance and spreading her creamy juices over her smooth, shaved flesh.

"I need an answer," he growled.

She brought her legs up, pressing her thighs against his hard body and shifting herself so his cock was throbbing against her pussy.

"Yes, Jordan. I want you to be my husband."

"God, Amber!" He didn't hesitate but thrust deep inside her.

"I love you, Jordan Anton, so much," she cried out, and hoped he didn't expect them to start working tomorrow. Neither one of them would get much sleep tonight.

"I love you, sweetheart. I promised you I wouldn't let you go and I meant it." He pressed his mouth over hers, devouring her as he began moving inside her.

Amber clung to him, feeling herself slip over the edge immediately and knowing she would never come back. It might have started on a small island, but it would last forever under the endless skies of Montana, which was where she'd always belonged.